THE
BOTTOM
OF THE
LAKE

STEVEN STACK

Ten|16 PRESS

www.ten16press.com - Waukesha, WI

For information, please contact:

www.ten16press.com
Waukesha, WI

Edited by Lauren Blue and Maggie Stack
Cover design by Kelly Maddern

Dedicated to

Adam Thomas

A remarkable son, brother, husband, brother-in-law, and most importantly . . . a person who lived life the way it was meant to be lived. So many others were enriched by being in his orbit.

"Live in the sunshine, swim the sea, drink the wild air."

"The purpose of life is not to be happy; it is to be useful, to be honorable, to be compassionate, to have it make some difference that you have lived and lived well."

Ralph Waldo Emerson

Special Thanks to . . .

Alex Bledsoe

Yari Johnson

Lindsay Price

Matt Geiger

Kelly Maddern

Lauren Blue

Theatrefolk

TEN16 Press

Chris Stack, for those two VCR games that you gave me for Christmas when we were kids and for being an awesome brother.

To my parents, Ginny and Steve, for always loving me and always showing me that I mattered.

Chloe and Zoe, for being a source of constant entertainment, uncomfortable moments, love, and meaning.

And to Maggie, for always supporting me, loving me, and making me want to be a better person.

CHAPTER 1

Present

Dani found herself here once more, as she did every night. Deep in the woods. Alone.

She supposed it would make more sense for her dad to simply drop her off here in the first place, instead of paying a ridiculous amount for a summer camp she never got to experience since she always ended up in the same place anyway. Because the other campers sucked.

No, that's not accurate, Dani thought. At some point, she'd have to admit the truth: that it wasn't the other campers that sucked. It never had been.

She'd spent most of her life listening to people tell her that being different was a good thing. How being "outside the circle" allowed for freedom and growth. She remembered how her teachers, counselors, and parents constantly preached about how "normal was boring" and "things would get better." Evidence of this, though, had proven hard to come by. Unless you liked being rejected constantly and sitting in a bathroom stall at lunch every day because that was better than the alternative. What she wouldn't give to one day fit in, blend in, belong. Be *in* the circle instead of always just outside. She hoped it would happen, and despite the absence of any signs that it might, that hope held on. Barely, but it did. Because of her dad. He had once told her that when everything is telling you there's no chance of what you want happening, you keep hoping and working because that's all you have. Holding on when there's no reason to is a sign of being brave, he said. Or, as Dani was now starting to believe, a sign of being a complete dumbass.

Still, she persisted. Always like her dad, she guessed. Even until the tragic end.

CHAPTER 2

Six weeks ago, beginning of summer

Karla, who had graduated from high school three years ago and had apparently decided to forgo college to fulfill her dream of being Vanessa's taxi driver, had shown up late once again, thus ensuring that Vanessa would have little choice in where she sat on the bus. Karla honked the horn of her brand new purple Volvo (no doubt a gift from her dad) at Vanessa, who had been waiting at the curb for at least 75 years.

She got up, picked up her luggage, and walked to the car. Karla rolled down the passenger-side window.

"You wanna hurry up, Van? I'm supposed to meet Matt in an hour."

"Well, maybe you shouldn't have been late," Vanessa said, not missing a beat. She tugged the back door open and tossed her luggage on the seat, closed the door, then climbed onto the front seat, pushing aside numerous empty Starbucks cups and other garbage. "Besides, Matt sucks anyway. Total loser."

"Yeah. Kind of." Karla looked at her intently.

"What?"

"When are you going to do something about that?" Karla asked, motioning vaguely at Vanessa's head.

"My hair?"

"Yeah. You should dye it. It's the only thing holding you back. Well, not the only thing, but like the biggest one."

Vanessa sighed. "I like my red hair. I think it's nice."

"Yes, it is . . . nice. And with that bright orange camp shirt, you look like a Cheeto." Karla stared at Vanessa's Camp Kimi t-shirt. "By the way, why is your camp named after someone named Kimi?"

"It's not. 'Kimi' means 'secrets' in Algonquin." At Karla's blank look, Vanessa added, "It's a Native American tribe."

"That's stupid," Karla said dismissively as she drove off.

Karla had been "in charge" of Vanessa for five years now, starting when Vanessa was 10, basically serving as her faux mom and dad when her actual parents said they had too much to do for work or whatever the *excuse du jour* was. Vanessa, though, knew what was what and was okay with her parents being less than loving helicopter parents. They were quite the opposite. Oh, they had hovered once – and then they stopped. Stopped everything resembling parenting, really. All because of what happened six years ago, though no one acknowledged it. Vanessa had figured out quickly that it's the unspoken truths that count the most. Besides, Karla was cool. Somewhat. She wasn't smart though. She was one of the dumbest people Vanessa had ever met that could still manage to walk upright. Somehow, she was still able to make Vanessa feel like she was the dumb one. Always. How she did it, Vanessa had no idea.

"Are you excited about camp, Van?" Karla asked while darting back and forth between cars, never once thinking of a turn signal or the fact that she was going twice the speed limit.

"I am. If your driving doesn't kill me first," Vanessa said, clutching her seatbelt tightly around her as she watched Karla, who was seemingly unaware of the cascade of honking that followed every one of her poor driving choices.

"Oh, don't worry about that. I'm a great driver."

"As your eight accidents can attest to. If anything tells me how much my parents love me, it's the fact that they trust you with my life."

"Right?" Karla said, laughing.

Just then, Karla's phone rang. It was a one of those "be proud of who you are" pop songs that made Vanessa cringe. Fortunately, she answered it quickly.

"Oh, hello, lover boy."

Matt. Vanessa knew that this conversation would go on forever and get gross, so she looked out the window, watching as they raced further and further away from society as she knew it.

Camp Kimi, the most expensive camp in the state, was about 40 miles away from the nearest town, sign of humanity, or cell service, which was why the camp had designated points where parents (or random teenagers) could drop their campers off for a luxurious ride into the deep, dark woods. It was also a camp that lasted the entire summer, something that she was sure her parents were on board with. This suited Vanessa fine, as she liked "camp Vanessa" way better than "anywhere else Vanessa."

At camp, Vanessa was free because none of her school friends would be caught dead at a place where sleeping and playing in the woods was encouraged, and her parents didn't care what she did as long as she didn't get sent home. So, when she got back from boarding school, off she happily went to the place where she was free to be whoever the hell she wanted to be. The mask of Ms. Perfect was no longer forced upon her. Messy hair and unbrushed teeth? Sure. No shower for a couple of days? Why not? You smell more like nature. Junk food galore? Absolutely. Though she very seldom took advantage of the first two (a girl does have standards, after all), she would push the boundaries of what she could get away with everywhere else. If she ever crossed the line, she would turn on the charm and get out of whatever it was with a warning. She had also used that charm to keep her only two camp friends, Lindsey and Claire, from getting into too much trouble.

Lindsey and Claire. She had met Lindsey first, and then Claire joined the fold about halfway through that first summer. This year, Lindsey almost couldn't come because her parents had decided that this camp was doing bad things to her, whatever that meant, and that it was too expensive. Lindsey had called Vanessa and said she needed her help, so Vanessa told her parents that if Lindsey couldn't go, then she wouldn't either and that she would spend the whole summer with them.

One phone call later, and Lindsey was going back to camp. Vanessa should've been hurt that the thought of spending the summer with her was enough for her parents to pay another camper's tuition and, to be fair, she was. Though that, among many other slights her parents had gifted to her, would remain her secret.

"God! Matt is such a jerk sometimes!" Karla screamed, rolling down her window and throwing her phone out of it.

Vanessa, startled from her daydreaming, turned to Karla. "I take it the call went well?"

"No, it didn't," Karla muttered through her teeth.

"Maybe you could've thrown the phone down on the floor instead of, you know, out the window."

"Screw that phone. It's full of bad memories now. Besides, I got another one," she said, reaching into the glove compartment and pulling out another phone, a replica of the one she'd thrown out the window. She turned it on and then turned back to Vanessa, all the while somehow keeping them on the road. "And screw Matt too. I don't know what I see in him."

"His attractiveness, perhaps?"

"Yeah," Karla agreed. "But one day, one day soon, that won't be enough." Vanessa watched Karla stew for a moment until an excited look came over her face. "I have a question for you."

"Oh, God." Vanessa sighed. "Is this one of those questions that I'm going to regret answering when you use it to embarrass me later in front of all your friends?"

"Probably," Karla said with a smile. "But I think it will be worth it anyway for you."

"Cool. Shoot."

"You know how you and your dorky camp friends go out in the woods and tell those lame stories instead of doing, you know, normal things that 15-year-olds who are popular do?"

"Yes," Vanessa said, looking out the window and quickly regretting agreeing to answer Karla's question.

"I get why they do it, but why do you?" Karla asked, furiously typing out a text and steering with her knees. "You're like me, just a less popular, more . . . red-headed version, yet you spend all your time when you're home for breaks writing those stories that you only share with two other people. Why . . ."

"Light's red," Vanessa said calmly.

Karla looked up from her phone and slammed on the brakes, barely missing slamming into the car in front of them. "Thank God I saw that." The light turned green, the other car moved forward, and Karla returned to her texting, talking, and driving. "So?"

"We tell stories because it's fun." Karla rolled her eyes, and Vanessa reluctantly went on, trying to put it into words. "I guess it's also because we have complete control of the narrative since we all live lives that are pretty much written for us by a world which only marginally understands or cares about us."

Karla took her eyes off her screen and looked at Vanessa. "I have no idea what any of that means."

"Didn't figure you would," Vanessa said, feeling a pang of disappointment for some reason. She ignored it and leaned her head against the window. "And the reason I spent all that time on my story this year was because I had an idea where the story leaves the page and becomes real. The problem is that I know how to do it, I just haven't found the perfect story."

A big smile crossed Karla's face as she put her phone down. "No worries because I, as always, am the answer to your problems. Before Matt pissed me off, he did start talking about something that happened at a camp not far from the one you're going to. I remembered it too because I was going to go to that camp the very next year but couldn't because of what happened that summer."

Vanessa turned back to Karla, suddenly more intrigued than

she could recall ever being in any conversation with her. "What happened?"

"Oh, a couple of mysterious deaths and a body that was never found. Nothing big."

"How have I not heard this story?"

"Because it got covered up and called an accident. People love their secrets, you know? But I know what really happened."

"How do you know?"

"Because my dad was in on the coverup. I mean, he doesn't know I know but sometimes you just hear things late at night."

Vanessa stared at Karla. "That was loaded and clearly something I want to know more about later, but you have to tell me what really happened at that camp first. And spare no details."

Karla looked at her slyly, paying no attention to the fact that she was still driving. "Are you sure? It's pretty messed up, and you're going to be super close to where it happened."

"I have never been surer of anything in my life."

And after hearing the story, Vanessa knew that it was perfect. Now she would only have to get Lindsey and Claire on board, which wouldn't be an issue. If everything worked out as Vanessa hoped and they pulled it off, it would make the most memorable story – and summer – of their lives.

CHAPTER 3

Present

Dani stared up at the moon. The same moon that, as a child, she was in awe of. That's also when she believed in magic, believed anything was possible, including having a pet purple unicorn and that life would be full of promises that would never be broken. Even though she was now looking at the same moon, she no longer felt that awe. She felt nothing. She no longer believed in magic, she knew she would never have a pet purple unicorn, and life had proven incapable of keeping any promises. Now she was simply another broken one.

Dani laughed out loud. She wondered when she had become such a teenage cliché.

Ah, yes. It was the moment she found out that her mother was never coming home again.

Danielle Rose Malone was the most amazing person Dani had ever known, and she always dreamed of one day being exactly like her. She was someone who had managed to be amazing at everything she cared to be amazing at. As an advertising executive, as a person, as a wife, as a mother. That's what Dani wanted to be.

But she wasn't. She was more like her dad.

She loved her dad. He was wonderful. But he was also a dreamer, an outsider, a screw-up. Talented but not talented enough. Likable but not likable enough. Just not enough.

- - - - - - - - - - -

Claire tried to blow her brown hair out of her eyes with little success. She had been carrying the giant red cooler the entire time while Vanessa and Lindsey carried nothing more than their flashlights. Earlier that night, they had snuck out of their cabin and tiptoed to the counselors' cabin, where the lights were off because, as Vanessa had predicted, they were out in the woods hanging out and doing whatever college students did when they were the ones in charge and the kids they were responsible for were in bed. (Lindsey had said they were having sex parties and smoking crack, but Lindsey assumed that's what everyone did when they were unsupervised.) Lindsey and Vanessa had pushed Claire up through the counselors' back window where, once she recovered from her awkward fall of approximately eight feet directly onto her face, she had gone around to the front of the cabin and let Vanessa and Lindsey in. They found the cooler, Claire carried it out, and they headed to the cafeteria where Lindsey (who was being forced to work there because of her various infractions that Vanessa had failed to get her completely out of) had left a side door unlocked. They quickly and quietly filled the cooler.

After that was done, Vanessa led the way to their destination.

Lindsey followed close behind, leaving Claire to carry the now much heavier cooler alone. And she had. And it felt like they'd gone 10 miles. Claire, going against her nature, was growing annoyed. "Why am I the only one carrying the cooler? You both have arms!" she grumbled, struggling to find her way in the dark as she lugged the cooler and her flashlight.

"Well, my flashlight is heavier than yours, and I have to focus on finding this place," Vanessa said, not looking back and trying to sound serious through her suppressed laughter. "If I carried that cooler, we would get hopelessly lost and then end up dead. Or worse."

"I don't know what's worse than death, and that answer doesn't explain why Lindsey isn't carrying something."

"Oh, there's quite a simple explanation for that, my dear Claire," Lindsey said, walking back to her and placing her hand on Claire's shoulder. "It's because I don't want to. Now buck up, little camper, and keep taking care of that cooler." Lindsey bopped her on the chin lightly (causing Claire to scrunch up her face angrily), turned, and caught back up to Vanessa. "I suppose you're taking us out this far to kill us and dispose of our bodies in a place no one would ever find them?"

"Well, not at first," Vanessa said. "I figured I would torture you both a lot and then kill you."

"Oh good, I was hoping for a lot of torture first. Torture after killing always seemed pointless to me."

"Wait, what?" Claire said, dropping the cooler to the ground. She pointed her flashlight at Vanessa, who had turned back and was staring coolly at her.

"Look around. We're miles from camp in the middle of the

night. There are plenty of places to get rid of the bodies of two forgettable teenagers. Maybe stuff you in a tree or drown you in the lake."

"You mean like . . ." Claire stopped when Vanessa nodded.

"I do." Vanessa slowly walked in Claire's direction, her flashlight pointing directly at her. "Think about it, Claire. Why do you suppose I was so quick to take you in as a friend a couple years back? The goofy, smart girl who was, let's be honest, the weirdest camper ever? Lindsey, over there, didn't want you, but I did." Claire looked over to Lindsey, whose response was a bored sigh. Vanessa turned back to Claire. "But Claire, it wasn't because I was a good person. It was because I knew this day would come. And now it has." She quickly turned her flashlight on Lindsey, who squinted and turned away. "And you, best friend, the one who no one would sit with on the bus that day. I mean, look at you. Not to mention, you're rather mean and off-putting. You're the dog in the shelter that everyone skips over because you're snarling at them, daring them to come closer, all the while secretly hoping they do."

"That's pretty spot on," Lindsey agreed.

"And on top of that, why do you think I made sure that you would be here this summer, of all summers, even to the point of using my parents' distaste for spending time alone with me to make sure you were here?"

"Because you longed for my companionship?" Lindsey said, slowly becoming a little less indifferent.

"What's wrong, Lindsey? A little scared?" Lindsey didn't answer. "Well, you should be. And so should you, Claire," Vanessa said, turning back to Claire.

"Oh, I am."

"Good." Vanessa smiled. She reached into her pocket, and something in Claire snapped.

"She's got a machete! Run, Lindsey!" Claire turned and started running back through the woods in the direction they had come from. Lindsey almost took off too, but she couldn't make herself move. She would rather die than give Vanessa the satisfaction of knowing she got her, so she stayed and watched as Vanessa pulled out gum. She unwrapped a piece for herself and handed one to Lindsey.

"I feel like I almost got you."

"Well, out of the three of us, you are the most likely sociopath," Lindsey said, unwrapping the gum and popping it into her mouth. "On one level, the logical one, I knew you were messing with us. But on the other hand, as much as I like you, there was always something about your model-looking self that made me a little uneasy. The plan you came up with that we're carrying out right now feeds into this feeling. If you decided to hack both Claire and me to death right now, I wouldn't be all that surprised. Impressed, not surprised. In the end though, I would rather be hacked to death then let you get me." Lindsey looked where Claire had run off, her screams filling the night. "How far do you think she'll get?" Then they heard a loud noise.

"Ow!" Claire yelled from somewhere in the dark.

"That far," Vanessa said.

"You know you could come and help me, you jerks!"

Vanessa and Lindsey walked back to where Claire's flashlight shone, a weak beacon in the night. They walked through a clearing, the same clearing that Claire had avoided in order to run through waist-high brush. They found her lying down a few feet from it.

Vanessa pointed her flashlight. "Hey, look, I know you're a little tired, but now's not the time for a nap. That cooler's not going to get there by itself."

"I'm not napping! You and your stupid jokes. There is something wrong with you. Seriously wrong. I thought you were going to kill us."

"But you two are the only people I've ever liked. And I'm offended that you so easily believed that I was going to murder you."

"You shouldn't be. You're the most likely sociopath in the group."

"That's what I said," Lindsey agreed.

Claire smiled and then continued. "Lindsey's the angry one, I'm the human one, and you, Vanessa, are the one without feelings."

Vanessa had heard that many times before. So many times, in fact, that perhaps it was becoming true. Feelings were overrated anyway. Sure, they might provide happy moments, but all the other times were bad enough to justify not having them at all, or at least putting them all in a room and blocking the door so the dirty bastards couldn't get out.

"Wait," Lindsey said, looking offended. "I thought I was the one without feelings." The other two girls looked at Lindsey, dumbfounded. "Whatever," she mumbled, kicking at the dirt.

"Also, it looked like you were pulling out a machete," Claire said.

"A machete?" Vanessa scoffed. "How the hell could I fit a

machete in my pocket? It was gum. Besides, whenever I do kill you two, it will be with a pickax."

"Awesome," Lindsey said. "Can we continue on this ridiculous quest or do we need to hear more about what a psychopath you are?"

"The first one!" Claire yelled. "But can someone help me up first? I think I'm stuck."

Vanessa reached out, but Lindsey's hand got there first, and she pulled Claire up. "And I'll carry the cooler the rest of the way." When she turned around, Vanessa was staring at her. "What?" Lindsey asked, a little defensively.

"Feels."

"Shut up, dick." Lindsey quickly dropped Claire's hand, turned around, and began walking back. "This night is beginning to bore me. Where is this place?"

"Pretty close. Maybe. I mean, it's not like I've ever been out here myself," Vanessa said. She turned to Claire. "You okay?"

"Fine," Claire said, dusting herself off. "I still don't get why we had to come way out here. This is out of bounds, and yes, we're used to breaking the rules, but this seems a little much. Besides, I like where we usually do it."

Vanessa drew even with Lindsey as Claire hurried to catch up.

"I told you, tonight is the anniversary of the night it happened, and Karla told me how to get here," Vanessa said, the three of them now walking together again. "Sort of. She's really stupid. Anyway, do you know how cool it's going to be to tell our stories there?"

"I'm not sure if the coolness balances out the amount of effort – or the trouble we're going to get into. Especially if we die of exhaustion before we get there," Lindsey said.

"Oh, it will be worth it. Trust me. Even if we die." Vanessa smiled, leading the way.

Claire was about to say something to that last sentence but decided to let it pass because she knew what Vanessa was doing. Setting the mood. They had always done this, leave the campsite late at night to tell stories. Why this became their "thing," Claire could never figure out. She wasn't even truly a fan of ghost stories. Nor could she tell them. But she went along anyway. Tonight, though, as she looked around with her flashlight, she was regretting her decision. Earlier they had climbed over a fence that had to be erected around the abandoned campsite (super fun to do with a cooler, by the way), and they had started seeing the old camp's remains. Signs that something used to be but was no longer. Something fun, magical, and memory-making, now lying in state of disrepair, being reclaimed by nature. The happiness that once was, now only a relic of something that would never be again. It reminded her of those defunct amusement parks her dad always took her and her sister to. After they were done exploring and taking pictures, he would explain that this was the ending that awaited us all. He said it was to help them appreciate the moment, but all it made Claire do was cry and ponder the end of everything. She didn't cry nor ponder the end of everything tonight as she saw the old campsite. Because she was too scared.

The abandoned cabins were the creepiest: broken windows and doors, graffiti everywhere. Lindsey had wanted to explore them, so they did. Well, Vanessa and Lindsey did. Claire stayed outside. Then she saw an old dirty teddy bear lying partially buried under the cabin. She had reached down for it and spotted the name "Sam" on the collar. The years and the weather had taken their toll, but Claire sensed that at one point it was loved. She sighed and placed it back down gently. She then heard her dad's voice in her head. "All things end, honey. That's the way it's meant to be."

The camp's end, or death as Vanessa had gleefully called it earlier, had come rather abruptly several years ago. Having campers die in unexplained ways tends to do that to a place no matter the stories that were told, but at some point, this camp had been like hers. Full of kids and counselors, full of games and days and nights making memories around campfires while eating s'mores and telling ghost stories. She imagined how all the campers were thinking that the summer would never end and that they would be kids forever. But it did end, and Claire was now surrounded by that reality. Not to mention that some of those kids didn't get to grow up. Their stories ended up being no more than a novella. What was worse, though, was that Claire swore there were times, as the three of them walked, that she had heard sounds that belonged not to tonight but to a night long gone. Maybe she was imagining it, but whatever the case, it unnerved her even more. And not only because they were getting closer to the spot where it supposedly happened.

"Hey, Claire," Lindsey called, shocking Claire back to reality. "You want to, I don't know, stop walking at the speed of backwards, so that we can get to this godforsaken place before we rot away and die?"

"Sorry."

Claire ran to catch up. As the clock moved closer and closer to midnight, the girls walked deeper and deeper into the woods,

Vanessa and Lindsey walking side by side and Claire, clearly spooked, walking slightly behind them. Which was the way it had always been since Vanessa and Lindsey had met.

- - - - - - - - - -

Vanessa and Lindsey met four years ago when they were both 11, the first time at camp for both of them. Karla, who had somehow gotten her driver's license two days earlier, dropped Vanessa off at the camp pickup point because her parents were otherwise occupied that day, and of course they were late, and of course everyone else was already on the bus. Vanessa got out of the car and retrieved her matching luggage set while Karla stayed in the driver's seat, talking animatedly to her boyfriend on her phone.

Vanessa noted that there were several parents standing by the bus, waving at their kids, some of them with tears in their eyes. Strange. All she got was an empty house when she left and a "see you at the end of the summer!" as Karla sped off. Vanessa watched her leave for a moment before checking in with a clipboard-toting counselor who was wearing the most god-awful fluorescent orange and green camp t-shirt she had ever seen. Climbing on the bus, Vanessa knew finding a seat would be difficult, given her late arrival and the camp's popularity.

Her attention was quickly captured by some loud girl who was seemingly rejecting anyone who tried to talk or sit with her, though no one seemed to be doing either.

"What are you doing? Stop the words that are coming from your mouth that are directed at me."

"Did I give you a look or something that made you think I

wanted you to take residence in the seat beside me? 'No' is the answer you are looking for."

"If you continue this dialogue, I'm going to get out of my seat, walk over to you, and punch you in your big fat lips!"

Vanessa was not surprised to see this girl sitting alone. She wore cutoff jeans and a t-shirt that said "So's Your Face." Her dirty blond hair looked as if it hadn't been washed or combed in years. Vanessa began to walk by her, but the girl stuck out one of her legs.

"Hey, you."

Vanessa stopped and turned to look at the girl, who was smacking loudly on her gum. "Hey, you what?"

The girl took a moment – and then she smiled. "Hey, you . . . want to sit by me?" She moved her leg and shifted over to the window.

"Not particularly."

"Too bad then. 'Cause there are no other seats."

Vanessa looked around, hoping that there was just one other seat somewhere far away from this weird girl. There were none. "Perhaps I'll sit on the floor."

At that moment, as if on cue, the bus driver yelled, "No sitting on the floor!"

The girl laughed. "Guess that option's out."

Vanessa sighed. "I suppose." She sat down, facing straight ahead, noting in her peripheral vision that the girl had extended her hand.

"I'm Lindsey."

Vanessa turned to Lindsey and looked down at her hand. "Is that clean?"

"As far as you know."

Vanessa allowed a small smile as she shook Lindsey's hand. "I'm Vanessa." Lindsey then leaned in really close to Vanessa's face. "What are you doing?"

"Your eyes are awesome!" the scruffy girl said. "What color do they call that?"

"Blue."

Lindsey shook her head. "I knew that, dumbass. What I meant was what type of blue? Because that blue is outstanding."

"Thanks, and I don't know."

"My mom told me I have mud-colored eyes. God, I love that woman," Lindsey said sarcastically.

"Well, it's a nice shade of mud."

Both girls started laughing then. They had been inseparable ever since.

- - - - - - - - - -

"So, what are the chances that anyone else is out here?" Lindsey asked, jolting Vanessa back into the present.

"Not very likely, but you never know." Vanessa made a sudden small turn, and Lindsey almost bumped into her. "Look out there."

Lindsey looked and was about to speak when Claire crashed into her, making Lindsey stumble. "We've stopped, Claire."

"Sorry." Claire stuck her head between them and looked out, instantly drawn to the view of the lake, its water rippling in the wind and highlighted by the soon-to-be-covered moon. "What lake is this?"

"It's the same one we swim in, Claire. It's just the other side," Lindsey said as she put the cooler down, took off her shoes, and ran to the shore. "Time to get these sweaty dogs clean."

"Gross," Vanessa said, now crossing closer to the lake herself, followed closely by Claire. "This is the side of the lake that no one comes to anymore. Not even the locals."

"So, this is where it happened?" Claire nervously asked as she looked around with her flashlight.

"Nope." Vanessa shook her head. "This is where it ended. Right out there." She pointed beyond where Lindsey was wading in the shallow water.

Lindsey headed back to Vanessa and Claire. "How do you know if the story is even true? That drowning could have been an accident." She sat down on the sand.

"C'mon, Lindsey," Vanessa said, pointing the flashlight at her. "You know it wasn't. First, Karla isn't smart enough to make something like this up, and second, if it were simply an accident, people would've moved on. Not shut an entire camp down. Besides, they never even found the body."

"Whatever." Lindsey shrugged. "You know how urban legends are. Someone tells the story for the first time, and then more and more people repeat it until everyone starts to believe it. Then it becomes fact. You know, like God."

Vanessa turned away. "I'll remember that when I pray for you tonight."

"Please do," Lindsey said. She moved her flashlight, and the beam caught Claire, who had crossed away from the two of them and was sitting on a nearby rock, looking out fearfully. "What are you doing, Claire?"

Claire turned to her, shoving her shaking hands in her jacket pockets. "I want to go back. Now."

"What? No, we're not going back. We've walked too far to leave."

"I don't want to be here anymore. Something is off. I feel it. Something bad is going to happen tonight if we don't leave."

"Like what?" Lindsey asked.

"I don't know, but it won't be good."

That feeling she'd felt earlier had come back. Along with the voices. But this time they were screams. And laughter. And a struggle. She couldn't see who was screaming, but she could hear them. It sounded ridiculous, even inside Claire's mind, but she went with it anyway.

"We are not leaving," Vanessa said firmly.

Claire turned to Vanessa and then to Lindsey, trying to muster up the courage to say something. It was a long, awkward moment. "Fine. I'll go by myself then."

"Good luck finding your way back to camp."

"Shut up, Lindsey," Vanessa said, crossing over to the rock Claire was sitting on. She sat beside her. "Tell me what's wrong, Claire."

"It's that, looking out there, where . . . it's too real. To think her body's still out there. Somewhere. And, this is going to sound crazy, but I swear I heard screams. And I heard voices when we were at the old camp. I can't stay here on the beach."

"Well, you're in luck," Vanessa said, putting an arm around her. "We're not telling stories here."

"Oh my god!" Lindsey exclaimed, pulling herself to her feet. "There's more walking?"

Vanessa turned to Lindsey with a small smile. "A little more. If it were daylight, we'd be able to see the spot from here. Probably." She turned back to Claire. "Look, Claire, it's going to be fun. Promise. And besides, Lindsey's right. You don't want to have to walk all the way back to camp by yourself. You'll never make it."

"Yeah, I guess." Claire looked out at the dark water. It seemed to absorb, rather than reflect, the light coming from the moon and stars. She wondered if it looked like this on the night . . . she stopped that thought and turned to Vanessa. "Okay, I'll stay. Though, let it be known that I'm not happy about it."

"We'll be sure to note that in the records," Vanessa said, standing up.

"I still don't see why we're telling stories again in that spot exactly. Seems like we'd have a better chance of what you want to happen happening if, you know, we were closer to camp," Lindsey said, throwing a rock into the lake.

"Because the creep factor is huge, note Claire's response, and that's where it started. When you're after the perfect story, you must find the perfect place. And no place is more perfect than this one," Vanessa said before running off into the woods.

"Hey, wait up," Lindsey said, laughing and hurrying after her.

Claire, who was caught off-guard with the history of where they were going and Vanessa's sudden and inexplicable running, was left alone. She considered trying to make it back to camp alone, but quickly rejected the thought. She also considered that she might need better friends.

"Guys, must we run?" She sighed. "Fine." And she took off after them.

- - - - - - - - - -

Voices.

"That's strange," Dani said aloud. Voices were the last thing she'd expected to hear out here.

Well, other than her own.

Who would be out this far? And this late? Dani heard at least two girls, maybe three.

She thought of leaving, which was her go-to response for obvious reasons, one that had proven correct time and time again. And if history were any indicator, she knew what would happen if she waited around. Besides, was there any way that people out this late at night and in this part of the woods were up to something fun and wholesome? Doubtful – and Dani had spent a lifetime dealing with people like that. Well, not people that explored the woods late at night, but people who would do that kind of thing if there were woods nearby. One part of her mind told her that she was wasting time pondering whether to go or stay because the voices were getting louder, and they were heading in her direction. If she didn't move soon, she would have no choice but to stay and meet them. And if they found her here, like this, they would think something was wrong with her, which, of course, there was.

There was one part of her, though, that wanted her to stay, was begging her to stay. Maybe this would be the time that the stars all aligned, and Dani would meet people who wanted to hang out with her. The probability of that happening was quite low, almost nonexistent, but Dani fixated on the fact that there was a chance, no matter how small, and she couldn't walk away.

She was going to stay despite being terrified of what might happen.

She slowly got up off the log, dusted herself off, and walked to the clearing. She stood behind a tree and peeked out, like some predator watching her prey. The tree and its low-hanging leaves provided the perfect cover. Then she saw them. There were three of them, girls, and they all looked about the same age, Dani's age. Two were running together with another one behind them, trying to catch up. They were heading her way, laughing.

The confidence that she had found moments ago began to wane as she realized that this meeting was going to happen. Her legs almost began carrying her away, but they couldn't. Who knew when, or if, she would have another chance like this? She watched them run, unable to tell much about them because of the darkness and the fact that their flashlights were bobbing up and down. She could see that the one in front, clearly taller than the other two, ran gracefully. The one almost passing her seemed to be the shortest of the group and ran like some attack dog. The one in the back, the least graceful of the three, ran like a wounded duck.

She walked back to the clearing and thought about sitting on the log facing where the girls would be entering, but then she thought that would be a little much. She walked slightly off to one side, still facing the direction from which they would be coming, but more removed. In the shadows, where she might have time to run away still if the girls turned out to be psychopaths looking for a fresh kill. Dani took a deep breath and didn't move. Except for the smile that escaped her. This feeling was something she'd rarely had since her mom had died. There had been moments, but they were brief and quickly forgotten. She hoped that this one would last longer. This feeling.

Happiness.

- - - - - - - - - -

Vanessa came to an abrupt stop and said, "Here we are," as she entered a clearing that had at one time been used as a gathering spot of sorts. In the center were logs set up in that traditional "campfire" way. There were still charred remains of fires long past. She let herself be filled with thoughts of what that night must have looked like. Felt like. Even though the remains of what happened were probably long gone, there was something here. Vanessa could feel it, and it gave her the feelings that she had hoped for when she'd come up with this plan. The feeling of excitement mixed with terror.

That feeling of being terrified would only grow when Lindsey, bursting through with Claire behind her, found something unexpected in the beam of her flashlight.

"And there *she* is."

CHAPTER 4

Dani pulled her hoodie further down over her head as the three girls stared awkwardly at her. No one seemed ready to speak or move. The feeling that was spreading between the four girls seemed to be the same feeling you would have if you were hiding under the bed and discovered someone hiding with you who shouldn't be there. Dani tried to smile at them, but their flashlights caused her to squint – so her smile, which had never been that pleasant anyway, only served to frighten them more.

"Hi," Dani said, trying to adjust her smile but only succeeding in making it odder. The girls said nothing to her. They remained frozen with their flashlights continuing to blind her. "You know, flashlights are really bright when you're shining them directly in someone's eyes. Especially when there are three of them." No response. Dani put up a hand to block some of the light. "I think this is crossing the line into weirdness, so I'll try again." She stood up, causing them to jump back a little. "Hi."

Vanessa, gaining her courage back, took a step towards Dani while moving her flashlight from Dani's eyes. She stared at her some more, her expression unreadable. "Um, hello, person sitting in the middle of the woods. At night. Without a flashlight."

"Well, I'm standing now. And about my flashlight, I guess I forgot it."

"Seems like an odd thing to forget," Lindsey said, crossing to them and standing not beside Vanessa but right in front of Dani. They were almost nose-to-nose, which seemed rather odd to Dani but gave her the first impression that Dani supposed the girl had intended. She stared directly at Dani, who met her gaze evenly though she did have to look down a little. Claire timidly walked behind Vanessa.

Dani and Lindsey continued the stare-off. Then Dani answered Lindsey, "Or maybe I didn't want to be seen."

"Looks like you failed there," Lindsey said. She continued peering at her, trying to dissect her. Vanessa looked on with Claire pressed into her back, refusing to look. Then Lindsey walked over to a log and casually sat down. "I don't know you. Are you a local?" Dani didn't answer her right away. Lindsey groaned loudly. "So? Are you local?" she repeated.

"I guess," Dani said finally.

Vanessa continued to study the girl. It was strange enough that the three of them had come out here late at night, but at least they had each other. But this girl, who was wearing ragged jean shorts and a black hoodie pulled so tight that you could barely make out the outline of her face, was out here by herself without a flashlight. All in all, it seemed like the perfect setup for a horror movie, and if it was, Horror Movie 101 said that Vanessa, Lindsey, and Claire would soon end up dead, which would be highly unfortunate.

She seemed normal enough, though. Sort of. Except for being out here, of course. When she saw Lindsey getting annoyed, which meant that this conversation was about to go from bad to worse, Vanessa untangled herself from Claire, who quickly fell to the ground. She walked away, ignoring her fallen friend completely, and sat down across from Lindsey.

"Here, let me help you." Claire looked up and saw that the strange girl had extended her hand. Claire didn't know what to do. Her hand looked normal enough. Super pale, but maybe that was just in contrast to Claire's darker skin. There was also a cut across the top of her hand that looked fresh, even though it wasn't bleeding. If she refused to take her hand, Claire thought, that might make her angry. Or sad. Which were both bad. But if she did take the hand, she might get pulled into her mouth and eaten. That was probably not very likely.

"I promise I won't pull you into my mouth and eat you."

Claire gasped. "Can you read minds?"

Dani laughed. "No. That's what your face was saying." Claire smiled and reached for her hand, and Dani helped her up. Claire let go quickly and went to sit on the log between Vanessa and Lindsey. Dani remained there, not moving, until Lindsey forcefully decided for her.

"I hope you're not planning to stand there all creeper-like for the rest of the night because that would be irritating. Come on over. There's an empty log left just for you," she said. Dani slowly walked over and sat down. Lindsey got up and sat close to Dani.

So close that if someone walked up, they would've assumed they were conjoined twins. Dani turned to her.

"You stood close to me earlier and now you're sitting close to me."

Lindsey nodded. "That I am. I'm what's called a close stander and sitter."

"I've never heard of that."

"You should get out more. Being a close stander and sitter is the new thing. All the kids are doing it."

Vanessa sighed. "Hi, I'm Vanessa. What's your name?"

Dani turned to Vanessa. "Dani."

"Okay, Dani, what *are* you doing out here all by yourself?"

"There was no one else to come with me."

"Oh, that's depressing. I'm sorry," Claire said with a smile that said she understood that feeling.

Dani smiled at the obviously still afraid girl. "It's okay. Really," she said, trying to help Claire calm down. "Being alone is something I'm used to by now."

"You're some weirdo, aren't you?" Lindsey broke in. Vanessa and Claire both groaned. Lindsey shot them a look, affronted. "What? It's a very logical question."

Dani got up. "Well, it certainly was nice meeting you." She stopped and looked at Lindsey. "Not you, because you're mean and make me uncomfortable, but whatever. I've been picked on enough, so I will leave you three here to do whatever it is that you're planning to do and go somewhere else, I guess."

Dani turned and started to walk away. She had hoped that this time would be different, but it was heading in the same direction as all her other attempts. She didn't get far before

Vanessa stood up and moved in front of her. Dani stopped, avoiding eye contact.

"Hey, wait," Vanessa said, reaching for Dani, who pulled away quickly. She stared at Vanessa.

"Please move." Vanessa didn't but neither did Dani. "What?"

Vanessa took a deep breath. "Look, Lindsey there is a fairly unpleasant person. But she's *our* fairly unpleasant person, so we have to let her hang with us. I'm sorry for what she said, and I'm pretty sure she didn't mean it."

"Well, if you knew me," scoffed Lindsey, "you would know that I say everything I think about other people, so clearly I did mean it. No filter here. I wasn't being mean, however. I was being honest." Claire threw a stick at her. "Did you throw a stick at me?"

"Yes. Stop talking."

"I'm going to . . ."

"Sit there and stop talking," Vanessa said, cutting her off.

Lindsey looked between Claire and Vanessa. "You guys are so rude."

Vanessa ignored her and looked at Dani. "Like I was saying, she's not much of a charmer, but she grows on you."

"Like fungus," Claire said, laughing.

Vanessa smiled and continued. "And you're obviously stuck out here or something because something bad happened to you, so why don't you hang with us for a while, and then we'll help you get back to your camp. What do you say?"

Dani was stunned. This was the first time anyone had been nice to her in a long time. She considered her options. One, stay and see if this night could end well. Vanessa and Claire were nice, and Lindsey . . . well, there had to be something good about her. And Dani, always being someone who studied more than interacted with people, picked up a vibe that Lindsey wasn't the person she tried to make everyone think she was. Option two was . . . well, there wasn't an option two. Or at least there wasn't one that Dani had any interest in. She looked up at Vanessa and smiled.

"Okay. I'll stay. I mean, I didn't have a clue where I would go if I did leave." Vanessa nodded once, then walked back over and sat down on an empty log. Dani took a moment and then walked back to the circle. She looked at Lindsey. "But this time, I'm sitting over here," she said, pointing to the only empty log before sitting on it carefully.

Lindsey turned to Dani. "I feel like you're not sitting by me for a reason."

Dani looked back at her. "Go with that feeling." Vanessa and Claire laughed, and after a moment, Lindsey laughed too.

"I think I was wrong about you. I already like you more than I do Claire."

There was a little more laughter then. When it died down, it was followed by that silence that typically follows a group getting together for the first time, everyone trying to think of something to break the ice. Claire, known as a failed icebreaker, tried her hand at it anyway. "So, you're from around here?"

"Yeah," Dani answered.

"Cool," Vanessa said. "There used to be another camp besides ours. Camp Espantosa. On the other side of the lake from our camp. Which would make it here. It closed down after what happened one summer a few years back."

33

Dani leaned in. "What happened?"

Vanessa looked at the ground for a moment and then at Lindsey and Claire. Dani noticed an odd look in their eyes. Especially Vanessa's. "Ah, only stories, you know? Probably not even true."

"But what were the stories about?" Dani inquired.

"About a girl whose time at camp didn't end so well because . . ." Dani waited for Vanessa to say more, but apparently, they were moving on from that subject. "I'm glad you decided to stay with us."

"Well, when you consider the alternative, I suppose I made the better choice."

"Don't be so sure," Lindsey said. She then looked around the clearing. "Hey, where's the cooler?"

The girls looked around. It was nowhere to be found. Lindsey turned to Claire. "Where's the cooler, Claire?"

Claire looked nervous. "I don't know. You started carrying it after Vanessa scared me when she was pretending that she was going to kill us."

Vanessa turned to Lindsey. "And you put it down by the lake when you went to get your smelly feet clean."

Lindsey nodded. "Ah, yes. I do remember doing that." She then turned to Claire. "You should go get it."

"Why me? You were the one who forgot it."

"Yes, but remember, I was carrying it for you. So . . ."

Claire considered the point. "That . . . is fair," she said, sitting very still on the log, fearful of what she knew she would hear next.

Vanessa walked over to her. "Go get it, Claire. It's not that far." Claire looked up at Vanessa, who was standing over her.

"By myself? But I'm afraid of . . . stuff."

"I can help you if you want," Dani said.

Claire brushed off the offer of help quickly. "No, that's okay. I can go by myself, I guess."

"Still afraid of me?"

"I'm a terrible liar, so yeah. But just a little . . ."

"It's okay. If it were me, I would be too."

Claire smiled. "Besides, since Lindsey gave me a break carrying it, I feel refreshed and ready to finish the job." She got up. "Be back soon." And she headed back to the lake, trying to act like she wasn't completely terrified (she was) and hoping she could remember where Lindsey had left the cooler (she didn't).

The three remaining girls sat there in silence, listening to the forest sounds. There was a gentle breeze that left a nice chill in the air. The insects could be heard close to the edge of the clearing on all sides. It was almost as if they were spectators to whatever the night was going to lead to with the four girls. The sound of crows cawing was so loud at times that it drowned out all other sounds. Vanessa and Lindsey didn't acknowledge it, but Dani looked up and smiled a little.

"You like those birds?" Lindsey asked incredulously, still staring at Dani.

"Yeah," Dani replied. "They were my mom's favorite birds."

"Said no one ever until this moment." Dani shrugged. "They're getting on my nerves," Lindsey said, throwing a rock into the sky. "And you know what else is getting on my nerves?" She got up and stretched. "Being cold. I'll get the fire started." She walked over to the edge of the woods and started looking for sticks, leaving only Vanessa and Dani.

"So, you guys are having a picnic out here?" Dani asked.

Vanessa smiled. "Kind of." Lindsey came back, struggling with an armful of wood. "That was quick."

"Yep. There was a stack of logs sitting over there," Lindsey said, jerking her head toward the lake. "It was almost like it was waiting for us."

"Or it could've been left over from the camp," Dani said.

"I suppose." Lindsey moved to the center of their gathering space and dropped the logs down haphazardly. "Time to get this fire started." She knelt and started messing with the logs in no clear pattern. She stopped and then turned to Vanessa and Dani. "Either of you know how to get a fire started?"

"Did you bring the matches?" Vanessa asked.

"No."

"Then how were you planning on starting a fire?"

"I can do it," Dani said, standing up. She crossed to Lindsey, took the logs from her, and set them down on the ground right by where the old fires used to be. She walked over to some weeds and sticks that she had seen earlier. "This is kindling. We place it under the logs." As Vanessa and Lindsey, who had sat back down on their stumps, quietly watched on, Dani placed the kindling underneath the logs. She then turned to the girls. "Could I use one of your flashlights?" Lindsey handed her one. "Thanks."

"Are you like a Girl Scout or something?" Lindsey asked.

"No, my parents were . . . are . . . pretty outdoorsy. We lived in a cabin in the woods for a while. We weren't living off the earth or anything, but they taught me tons of stuff." Dani remembered how those three years were the best years of her life. Her dad spent his days painting outdoor scenes that were literally from out the back door, and she and her mom would hike until dark once she got home from work and then explore the creek in their backyard that stretched the entire length of their land. While she was recalling those memories, she walked around the edge of the woods looking for exactly what she knew was needed. After looking for a while, she saw them. Two perfect sticks. She reached down and picked them up, then turned back towards the girls. "These are perfect."

"Wait," Vanessa said. "You're going to start a fire with sticks?" Dani nodded. "I thought that was made up."

"Nope." Dani knelt and went to work rubbing the sticks together underneath the kindling. In mere minutes, she had a spark, then the kindling caught. She blew on it gently, and in no time, she had a small fire started. "It'll get bigger pretty soon. We'll need some more logs to keep it going."

"There's plenty of logs over where I got these," Lindsey said. "And if we run out, I imagine you can fashion an ax out of vines and butterfly remains."

"I wish," Dani said, laughing. "But my mom never got around to teaching me that." The three girls sat around the growing fire.

Vanessa turned to Dani. "This fire is awesome. You'll have to teach me how to do this sometime."

"I will," Dani said, trying to hide how happy that last statement made her.

At that moment, Claire came back, lugging the cooler and out of breath. Lindsey looked up at her.

"You ran the entire way, didn't you?"

"I did, and somehow, I managed to not get lost, not fall, and find the cooler."

"That is shocking," Lindsey said as she turned back to the fire. "We have a fire."

Claire faced the now blazing fire and instantly dropped the cooler. "A fire! We've never had a fire before. I mean, I know you guys said we would this time, but you say that every time, and we never had one before, so this . . . wow!"

"Dani made it," Vanessa said.

Claire turned to Dani, a shocked look covering her entire face. "You can make fire?"

Dani laughed at her expression. "Well, I didn't make it. I started it."

"With the logs I found, lest we forget," Lindsey added.

"Yes, Lindsey found the logs," Dani said, using a stick to move some of the logs around. The fire roared up even bigger than before.

Claire picked the cooler back up and brought it over to the campfire. Lindsey walked over and opened it up. The food, which had been stuffed in far past the maximum food occupancy level, exploded out of the cooler like a jack-in-the-box. Vanessa noticed Dani looking at the cooler rather suspiciously. Vanessa laughed. "It's not beer or anything like that."

"Nope. And the heroin is at the bottom," Lindsey said. Then she looked at Dani. "You know, the kind you keep in a cooler."

Dani smiled and shook her head. "I didn't think that."

"Of course you did – but we're not that kind of cliché teenagers. Except for the kind of cliché teenagers that steal because we did steal all this from camp," Lindsey said, reaching in and pulling out a can. "Here, have a can of some foul-tasting generic shit." She tossed the can to Dani, who caught it with one hand. Lindsey let out a low whistle and said, "Nice. These two losers can barely catch a cold."

"Nice joke, grandpa," Vanessa said, grabbing a soda.

"And I can too catch!" Claire said. Lindsey raised an eyebrow and tossed her a soda. It went through Claire's hands and hit her in the forehead. "Ow, jerk. Didn't say I could catch cans."

Lindsey grinned as she opened a drink. "Should've given you the chance to say that, I suppose."

The girls slowly sipped their sodas as the sounds of the woods and the light of the fire helped them all loosen up, and their chatter filled the night. They were talking and laughing and, for a moment, none of them had a care in the world. Not even Dani, who had had very few moments like this. Moments where she was part of something. Vanessa reached back in and started pulling out a variety of foods from the apparently bottomless cooler.

"You stole all of this?" Dani asked.

"If taking it from the camp cafeteria without asking is stealing, then yes," Vanessa answered.

"Oh," said Dani. She watched as the three girls started ripping various packages open and eating like they hadn't seen food in ages. "And you're not afraid of getting into trouble?"

"The time to be afraid of getting into trouble was when we were deciding whether or not to steal all the food. Once we decided and did it, well, the trouble will find us anyway, and Vanessa will use her undeniable charm to get us out of it, so why worry about it?" Lindsey said, noticing Dani watching them. It seemed like she wanted some of the food, but she wasn't eating any. "Dig in, Dani. You're part of us now." The food fell out of her mouth as she spoke, but Lindsey was unconcerned. "Besides, even if you didn't eat any, or steal it for that matter, we would say you did." That comment brought back an old memory, which Dani quickly buried. Lindsey noticed Dani's expression change. "I'm kidding. We'll blame it all on Claire. Now eat up!"

Dani smiled. She reached for a peanut butter and jelly sandwich, unwrapped it, and took a huge bite. She hadn't eaten for so long, and the sandwich was, well, a camp sandwich made with the cheapest stuff possible. But in this moment, as Dani looked around at the three girls she was sitting with, who wanted her there, the big fire blazing . . . it was the best sandwich ever. She wished her dad could be here in this moment. To see how happy she was.

Lindsey pulled her hand up from the cooler with a cookie. A look of disgust came over her face.

"Seriously, Vanessa. Oatmeal raisin cookies? I told you not to get any of these abominations."

"I like them," Vanessa said as she scarfed one down.

"You would," Lindsey said with disdain. She threw the cookie into the fire and settled for yet another bag of chips. As she sat down, she continued sharing her thoughts on the cookie.

"Those cookies are the worst. I thought you had taste. Oatmeal and raisins together in a cookie . . . what a stupid ass idea. Oh, look, we're healthy cookies but not really. We're just tasteless chocolate chip cookie wannabes."

"If they had feelings, I bet you would be hurting them right now," Vanessa said through mock tears.

"Good," Lindsey reached into the cooler and then threw another one into the fire. "Because they're dumb. Like iceberg lettuce." She sat back down on the log, shaking her head. She had hated oatmeal raisin cookies for as long as she could remember, with the main reason being that her grandmother, whom she despised, was convinced that they were her favorite and brought them for her every time she visited. She would also make Lindsey eat them in front of her every time. On some level, Lindsey figured Grandma knew she hated them but was punishing her because she wasn't the little God-fearing grandchild like her brother. Whatever, she was dead now, and Lindsey would never eat one of those stupid bastard cookies again.

Dani finished her sandwich. "So, there's food and drinks, and you came all the way out here for what? A late-night snack?"

"Can I tell her?" Claire said, jumping up and almost spilling her drink. Lindsey was about to say something, but Vanessa cut her off.

"Sure, why not."

Claire smiled. "Well, Dani, we do this kind of thing several times a summer. Usually not this far out . . ." She stopped to consider. "Never this far out, but Vanessa, our fearless and obsessive leader, wanted us here for a reason that only she has completely bought into at this point. Anyway, we come out here to tell ghost stories!"

"Well, Vanessa and I tell ghost stories. Claire tries and fails miserably," Lindsey said.

"Not this time. I've got the perfect story."

"We're sure you do," Vanessa said, laughing. Dani stared at the three of them. Vanessa caught her dumbfounded look. "What?"

"Seriously? You come all the way out here to tell ghost stories?"

"No one ever said we were cool," Lindsey said. "It's something we do to get away from camp and the other campers who don't appreciate how awesome we are."

"Yeah, we're like sisters," Claire added. She looked at Lindsey. "Yes, Lindsey, with me being the adopted one." Lindsey smiled at Claire, who had stolen her go-to joke. The girls laughed as Dani watched them. Then she laughed too.

"I mean, I guess it's cool and all," Dani said. "Little strange, but a cool strange." She turned to Vanessa. "So why here?"

"Oh, you'll find out later," Vanessa said, looking out in the direction of the lake.

Dani laughed uncomfortably. "That was loaded."

"Yep," Vanessa said. "And now that you're a part of us, you get to tell ghost stories too. If you want."

"Well, I'm not a big fan of ghost stories."

"Really?" Vanessa asked. Dani nodded. "Is it because they scare you?"

"Maybe. I mean, after my mom . . ." Dani grew silent.

"What?" said Claire.

"Never mind," Dani said, looking down.

"Oh, a secret," Lindsey said happily. "I'll get that out of you before the night ends."

"And maybe we'll get yours out of you, too. Because we know you have a big secret," Vanessa said, trying to shut Lindsey up. It worked. Lindsey stared a moment at Vanessa before dismissing her.

- - - - - - - - - -

Lindsey hated when Vanessa did that to her. Sure, she brought these things on herself by constantly making fun of other people and exposing their secrets, but that's who she was. Or the part she played. So it wasn't super fair for Vanessa to turn around and do to her what she did to others. Lindsey remembered a commandment from her biblical days that said exactly that, or something close. And Vanessa had started doing it a lot lately. Especially this year. Lindsey figured that it probably had something to do with the fact that Vanessa's parents paid for her to come to camp, something Vanessa jokingly brought up. All the time. And the way Vanessa said "big secret." Like she knew. Did she? She couldn't, because Lindsey never shared anything with anyone because people suck and can't be trusted. All of them. Including her. Sort of. Most of the time. Besides, if she told anybody, it wouldn't be Vanessa, the heartless wonder. It would be Claire because she was Claire. And Claire was . . . God, she couldn't even think about that in her mind. Stupid, stupid mind. Claire was different from her and Vanessa. More human. And like an abandoned puppy. That's what made Vanessa and Lindsey bring her into the group in the first place. They wanted to protect her. And yes, Lindsey did make fun of her all the time, but that was to toughen her up because she was so nice, and the vultures always take advantage of someone like her. Thus, Lindsey played the role of vulture to help her. Also because she was a vulture. Better to be the one picking apart than the one being picked apart. She saw a lot of Claire in this new girl, Dani. Maybe that's why she started to circle.

- - - - - - - - - -

"Are you sitting there thinking about your backstory, Lindsey, to keep from getting mad at me?" Vanessa asked.

Lindsey looked up at her. "You know me too well."

"Look, I didn't mean anything by it. I did it to shut you up before you Lindseyed the night." Lindsey merely stared at Vanessa, who could tell by the look she was getting that Lindsey was pissed but also that she wouldn't bring it up. Until later. "Are we good?"

Lindsey picked up another cookie and threw it at her. It hit her in the face. "Terrible to eat but wonderful to throw. And yes."

"Stop wasting the cookies because you don't like them!" A cookie smacked Claire in the face as well.

"Well, there's one for you too . . ." but before Lindsey could finish her sentence, she was hit by a sandwich. She looked in the direction it came from and saw Dani's smiling face.

"Dani?"

"Well, you did say I was part of the group, right?" Dani said, moving away from the cooler. "Plus, I've never thrown food at anyone before, and you seemed like a perfect first target."

"Thank you," Lindsey said, wiping peanut butter and jelly off her face. "By the way, well played taking the time to open the sandwich. It looks like you're the only one who hasn't been hit by food yet."

A bag of chips then landed by Dani's feet. The three girls looked at Claire, who smiled meekly.

"Potato chip bags don't fly that well." Claire continued looking at them and then calmly got up, walked over to the chips, picked them up, struggled to open them but eventually succeeded, and then dumped them on Dani's head. Then she turned around and walked back to her seat. The four girls looked at one another and laughed. Then they started throwing the rest of the food at each other.

After their food supply was exhausted, they looked at the mess they had made.

"Perhaps this wasn't the best use of our food," Vanessa said.

"Not to mention, this may be the first food fight that happened in real life," Lindsey said. A look of alarm came across her face. "I had a thought."

"Two firsts in one night. Wow."

Vanessa turned to Claire. "Make it three firsts. Claire with the burn. Nice." Claire smiled.

"Anyway," Lindsey continued, though clearly impressed, "with all this food lying around, should we worry about, I don't know, bears or something?"

A terrified look came over Claire's face. "Bears? There are bears here?"

"Oh, there are bears here," Lindsey said menacingly. "There are bears everywhere. Grizzly, brown . . . other bears I do not know the names of because my knowledge of bears is quite limited. But I do know one thing, Claire. They are all in these woods, and they love eating food that got scattered in a food fight. And then they like eating innocent girls who fear them. I mean, if you look behind you . . ."

Claire slowly turned, and Vanessa jumped at her, growling. Claire screamed and almost fell but Dani caught her. Claire turned to her.

"Thanks for catching me." Claire looked at Vanessa. "And how did you get behind me without me noticing?"

"Maybe I'm a ghost," Vanessa said, laughing and walking away. She turned back to Claire. "And there are no bears here. There are, however, ghosts." She faced Dani. "Which brings us back to you, Dani."

"What?"

"Well, you're not a fan of ghost stories, which we were talking about before we engaged in some random food fight. Anyway, you haven't heard or read one in a long time, I assume, if ever, and according to you, you're a little . . . or a lot scared of them. Which makes you exactly the person we're looking for." Dani looked at her, confused. "To tell ghost stories to. Scaring Claire is too easy, as you saw, so some new blood is exactly what we need. Especially tonight. I mean, look around you. The setting is perfect. Middle of the night, deep in the woods, an abandoned camping area that used to be a place of so much fun but has now gone silent, and of course, the lake, with a sordid past and dark water, night or day. You couldn't find a better place to get scared . . . to death, right?"

Dani shuffled nervously. "I suppose."

"You suppose?" Lindsey asked.

"Well, I mean, we were having so much fun and maybe we could do something different."

"Like shuffleboard?" Lindsey said mockingly.

"Or talk about our feelings?" Vanessa said. "Lindsey would be all over that."

"Oh!" Claire said, getting an idea. "What about we talk about our feelings while playing shuffleboard?"

Lindsey turned to Claire. "Shut up, Claire." She then turned to Vanessa. "I would love to talk about my feelings if I had any that I didn't suppress completely, but I don't." Then she turned to Dani. "And no, we are not going to talk about our feelings or play shuffleboard because we are here to tell ghost stories. If you don't want to hear the stories, we could go somewhere else and leave you here . . ."

Vanessa looked at her. "Why must everything lead to a threat of leaving?"

Lindsey shrugged. "I don't know. I figure going DEFCON 1 at the beginning limits discussion."

"I don't want you guys to leave anyway," Dani said. "I totally want to hear ghost stories. I mean, they're only stories after all."

"Well, most of them," Vanessa added.

Dani chose to ignore that last comment. "I'm not sure if I have one though."

"You have time," Lindsey said, standing up. "Because I'm going first."

"I thought I was first this time," Claire said.

"Why would you ever go first?" Lindsey asked, dismissing her.

"Because after last time, you said I could go first."

Lindsey looked at her for a moment and then walked over to her. She knelt in front of her rather dramatically, which caused Claire to make the "I know what's coming" face that Claire always made when Lindsey was about to mock her. "I don't remember that happening, dear Claire, but that doesn't mean it didn't happen." She touched Claire's head. "In there."

Claire was about to say something back when Vanessa, ready to start the night, said, "What's your story, Lindsey?"

Lindsey turned to Vanessa. "Yes, what is my story?" She stood up and placed the flashlight below her chin, casting a ghostly light on her face. "Once upon a time, in a nice, quaint neighborhood, where the houses were perfect, and the children played happily and safely in the streets, where the neighbors were always friendly, sharing casseroles, and . . ."

"Geez! Get to the story already," Vanessa said.

"It's called exposition, Vanessa. Which you would know if you could read," Lindsey said. "Anyway, in this delightful neighborhood, there was one house that didn't belong. A splotch on the otherwise perfect canvas. The house that everyone avoided and pretended didn't exist. Because of its dark history and the fact that it was said to be haunted by . . . the Lady in White."

CHAPTER 5

Lindsey's Story

The two-story Victorian house had sat high on the only real hill in Willow Parks for years, slowly succumbing to the wears of time. Gated and boarded up, with very few windows that remained intact, it cast a long shadow on an otherwise idyllic neighborhood. Neighbors who had to walk by the house would hurry past it, always looking the other way, and the children were never allowed to play near it. Though the people tried as hard as they might, the house could not be forgotten because in Willow Parks, this was the house that didn't belong. The place where it happened: 12 children caught up in a fire from which they weren't allowed to escape. Or at least that's how the story went. And as the years passed, the story has become darker and darker, invading the dreams of the children and adults who live there now. Children have claimed to be visited by her. Floating above them at night. Threatening to burn them if they aren't good little girls and boys. Like a modern-day Santa Claus. Their parents say they have nothing to worry about. She's dead and can't hurt anyone anymore.

Yet the stories remain. And the legend grows. The legend . . . of the Lady in White.

- - - - - - - - - -

"Here it is," Hayley said, pointing her flashlight at the rusted gate that held the target of their quest. "Pretty crappy looking. No one has lived here in over 70 years."

Alexis edged closer to the gate and looked up at the house, perched high on the tallest hill she had ever seen. She noticed that the house somehow managed to look both on the edge of collapsing and completely indestructible at the same time. "If people are so freaked out by it, why haven't they torn it down?"

"My dad said they tried over and over again, but something always happened. Like the house was protected or something," Derek said, adjusting his glasses and hanging slightly behind Alexis and Hayley. "Equipment broke, horrible storms came out of nowhere, people got hurt, and one guy . . ." Derek trailed off as if he was afraid to say what happened.

Alexis turned to him. "What?" Hayley laughed and cut in.

"He got cut to bits," Hayley said. "Like a chainsaw went crazy on him. The story was that he fell, and then the chainsaw fell on the wrong spot. Him. Ripped his body to shreds. But here's the thing: the unpublished story was that the guy started cutting himself up while a figure, a woman, watched from inside of the house, smiling. After that, they decided 'screw this' and boarded everything up. They then put this lovely gate around the place to keep people out."

Derek walked over to Alexis. "And they were right to keep people out. You shouldn't do this, Alexis. I have a bad feeling."

Alexis smiled. "I think I'll be all right. It's only a house."

Hayley looked at Derek. "Besides, Derek, the only reason you have a bad feeling about it is because you have a 'good feeling' for Alexis."

Everyone well knew that Derek did, in fact, have a "good feeling" for Alexis. He had casually, yet very seriously, told Alexis and Hayley that very fact over lunch one day. Then, of course, Kyle, the boy who made Derek's school life a living hell, announced it to the cafeteria, which at the time was filled by almost the entire school. The response, however, was not the one Kyle had expected. Everyone looked up for a moment and then went back to eating whatever delicious awfulness was being served that day. Kyle was shocked as well – until Hayley, in a full-on Hayley manner, explained that everyone already knew. And they did. Everyone but Alexis, who had stared at Derek for a moment, trying to figure out what to say. But she didn't have to worry because Derek, now covered in his lunch which Kyle had dumped on him while trying to cover up his embarrassment, told Alexis that he was never going to act on those feelings unless one day she returned them. If she ever did.

"That's part of it," Derek said nonchalantly. "But the other part is, unlike you, Hayley, I've studied the supernatural in a quite in-depth manner along with this house. Based on my research, my bad feelings are quite warranted because this is not only a house. This place . . . is evil."

"It is not," Hayley said. "I don't even think it looks that bad. I mean, when you look past the fire damage, the rotting wood, the peeling paint, broken windows, a couple of bullet holes, what appears to be blood splatter . . . a lot of blood splatter, and . . ."

Hayley dropped her flashlight and suddenly jumped back from the gate. "Did you see that?"

Alexis and Derek turned towards the house.

"See what?" Derek asked.

"In the upstairs window, on the right side, by that giant hole."

"What was it?" Alexis asked, aiming her flashlight at the window, illuminating it faintly.

"It looked like a lady. A lady in white."

"Stop messing around, Hayley."

"I swear to God, I'm not lying!"

"To be honest, Alexis, she might have seen it," said Derek. "Tortured souls do tend to stay where they died. And she was wearing a white dress, according to the legend. That would give credence to the constant sightings that have been recorded."

"And the festive chainsaw chop-up," Hayley said happily. Alexis turned to her.

"There is seriously something demented about you, so we're clear. Anyway, it was probably the drapes or something," Alexis said, hoping she sounded surer than she was. She was, by nature and upbringing, a skeptic of anything that couldn't be proven. And despite constant so-called "sightings," the existence of the supernatural had never been proven. Alexis's parents told her that people wanted to believe in the supernatural because that would give them hope that there was something after they died. That being said, as she looked at the house, fear was growing inside of her, and a quick glance at Derek showed the same thing. Her anxiety, which had grown worse as she had gotten older, was now bubbling up. "So, for the sake of a good story and to delay this as long as possible, who is this Lady in White anyway?"

"How do you not know this story?" Hayley asked, sitting down and leaning on the fence, her back to the house. She pulled out a bag of chips and opened them.

"I don't know," Alexis said, sitting down beside her and taking a chip. "I guess I haven't lived here long enough to get the goods."

"Well, Derek knows more of the story because he finds these kinds of things fun."

"I do not find them fun, as I've told you many times. I find them important," Derek said, now standing slightly behind a tree. "So I can save others. And myself, if needed."

"Great. Now stop hiding behind that tree and come sit with us and have some chips."

"I'm not hiding! And who has a snack in a front of a house where 12 kids were murdered?"

"Us?" Hayley said. "Or me. Besides, if you don't come over here and tell the story, I'm going to tell it and will no doubt get something wrong that will lead to Alexis's inevitable death."

Alexis turned to her. "Thanks for that."

"You're welcome."

Hayley and Alexis then both screamed as Derek appeared in front of them and sat down.

"Holy crap, Derek!"

"What? Oh, I've learned to move quietly in case someone's after me. Anyway, I'll tell the story, but I'll need you two to sneak a peek at the house now and then just to be safe."

"Will do, dork," Hayley said, laughing.

"Anyway," he began, ignoring the slight, "the Lady in White's real name was Abigail Caldwell, and the house behind you is the place where she was born, lived, and died. As a matter of fact, she apparently never left. Once she got older, she turned it into an orphanage."

"Why would she do that?" Alexis asked, grabbing another chip.

"To murder children, clearly," Hayley offered.

"No, that's not why," said Derek. "From what I've been able to determine, her original intentions were good. Because her childhood sucked so bad, she wanted to help other children avoid having a childhood like hers."

"By killing them."

Derek turned to Hayley. "Stop it, Hayley. She wasn't always bad."

"How do you know? Were you like childhood chums or something? Sharing milkshakes? One cup, two straws? Or maybe one straw?"

"No, clearly we were not. She is quite older then I am – and I'm lactose intolerant. The reason I said she wasn't always bad is because people don't normally start off bad. They start off normal as babies, and then stuff happens that makes them who they are. The whole nature versus nurture thing. And in her case, what happened to Abigail as a kid was too much to overcome."

"What happened to her as a kid?"

"Her parents were really old school and strict. Ultra-religious too. And on top of that, they were into some odd stuff. Cult-like. Never let her out of the house. No school, no friends, no nothing. Except for her dolls."

"Creepy."

"Yeah. As she got older, she would either play with them

or look out the attic window, where she could watch the other children play. A lot of the older people who've lived here all their lives talk about seeing the 'little girl in the window.' But when her parents caught her doing that – or anything that they decided wasn't proper – they would lock her in a basement closet for days."

"Oh, man," Alexis said. "How do they know what happened inside the house if they were so . . ."

"Bam, I can answer this one," Hayley said happily. "They had a nosy housekeeper who was the town gossip."

"That's right," Derek said. "Anyway, when Abigail was in her twenties, her parents died under suspicious circumstances. It was ruled accidental, but the bodies were found in the very closet where they used to lock Abigail in as a child. But I think people were glad to see them gone, and they felt sorry for Abigail, so no one questioned anything. They simply turned their heads and went on with their lives."

"A few months later," continued Hayley, "Abigail turned her house into an orphanage. The townsfolk here supported it because they could see that Abigail was trying, and there . . . were a lot of orphans here? I don't know. Anyway, they helped redo the house and made sure that she got the right paperwork and stuff."

"And they did all of this even though they knew something was off about Abigail. I mean, how could it not be?" said Derek, who seemed to be relaxing as he told the story. "Her childhood was so messed up. For a while, everything seemed to be going well. She would take the children around town, and I think she even joined some clubs and stuff. Never took them to church though. She was apparently done with that. But everything else was fine. Until the rumors started."

"Rumors?"

"Yep, rumors," Hayley said as she took a bag of cookies, chocolate chip, not oatmeal raisin, out and tossed it on the ground for everybody to share. "See, kids from her house started acting weird, scared, you know? Certain kids who used to be loud and goofy became sullen, not saying a word. And bruises started showing up on them. Then . . . poof . . . no one saw them anymore. They didn't see Abigail anymore either. They'd send cops to check on them, but they never really found anything, and the kids wouldn't talk. Everybody started getting scared that she'd finally lost it and that the kids were in serious jeopardy. But on the night they came to take the kids away . . ."

"The fire broke out and . . ."

"I wanted to tell the fire part!" Hayley interrupted.

"You don't even know the fire part," Derek protested.

"Yes, I do," she said. "In 1933, a fire broke out in the house, and all the kids died. Burnt to a crisp. Like the chicken Derek's mom makes. To top it off, the fire department found Abigail rocking on the porch as her house and the children burned and screamed behind her."

"Holy crap," Alexis said.

"I guess you do know what happened. And my mom's chicken is not always burnt. I mean, most of the time it is, but still," Derek said.

"What happened to Abigail? Did she get arrested?"

"No," he said. "Well, sort of. The fire was ruled an accident, but she was committed to . . ."

"The nut house," Hayley broke in. Derek frowned at her and shook his head, then waved for her to continue. "A couple of months after that, after being deemed somewhat sane, Abigail was released, and she moved back into the charred remains of her glorious childhood home. And a few weeks later, she was found dead! Locked away in that same basement closet. Bloodied and burned and wearing a white dress."

"What happened?" Alexis asked.

Derek shook his head. "No one knows."

"Bull crap," Hayley said, standing up. "My dad said that there were some townsfolk who wanted their own kind of justice. And they took it. Made her pay." She turned towards the house. "And now, she haunts her house. Think, Alexis, maybe you'll be able to join her."

"I think I'll pass," Alexis said, mustering some bravado. "Besides, ghosts aren't real. Abigail Caldwell is dead and buried. Or at least dead. There's nothing in the house now but cobwebs, old furniture, and bad memories. Nothing else." Alexis zipped up her jacket a little even though it was a warm night. "So I go in and what?"

"Take one item that belonged to her. In and out in no time."

"And it can be anything?"

"Nothing lame," Hayley said. "Try to get one of her dolls."

"No!" Derek said, a little louder than he intended. He lowered his voice, almost to a whisper. "Her spirit could be inside of it." He turned to Alexis. "You know what, Alexis, don't do it. This is a really bad idea."

"A bet's a bet, Derek," Hayley said as she got out some batteries from her backpack. She turned to Alexis and handed them to her. "Take these and put them in your flashlight. They're brand new."

Alexis took them. "Thanks."

Derek began pacing and talking to himself. Hayley stepped in front of him. "Are you losing it? Because I feel like you're losing it." Derek stared at Hayley for a moment and then walked over to Alexis, who had finished putting the batteries in her flashlight. Derek took Alexis by the shoulders and stared at her. Alexis looked at him.

"Yes?"

"Please don't go into that house."

Alexis smiled. "I'll be fine. You worry too much. I'll be back before you know it."

"No, you won't be. This doesn't feel right." He took a deep breath. "I'll go in your stead." Alexis looked at him. "In your place."

"You didn't make the bet."

"I know, but I'll be more likely to make it out alive."

"Because you're a man?"

Derek, despite himself, laughed loudly. "God, no. I'm the least manly of the three of us. It's just, with your anxiety being what it is, putting yourself in a situation such as this is not a good thing, and since I know a lot about the supernatural, I might be a little more prepared if something does happen. Besides, I know we're not dating, and we're only friends right now, but if you go in there and die then I'll never know how you actually felt."

It was true. Alexis had never responded yea or nay to her actual feelings about Derek. And the funny thing was, despite his completely dorkish ways, she did like him. That way. A lot. She was going to tell him tonight, until she'd lost the bet and the three of them had ended up spending their Halloween at a dilapidated old house instead of at Hayley's watching musicals.

"That's super sweet, but I'll do it, and I'll be fine." She smiled. "And about the other thing . . ." Alexis took a deep breath and then kissed Derek on the cheek, causing him to turn a shade of red that the world had never seen. She leaned in, and then Derek gave her a tight hug as if it would be the last time he would ever see her. Derek, perhaps realizing that he was making this awkward, pulled back.

"Godspeed, then."

Hayley looked at Derek. "Wow. You are so smooth."

Alexis, feeling braver and something else that she couldn't quite place, walked to the gate and tried to open it. It was locked.

"Can't get in. The gate is locked up, and there is no way that I'm climbing that fence."

"Too bad," Derek said. "Guess we have to go back to Hayley's. I've got a hankering for some singing in the rain."

"Stop right there," Hayley said, pulling something out of her bag. "Never leave home without it." Alexis noticed what it was.

"You have a lock picking bag?"

"Several. Never know when . . ." The lock popped. "It's like Mama always said: 'Baby girl, you must know how to pick a lock.'" Hayley stood up. "In you go."

As Alexis stared at the gate and then at the house that loomed at her from seemingly miles away, fear started coursing through her. There was a voice inside of her telling her that she was about to make the worse decision of her life. She laughed a little and did what she normally did: ignored whatever she feared and did it anyway. She pushed on the gate.

It didn't move.

She pushed harder, but nothing happened. "It won't open."

"Clearly," Hayley said. "Watch out." Hayley moved Alexis aside and sized up the gate. Derek crossed over to them.

"What are you doing?"

Hayley kicked at the gate as hard as she could. The gate door didn't move, but as they watched, the fence surrounding the door fell like dominoes, leaving only the gate door standing. They stood there for a moment, and then Hayley turned to Alexis.

"Well," said Hayley. "You can go in now."

Alexis nodded. "That was a really powerful kick there."

"Yes, it was. Good luck. We're rooting for you not to die."

"Cool." Alexis zipped up her coat even tighter and doubled-checked her flashlight. She turned to Derek and smiled. He smiled back. Alexis knew that the first thing she was going to do when she got back was to apologize to him for not being honest about her feelings and see where it went. She turned to Hayley, who gave her the "hurry-it-up" gesture. "Charming," Alexis muttered.

Then she turned and slowly picked her way over the fallen fence, beginning the long journey to the house as Hayley and Derek watched her go.

"It's only a house. It's only a house," Alexis said to herself, trying to convince herself of something she was starting not to believe.

- - - - - - - - - -

She watched the girl from her attic window. It had been so long since anyone had come to visit. So, so long. The last time was when those hateful people had tried to destroy the only thing she had left. And she'd made sure those people paid for what they did. But this girl could be different. She could be the one. The one to help her finally be free. And she deserved to be free – because, after all, she wasn't bad. She had done bad things, but only because bad things had been done to her. This girl, this, Alexis, was sure to understand. She was coming to take something, to steal it, so maybe she would be willing to give something as well. Abigail was sure she would. She had to make sure the house was ready.

The walk to the house's steps felt incredibly long to Alexis. It seemed that no matter how many steps she took, the house never got any closer. It had rained for the last several nights, so the ground was super saturated and muddy. With each step, she felt that she was moments away from falling and sliding back down the hill.

She paused for a moment and looked up at the house. It was amazing how huge it was. When Alexis passed it riding her bike on the way home from school every day, it looked like just an abandoned house, but seeing it up close like this, at night, well, it didn't exactly lessen the sense of foreboding that was spreading throughout her. She also couldn't believe that it was still standing. She noticed where the fire had done the most damage, an upstairs window closest to the park. That room looked almost hollowed out. *That must have been where the kids' bodies were discovered,* Alexis thought. She also saw signs of the attempts to tear the house down: large holes along the walls as if they'd been hit with a sledgehammer. Alexis looked down and saw where it looked as if they had tried to dig out the foundation of the house in the hopes that it would collapse. It didn't. Though it looked like it could at any time.

Then she saw them. Inches away from her.

Children. But not children from today. Children from long ago. Standing there. Staring at her. Well, staring was not possible. Because they had no eyes.

And then the bodies disintegrated in front of her.

Alexis screamed and shut her eyes.

"Are you all right?" she heard Derek yell. Alexis opened her eyes and looked where the children were before. They were gone, and she realized that somehow, she was standing at the front door of the house.

"Alexis!"

She turned to her friends. "I'm good. I . . . uh . . . got bit by a snake." *Bit by a snake? That's what she came up with?* She decided to go in before they could ask any more questions. She turned back towards the door, ready to open it. But she didn't have to worry about that.

As Alexis watched, the door slowly opened by itself.

- - - - - - - - - -

"Well, took forever, but she's at the house. Let's go," Hayley said.

"Did she say she was bit by a snake?" Derek asked.

"No, she said she stepped on a rake. Probably." Hayley turned around and began to walk off. Derek grabbed her arm.

"Wait, where are you going? We have to wait for Alexis to come back."

"I'm going trick-or-treating at a few close houses."

"You're too old for trick-or-treating."

Hayley looked at him, offended. "How dare you bring that up again! I've already told you that you are never too old for trick-or-treating. You can come with me if you want."

"I don't want to. Alexis won't be in there long, and she may have been bitten by a snake, so I'm staying."

"Cool, but I'm going trick-or-treating."

Derek sighed. "I guess I'll wait here by myself then."

"Guess you will. I promise I'll be right back. I've got a hankering for some chocolate." Hayley started to leave but then turned back. "You want me to get you anything?"

"Maybe a toothbrush if someone's giving those out. Mine is getting a little old. Soft bristle though."

Hayley stared at him incredulously. "You are so freaking lame." She started to walk away, then looked back. "By the way, congrats on Alexis liking you. I guess I'm now the third wheel, which has always been my dream." Hayley laughed and turned away again. "See you in a few," she tossed over her shoulder as she walked away.

"Yep," Derek said, sitting down to keep watch on the house that Alexis had entered, hoping beyond hope that she wouldn't end up dead. That she would be fine. There were so many things that could happen inside a house like that, even if there wasn't a supernatural entity. Which there was. Of that, Derek was sure. He only hoped that Abigail wasn't out for vengeance. That she had somehow come to peace with her life. Or her afterlife, as it were. That was doubtful, but that was what Derek had to hang on to. Because he liked Alexis. And she liked him. She liked him! The thought made him quite giddy because no one had ever "liked him" liked him. When she got out, they might be a couple. And then later, go to college, graduate school, get high-paying and life-changing jobs, and then get married and have three children. Or as many as she wanted. The perfect life.

If Alexis did not die. The thought of Alexis dying made him shudder and forced his daydreaming to a halt. It almost made him go in. But he didn't. Whether it was his own fear of the house or worse, the fear of being considered a sexist, Derek couldn't quite be sure. Or maybe it was neither of those things. Maybe he didn't want his first act after finding out that Alexis liked him to be doubting her ability and making her think he thought she needed saving. This was getting way too complicated, so Derek put all his focus on looking for signs of trouble coming from the Caldwell house. He watched as Alexis stood on the threshold, just outside the open door.

If there was any trouble, Derek would rush in and hope he knew as much as he thought he did.

- - - - - - - - - -

Alexis took a tentative step, which took her barely inside the house. She shone her flashlight in various directions, not to get a layout of the room or anything, but more to see if something would suddenly jump out at her and perhaps kill her. Fortunately, Alexis discovered no murderous lurking presence other than the overwhelming sadness that permeated every part of the house. Physically, though, it was only an old, old house that had been through a fire. She turned around to let her friends know that she was okay. She stepped back halfway out the door and looked out, only to see Hayley walking away and Derek sitting down, watching the house.

"Oh, Derek." She waved to him, and he waved back. She imagined that Hayley had probably decided to go trick-or-treating because earlier she had given them the pleasure of a long rant about how she would never be too old to go trick-or-treating.

Alexis walked back inside the house and looked at the door for a moment, thankful that it didn't do anything creepy like slam shut once she got inside. No horror movie clichés here. Except for the disintegrating children and the door opening slowly by itself. No explanation for the children, but the door could've been opened by the wind. She had walked a bit further in when she heard something creaking. Alexis quickly turned back and pointed her flashlight at the door. The door that was now slowly closing. She watched it, fighting back the growing concern which would soon lead to anxiety if left unchecked, telling herself there was a draft inside the house that was causing the door to close.

Then the lock on the door turned and locked.

"Well, I guess that rules out the wind. And the lack of horror movie clichés."

Alexis decided she'd had enough. She went to the door and

tried to unlock it, but it wouldn't budge. She turned harder and harder, but it was as if she were fighting against a force that was determined to keep her there. She grabbed the doorknob with both hands, finding it hot to the touch. Burning, actually.

"Ow!" Alexis jumped back and looked at her hands. Her skin was bubbling up from the heat from the doorknob. The smell of burning flesh filled her nostrils. She screamed in pain, but then she noticed scratches and handprints on the door. Tiny handprints, and scratches as if someone were trying to get out. Not someone. Many little someones.

Alexis looked down at her hands. They were no longer burning. Then she looked back to the door.

The handprints and scratches were gone.

She took a deep breath to steady herself. "Everything is fine, Alexis. Your imagination is getting the best of you, that's all."

The self-locking door flashed in her mind. "Well, not everything is my imagination." She paused. "Which may mean that nothing is my imagination." She shut down that thought and began walking down the hall, determined not to "explore" this house too much, just to get something and then get out.

The hallway at the entrance showed few signs of the fire, mostly age and disrepair. Alexis noticed lots of pictures hanging on the walls. Most were askew, some were barely hanging on, and some had already met their fate by crashing to the floor. Alexis stopped and looked at them. They were like class photos. Or orphanage photos, she supposed. Each one was marked with the date it was taken and showed the children in the orphanage. And right smack in the middle of each one was Abigail Caldwell. Alexis noticed that in the very first picture, dated 1923, Abigail looked young and even pretty. Almost happy. So did her kids. Everyone was nicely dressed, and if Alexis didn't know this was an orphanage, she would've sworn that it was an actual family picture.

But maybe they were a family. The one Abigail never had.

As she went down the row of pictures, something changed. It was gradual at first, but the changes were more pronounced in the later years. Abigail looked older and angrier in each one, and the kids stared blankly at the camera. Like they were dead. Or empty. And the number of kids started decreasing. Maybe they were adopted, Alexis thought hopefully. Something told her that wasn't true, though.

She got to the place where the last picture was supposed to hang. There was a small label with the date: April 6th, 1933. Wait . . . that was the same year as the fire. Alexis pointed her flashlight down and saw that the picture had fallen. She carefully reached down and got it, pushed the broken glass aside, and took a good look.

Alexis supposed she would've gasped if she were the kind of girl who gasped at seeing truly disturbing things. And this was disturbing.

Where there had once been 20 kids, there were now only 12 . . . and they looked terrified. They were smiling in a special way that screamed to Alexis that they were facing their executioner and that executioner had yelled moments before the picture was taken, "Smile for the picture, or I'll make sure you never smile again."

Caldwell wasn't in this picture. Alexis assumed she was the one taking it. She was about to put the picture down when she noticed how the kids were dressed. They weren't dressed like kids anymore. More like . . . dolls. And they all had bright blush on their cheeks, and their hair was plastered down. Even the girls.

"Well, that's certainly not unsettling."

Then she heard it.

The laughter and whispers of children.

The noise was faint, but it was there. Well, not there. More like everywhere. Inside every room. The walls. Even inside her head.

Alexis had never been a huge fan of horror movies because she always felt that the characters made horrible choices: splitting up when they shouldn't, hiding in a place that screamed "this is where you are going to die," or exploring a sound that they had no business exploring.

Which, unfortunately, Alexis found herself doing as she walked to where she thought the sounds were coming from the loudest, which even in the moment seemed like a horrible idea.

"Guess now I understand."

As she walked deeper into the house, the children's laughter and whispers grew louder and louder. She rationalized that perhaps the children were trapped here and needed help. And they were asking for that help by . . . laughing and whispering at her? That didn't make any sense. Wait. Now she knew what was going on. Why didn't she think of that first? She had even watched her walk off.

She stopped moving and looked around. "Very funny, Hayley. Very funny." It had to be her.

Only it wasn't, and Alexis knew it. Hayley could never have made it up here in time. Whatever was laughing and whispering was here inside the house with her, and she had to find out what it was. She started walking again and soon reached the end of the foyer. Straight ahead was the kitchen, to her left a doorway with stairs that led down to the basement, a place Alexis had no intention of going near. The noise wasn't coming from there anyway, thank God, so no need to even consider going down there. The laughter suddenly stopped, and only the whispers remained. Alexis listened closely but couldn't make out what was being said. One thing she now knew though was where the whispering was coming from. After the laughter had stopped, so had the idea that it was coming from various places. Now it was only coming from one. And the whispers were growing louder and louder. She turned and saw the entrance to what she thought had to be the living room. Or perhaps it was considered a parlor? Not that Victorian room nomenclature mattered much at the moment. With her flashlight held firmly in front of her, casting a light that somehow created more shadows than light, she walked into the living room/parlor thing.

When she entered, the whispering stopped. This was where it was coming from, though, because the remains of the sounds still echoed in this spacious room. Alexis scanned it, noticing that she was in the back of the room. For the most part, it looked like what she imagined any old burned-out old house that everyone was terrified to enter would look like, including what appeared to be blood covering the floor and cut rope hanging from the rafters.

"Pleasant," Alexis said aloud.

When she moved her flashlight off the floor, she saw them. All of them.

Dolls.

All over the room. Set up as if they were on some bizarre playdate. And they were all pointed in her direction. Alexis gasped and then tried to move to a place that was doll-less. She hoped that the dolls' heads were not all turning to follow her. She didn't want to check but found she couldn't stop herself. She found no relief in the fact that not all of them had.

She finally found a place in the corner of the room and faced the wall to prepare herself because, and Alexis had never told anyone besides her parents this before, she was deathly afraid of dolls. Of all types. Even the soft ones. She wasn't sure when it started or why, but she did remember ruining Christmas when she was seven. Her grandmother had given her a new doll, and she'd started yelling and screaming about how terrible it was. That was bad enough, but then . . . Alexis had grabbed the doll and thrown it into the fire.

That marked the day that Alexis was no longer Grandmother's favorite.

And now, she was in a room surrounded by dolls that belonged to perhaps a deranged killer. Awesome. And these dolls were real enough, looking with their acrylic faces to be almost human – but not quite. As Alexis felt her heart begin to race, she swore that the dolls were all looking at her in their smug Victorian way. Were they the ones that were laughing and whispering?

"No, stupid, they're dolls. They can't laugh."

She forced herself to turn away, and she screamed again. Eyes that hadn't been on her now were. Not all, but enough. And even though she didn't want to see, she knew that being alone in the dark with head-turning dolls would be even worse. Her flashlight going dark in this horror hell place was the last thing she needed to happen. Thank God it didn't.

Oh, wait.

"Are you freaking kidding me?" Alexis said, now standing in a terrifying house surrounded by dolls as her flashlight flickered once and went dark. "Seriously?"

She wanted to run, but for whatever reason, she didn't. Well, she knew why. Running with her current lack of visibility would undoubtedly lead to her falling, hurting herself, and getting pounced upon by all those stupid dolls.

"My God, I'm becoming Derek." She tried to laugh at that, but it came out like her Uncle Leo, a guy who had made smoking cigars his profession.

In the darkness, Alexis focused on her breathing as she tried to slow her rapidly beating heart. What did her mom suggest when her anxiety kicked in? Self-talk. Right. She had never tried it before, but her mom, another sufferer of panic attacks, swore by it. So, as she took breaths, Alexis attempted to have a delightful conversation with herself.

"You're okay, Alexis. It's only an old house. An old, dusty, decrepit house. There's nothing to fear. Well, besides the self-closing and locking door and the dolls that are currently surrounding you and trying to steal your soul. And, oh, the laughing and whispering dead children."

She felt like her self-talk technique needed work. Her anxiety was growing to the dangerous level that her mom had calmly warned her about. She took a deep breath and slowly started moving toward the back of the room, looking for the door.

"We are going to slowly make our way through the door and

back into the hallway, Alexis. There is nothing to be . . ." She bumped into something.

"Mama."

"Dammit," Alexis squeaked, jumping back and falling over a table of some sort. "Ow." She slowly got up and noticed that she had tweaked her ankle, her "trick ankle" as her Uncle Leo said every time she started limping. Fortunately, the crashing to the floor had caused her flashlight to come back on.

The "Mamas" continued and Alexis, struggling to control her breath, noticed that the voice had a very doll-like quality. She pointed her flashlight in the direction of the noise and saw that it was one of those old cloth dolls with the pull string. She avoided asking herself who pulled the string.

"Well, thank God for that." Alexis gingerly moved to what she thought was the exit from the room and paused. "Maybe I should take a doll. There are about a billion of them. I'm sure that a dead woman wouldn't miss . . ."

The cat's meow stopped her.

"Oh, hey kitty, kitty." She felt something rub against her leg. Alexis loved cats, and she felt her heart rate instantly slow down. She knelt, half expecting that the cat would be missing an eye and covered in blood. And perhaps dead.

It wasn't. Well, it was missing an eye, but Alexis found the gray tabby adorable, and she needed the company. She gently petted the attention-craving cat. A small smile crossed Alexis's face as the cat purred loudly.

"Well, it looks like it's you and me, kitty. Do you have a name?" She found a tag on the cat's collar. "Tippy. That's a great name." Then Alexis had a great idea. "Tippy, how about if you're the thing I take out of this scary house? My house is way nicer." Tippy's one eye narrowed as she looked over Alexis's shoulder. The cat growled and arched her back. "Or not. I mean, if you're happy here, I could . . ."

Tippy started hissing and backing away.

"What is it?" Tippy ran away. "I'm thinking something bad." Alexis got up and tried to find the cat. She scanned the room, finally spotting her hiding underneath a dresser of some sort. On top of it was an old phonograph. Alexis walked over to the dresser and knelt in front of the terrified cat.

"It's okay, girl. You're okay. Come here, and let's get out of here."

Alexis reached for her and was greeted by a hiss and a sharp claw to her hand.

"Ow!" Alexis said for the second time in this godforsaken house. She dropped the flashlight, which stayed on. Alexis picked it up as Tippy took off again, shining it on her hand. It was quite an impressive gash, bleeding badly. "Great. Now I probably have feline leukemia. I have to get out of here before I bleed to death." She grabbed a random doll and started for the door.

And then everything happened at once.

Her flashlight went out.

Again.

The phonograph came to life and started playing charmingly old-timey, sinister music that Alexis couldn't imagine at any time would *not* be frightening.

And then the children's laughter started again, followed instantly by the onset of another panic attack.

"Screw this."

Alexis started running to the hallway, which she'd seen before the flashlight went out. She was almost there when the door separating her from her freedom, one she hadn't even known was there, slammed shut.

Alexis stared at the door. "I have to get out of here."

"Oh, I don't think that will be a problem."

Alexis stopped cold as she heard the voice behind her. This could not be a good thing. Her flashlight came back on, and it could be debated whether that was a good thing or not as well. Alexis took a deep breath and slowly turned around.

There she was. Standing in front of her. Alexis almost passed out at that moment but somehow remained standing. The figure, a lady, was dressed in an ancient white dress that was torn and dirty. There was a stab wound to her chest. She wasn't wearing shoes, and her feet looked as if they had been branded. Alexis stared at her face and saw a line across it, a cut, right below her left eye. And then she saw the wound around her neck. Whoever, or whatever, killed her had wanted her dead. Alexis's thoughts were cut short when the figure slowly walked, perhaps floated, towards her and her trembling self.

The woman stopped when she was inches away. Alexis noticed that the music and laughing had both stopped, but when, she couldn't say. Then the figure spoke.

"Did you come to play?"

Her voice was soft, childlike, and oddly hopeful. Alexis found she had lost the ability to speak, which seemed logical, considering she was face-to-face with a ghost.

"I asked you if you had come to play." This time the tone was less childlike and more . . . threatening.

"Uh . . . no." Alexis managed to get out.

"That's too bad."

"Are you . . ."

"I am," the ghost answered.

Alexis's eyes grew even wider, which shouldn't have been possible. "Holy crap."

The figure, the dead Abigail Caldwell, laughed bitterly. "I assure you, there is nothing holy in this house." Abigail moved even closer to Alexis, to the point where, if she needed to breathe, Alexis would have known what the breath of the dead smelled like. And what she had eaten last. "You're afraid."

Alexis tried to back away but fell in the process, her ankle giving way again. Or she tripped. Who knew or even cared at this point?

"It seems . . . like a natural feeling . . . considering," Alexis muttered.

"I suppose," Abigail said, moving away from Alexis and to the window. Alexis struggled to get up, desperately trying to figure out a way to get out of this house. Away from her.

"I'm sorry to . . . you know . . . be here."

"That's quite all right," Abigail said, not looking back. "I haven't had guests in so long. So, so, long."

"Well, I just came to . . ."

"Take something. I know." Alexis looked at her, stunned. Abigail turned to face her. "It wasn't the drapes."

"Oh."

"Even though you came to steal from me, I'm rather glad you're here. I've been so lonely. You would think I would be used to it by now, the loneliness, since I spent most of my life that way, but oddly, I never grew accustomed to it. Silence grows much more unbearable over time. The only company I have are my dolls. My children. But they've already greeted you, haven't they?"

"Yeah," Alexis said, finding a wall to lean on while attempting to distance herself from Abigail, her ankle continuing to throb.

"When they laugh, I relive it all again. The joy of having them here, of finally mattering to someone . . . of being a mother. But nothing is meant to last, I suppose. Seeing them burn again and again. Hearing them cry out for mercy. But their laughter is worse. It's pure torture." Abigail looked at the dolls that surrounded her, watching images that Alexis could not see. "They said I murdered them. That I let them burn."

And then, somehow, Abigail was right in front of Alexis again, her face afire with anger.

"But how could I kill the only things I ever loved? The only ones who ever loved me? How?" She moved away again to one of her dolls, a girl with a bright (or used to be bright) purple dress. Abigail tried to touch it, but her hand went right through it. "They were damaged like me," she said, slightly above a whisper.

"Then why did you let them die?" Alexis asked before considering the possible ramifications of such a question. Abigail turned back to her with a look that terrified her.

"What did you say?"

"I . . . I . . . uh."

"How dare you come into my house and accuse me of such things!"

"I'm sorry. I didn't mean anything by it," Alexis said and, now fearful for her life, struggled to move as far away from Abigail as she could. "I heard that . . ."

"You shouldn't believe everything you hear, little girl. Now sit down while I share the truth of what happened."

"I would rather leave."

"Sit!" Abigail said as books flew off the shelf, barely missing Alexis's head. Alexis yelped as she felt herself fly into a chair. She was sharing it with a rather grotesque boy doll, whose flesh looked burned. While having done a reasonable job of controlling her anxiety since meeting Abigail, Alexis now found her heart beginning to race again. Abigail smiled.

"You need to breathe. Wouldn't want you to have another attack, now would we?" When Alexis said nothing, Abigail continued, "I won't hurt you. I'm sorry that I lost my temper." Abigail floated, not walked, to some pictures on the wall that Alexis had not seen before. Of a family. Abigail looked at one of them for a moment and reached out to touch the face of the girl in the picture, then stopped suddenly. "Now, about that night. The children had become naughtier, not listening, and I had finally had enough. So, I locked them in their room until they learned to respect me. Unruly children need to be punished." Alexis watched Abigail slowly float around the room as she spoke. "When the fire started, I rushed upstairs. The doors were so hot, and flames were everywhere. I could barely breathe, and the next thing I knew, I was sitting outside in the rocking chair. Rocking back and forth. Back and forth. I tried to get back in, but it was too late. So, I sat back down and waited."

"No one came to help?"

"Oh, they did, but the children were dead by then. And the people's need to save was replaced by something much more fearful. A need for vengeance. You see, by then, the people had turned against me. I had heard that they were planning on taking the children away that very night. I wasn't going to let them, though. And I didn't." Abigail paused and then laughed. "That last sentence sounded like I meant for them to die, didn't it?"

"A little."

"Well, I didn't. Sometimes accidents do have benefits, although the townsfolk never believed it was an accident. I was taken away that night, deemed insane, and locked away. How long, I don't remember. When I got out, I came back here. To the only home I've ever known."

Despite her best efforts, Alexis found herself enthralled in Abigail's story and noticed that she was no longer afraid. Well, maybe still a little. "How did you die?"

"After I'd been home a few days, the townspeople started to come by my house. They would shout hateful and threatening things while throwing rocks through my windows. Then one night, after the taunts and desecration of my home, or what remained of it, fulfilled them no longer, a group came back late at night, after the rest of the town had fallen asleep. They came through the back door, wearing masks, and found me sleeping in my bed. They violently pulled me from the bed and then proceeded to beat me with various implements they had brought. Mrs. Clearwater, who had always hated my family, was the one who stabbed me in my chest. It went in clean. Hate and fear must make one stronger than they appear. Since I wasn't dead yet, they wrapped a rope around my neck and hung me from the highest rafter." She pointed up, and Alexis's eyes followed to a rafter that still contained the broken noose. Well, now she knew what the rope was for. "All the while they were saying that

I was getting what I deserved. But as I hung there, swinging back and forth, I still didn't die. I merely laughed at them. Because I knew things that they didn't. Without touching them or moving a muscle, their necks began snapping one by one by one. I thought the remaining ones would run, but they did not. They cut me down and tied me up so that I could no longer move. They put a bag on my head, and I could see nothing. I tried to stop them but, for reasons that I have never discerned, I could not. They carried me down to the basement and locked me in the closet. Even though I couldn't see, I knew which closet I was in. The same one I had been locked in as a child. The same one my parents died in. I was once again reduced to that five-year-old girl who had pleaded with her parents, always to no avail. This time was no different. Then they threw some liquid on me and set me on fire."

Alexis watched in horror as flames ravaged Abigail's body, and the older woman screamed out in anguish. She began thrashing about, and Alexis saw the dolls catch fire as well, their screams joining with Abigail's. Alexis tried to run away from what she was seeing but couldn't move. She covered her eyes and ears, and when she opened them, the charred remains of Abigail stood before her. It spoke in a raspy voice.

"I only wanted someone to love me. That's what I, what we all, wanted. Nothing more. And we burned because of it."

"I'm so sorry," Alexis said truthfully.

"You're lying!" Abigail screamed. "You're like them!"

"No!" Alexis yelled back, shaking her head. "I'm not. I truly am sorry that this happened to you!"

In an instant, the burned Abigail was gone and the dirty,

bloody, and slightly less terrifying Abigail was back. She smiled gently at Alexis.

"Are you?"

"Yes."

"Then perhaps you could do me a favor."

There comes a time in your life where something happens and you say, "What have I gotten myself into?" This moment wasn't exactly one of those times because, for Alexis, that had happened when the door first closed behind her and oh, like a thousand times since she'd been in the house. This moment did, however, feel like one of those life-defining (or life-ending) moments. Alexis, gathering what little courage she had left after what she had just seen, spoke.

"A favor?"

Abigail smiled. "A small favor. A teeny, tiny favor."

A teeny, tiny favor? When has a favor described that way ever been teeny tiny? Alexis thought. "What?"

Abigail started gliding around the room as if what had happened moments before hadn't happened. And maybe it hadn't, Alexis thought, now doubting her ability to separate reality from her imagination.

"You see, my little one," Abigail said, "due to circumstances beyond my control, and believe me, I've tried to control them . . . I am bound here. As well as the children. Trapped in this house. With all these memories. The suffering. For eternity." She turned back to Alexis. "Unless we are set free."

Alexis shuffled her feet uncomfortably. "I . . . uh . . . have never been good at freeing ghosts and things. I failed that class in school, so . . ."

"I'm sure that you can do it."

"Yeah, I would like to help, but my friends are waiting for me."

"Then you should go." At that moment, the parlor door slid open, and Alexis heard what had to be the front door unlock and open as well. Alexis looked at her now-clear escape route and then turned back to Abigail.

"Seriously? Just like that?"

"Of course. I asked you to help me, and you could not. I understand. Thank you for providing me company, even for such a brief time."

Alexis, feeling relieved, but still wary, smiled. "Of course, and maybe I could come back and . . ." She let the rest of the sentence die out, deciding it was best not to lie to a vengeful ghost. "All right, it's been . . . fun." Alexis got up from the chair and started backing away as a creepy smile appeared on Abigail's lips. *If that was her goodbye smile when she was alive,* Alexis thought, *no wonder people were afraid of her.* Alexis turned around and headed for the exit as fast as she could. She made it through the door to the living room, believing completely that it would slam closed on her. But she made it through and headed for the gloriously now-open front door. She looked through it and saw the faint outlines of Derek waiting and Hayley returning. Boy, would she have a story to tell them.

Alexis had one foot across the threshold when she felt herself flying backwards. She watched in terror as the door closed . . . slowly? She thought if there were ever a door slamming moment, this was it. Then she remembered that she was currently flying backwards through the air. Alexis closed her eyes and screamed.

"You can stop screaming now. And open your eyes."

81

Alexis did as she was told. She was back in the living room with Abigail standing in front of her. *Predictable*, Alexis thought.

"I thought you said I could leave."

"It wasn't a favor."

"Then why let me think I was leaving?"

"Theatrics. And you will be able to leave after you help me. If not, you shall remain here with me and my children in eternal torment."

Alexis, heart rate increasing to the point that if her heart burst from her chest she wouldn't be surprised, tried to take a deep breath but couldn't. She was well past that point. She looked Abigail in the eyes.

"What do I have to do?" she struggled to get out.

Abigail smiled and touched her cheek. Her breathing instantly became normal. "Can't have you dying right now, can we?" Alexis took a deep breath as she watched Abigail move to a bookshelf. Abigail raised her arm up and a book flew into her hands. The book looked ancient and covered in . . . flesh. Probably human flesh. Fantastic.

"It's true what they said about my parents. They had . . . certain hobbies. Dark hobbies. They practiced on me when I was a child. It wasn't pleasant. But when they died, I began exploring the book that granted them such power. This book."

"I figured," Alexis said. Abigail cut her a look.

"Don't be petulant, child."

"Sorry."

"As I was saying," Abigail continued, "I found certain things useful in this book. Like snapping necks. Avoiding death by hanging. But not by fire." The pages of the book began turning quickly on their own. "After my unfortunate demise, I happened upon a spell that sets bound souls free." Abigail turned to Alexis. "And, my dear, that is the only thing you must do. Read it aloud, and both of us shall be in this house no longer."

"That's all?"

"Of course."

"Why can't you read it?"

"The spell only works if read by one of the living. And you're the only living being who has dared to set foot in this house besides that wretched cat."

"Lucky me," Alexis said, shaking her head. She looked back at the book. "I'll do it."

"Good." The book lifted from Abigail's hand and floated towards Alexis, landing gently in her hands. She shuddered as she felt its leathery, somehow warm cover settle into her palms.

"I would like to say that that was cool, but considering . . ." Alexis stopped talking as she looked at the book. She looked up at Abigail. "I can't read this. It's like in Latin or something, and I took one class, but I ended up with a C . . . maybe a C-."

"You'll recall that your life depends on it."

Alexis gulped and took another deep breath, then looked back up one more time. "And you promise that if I do this, you'll let me go?"

"I don't make promises, little one, because, in my experience, promises are only meant to be broken and die. Therefore, I won't promise, but I will tell you that if you don't aid in my receiving my deserved freedom, you will never leave this place. Therefore, it seems you have but one choice."

She was right. Alexis still doubted that a vengeful ghost

would keep her word, but what choice did she have? She looked back down at the book, cleared her throat, and began reading.

"In vicis illae moment. Permissum thy vomica obduco. Silenti etc fio victus victus fio silent etc."

Alexis looked up and saw Abigail watching her. She appeared calm, except for her eyes, which glinted darkly. "Guess it didn't work. Maybe someone . . ."

"You must repeat it over and over until it does work."

"Maybe it doesn't . . ." The look that came from Abigail, clearly one that only a person who had perhaps burned children alive and then herself been burned alive could generate, shut Alexis up.

She began reading the spell again. Over and over. Sometime around the fifth reading, the children started laughing again. Or crying. Sounds and lights began radiating throughout the house. The walls came alive, shaking violently. It was almost as if the entire history of the house was coming alive in that moment. A blinding light appeared in front of Alexis. She looked up and saw that it was coming from Abigail, who was floating high above her, almost to the ceiling. Alexis stopped reading for a moment as she took in all that was happening.

"Keep reading!" Abigail yelled above the noise. It was really loud. Alexis continued. The world around her grew more and more chaotic, and her heart rate tried to match it. Then, Alexis felt something inside of her. A pain. A pain that began in her chest. She clutched her chest as that feeling, at first only a pinprick, began spreading throughout her entire body. She looked around and saw that the bright light was now fading. Darkness was spreading through her.

"What's happening?"

Alexis never heard a response. She collapsed to the floor at the same moment that Abigail collapsed to the floor.

A silence spread over the house. The girl who had entered only to satisfy a dare lay still, no breath noticeable. The ghost also lay still. The only things that seemed alive in some form or another were the children, the dolls, who had turned their eyes to the fallen as the silence grew.

A faint sound was heard from outside. Voices. Two teenagers who had seen their friend for a moment when the door opened, only to see her ripped away from the door as it closed slowly. Now, recovered enough to check on their friend, they had run to the house and had begun calling out her name. Their efforts to open the door, though intense, were futile.

Then Alexis's eyes opened. She slowly got to her feet, stretched, and looked down at the body beside her, the ghost. A brief smile escaped her lips as she headed for the door.

- - - - - - - - - -

"Why isn't she coming out?"

"I don't know, Derek!" Hayley said, unable to play her role of 'sarcastic friend who isn't affected by anything' anymore. "Why won't the door open?"

"Something bad happened. I told you it would. We have to break the door down and go get her!" Derek said.

"I'm not going in there!"

Derek turned to her. "What?"

"I'm not going in there for two reasons. One, our shared history would make it abundantly clear that I like to get other people to do stupid things while I sit and watch them do it. And two . . ."

Hayley went silent. Derek looked at her, confused.

"And?"

"And two . . ." Hayley continued looking towards the door as if hoping for something. Then she watched as it slowly opened and Alexis walked out. "And two, Alexis is here."

Derek looked and saw Alexis. He ran to her and hugged her.

"I thought you were dead!"

Alexis smiled. "I am not."

"Clearly," Hayley said, crossing to them. "What took you so long?"

"I'm sorry. Was I gone for some time?"

"Yeah. And we saw you, like, floating in the air. And the door shut really slowly. We were worried."

"But not worried enough to come in?"

"Well, I was about to. And earlier . . ." Derek stuttered.

"I wanted to, but Derek wouldn't let me," Hayley blurted out. Derek turned to her, and Hayley smiled. "I'm kidding. I wasn't going to go in. I was worried, though."

"It is very sweet that you were both concerned for my well-being," Alexis said as she began walking away from the house.

"Hey, wait up," Hayley said, running to catch up with Derek close behind. "What did you take?" She looked at Alexis and saw that she had nothing in her hands, and it looked like her jacket was empty. "Wait, you didn't take anything, did you?"

Alexis turned and looked at them. "Oh, I wouldn't say that." She smiled, then turned and walked away, leaving Hayley and Derek staring at her. Hayley turned to Derek.

"Was it weird how she said that with a creepy, non-Alexis-like smile? Because I feel like it was."

"Yes, yes it was. And not the good weird," Derek said.

"It might be because of her newfound feelings for you."

"I don't think so."

Derek and Hayley began walking but made little attempt to catch up with Alexis.

Alexis opened her eyes and looked around, seeing the house that she had spent the past hour in. She pushed herself up, and that's when she noticed that something felt different. Off. She looked at her arms. Where was her jacket? She looked down at her body and was shocked to see that she was now wearing a long, torn, white dress. She gently touched the hole in her chest.

Panic overtook her.

She rushed, or rather floated, to a mirror hanging on the wall by the entrance to the hall. Alexis frantically wiped away the years of dust that had accumulated and looked into it.

Then she screamed. Her face was not her own.

Abigail Caldwell stared back at her.

Alexis (Abigail?) continued screaming until she broke down into sobs. She collapsed, her hands covering her face. Then the realization hit her.

If she was now in the body of Abigail Caldwell, that would mean . . . she quickly rushed to the door. Her friends were in danger. She got to the door but could go no further. No matter how hard she tried, she was stuck here, in this house.

Bound. Forever.

She flew upstairs and looked out the window. There she saw them. Derek and Hayley were walking behind, far behind, Alexis. Or Abigail.

The children of the house began laughing as Alexis stared out the window, wishing desperately that she had never taken that stupid bet. Now she would be stuck here. Until . . .

"Just go in and take something. What's the worst thing that could happen?"

CHAPTER 6

"Wow. That was almost good," Vanessa said as she looked for any remnants of food that hadn't been destroyed in their food fight.

"Almost, my ass," said Lindsey. "Mix of comedy, coming of age, mocking the cliché elements found in most ghost stories, and on top of that . . . it was scary. Best story that any of us has ever told."

"Well, the night's still young," Vanessa contradicted. "Who knows what will happen? Right, Dani?"

"Sure," Dani said. She turned to Lindsey. "That was awesome. I don't think I'll be able to sleep tonight. Or possibly ever again." Lindsey took a mock bow. "Did you make it up?"

"Maybe, or it could be true." Lindsey noticed Claire staring off with a look that she and Vanessa knew well. "You're doing that thing again, Claire. Where you stare off with that dumb, pondering look. What don't you understand?" Claire didn't reply. "Claire?" Lindsey said, louder this time.

"What?" Claire said, leaving her baffled fog for a few moments. "You're confused."

"I am."

"About?"

"About why Alexis was acting all weird at the end."

"Because it wasn't Alexis," Dani said. "It was Abigail in the body of Alexis."

Claire gasped. "What? Are you serious?" All the girls nodded. "What happened to Alexis?"

Vanessa shook her head. "She's now in the body of Abigail." Claire stared at her, confused. "Because they switched bodies."

"That makes no sense," Claire said dismissively.

"No," Lindsey said. "The fact that you're not getting it makes no sense."

"Well, you never said they switched bodies."

"Because good stories don't spell everything out. They hint at things and then let the audience put the pieces together."

"No, good stories," Claire said, standing up, "are told in such a way that the audience understands what's happening."

"I'll keep that in mind for my next story: 'A Story That Is So Scarily Clear That Even Claire Can Understand It.' You know, for someone smart, you can be super dense sometimes."

Claire smiled. "Thanks for calling me smart," she said, starting to fidget awkwardly.

"So . . ." Lindsey began, "trying to turn this night into a dance party again, I see."

"No. I have to pee. I'm about to burst."

"Why didn't you pee when you were getting the cooler?"

"Didn't have to then. I do now."

"Then go pee," Vanessa said.

"Who's going to go with me but stay fairly far back?" None of the girls said anything.

"Why can't you go . . . ?" Dani asked.

Claire started to answer but was cut off by Vanessa, who raised a hand at her. "I got this, small-bladdered one. See, Dani, Claire pees all the time. Like, all the time. But she can't go if people are around her and can hear. Being out here, though, poses a problem, because she's also afraid of the dark."

"I am not afraid of the dark. I'm afraid of being alone in the dark," Claire said, momentarily forgetting the crucial thing that one must do when needing to pee badly and being unable to. She remembered quickly. Not quickly enough, though. "Oh, man."

"You peed yourself, didn't you?" Lindsey said.

"A little. It'll dry," Claire muttered. "And now I will go . . . alone deep in the woods because I'm not scared . . . to pee because I don't want my kidneys to explode, thus releasing toxins into my entire body and killing me. So there," she said defiantly, beginning to walk away awkwardly.

"Don't think of water-related things," Vanessa yelled after her. "Like waterfalls, running water, rain . . ."

"And don't let them get you!" Lindsey yelled after her.

"Not helping!" Claire yelled back as she headed into the woods with her flashlight.

"Who's them?" Dani asked.

"No one. Just messing around," Vanessa said. Then she looked to the woods. "Claire, we'll wait for you to tell the next story!"

- - - - - - - - - -

Claire walked quickly yet gingerly through the woods, the sound of her friends' voices becoming fainter and fainter until they were nothing more than echoes in the night.

As she looked for the perfect spot, she began to think about what would happen if her kidneys did explode. As one who was labeled as "the quirky nerd" in school who did, in fact, pee a lot, she had done a lot of research on the effects of "holding it" but had not yet figured out exactly how much time she had before her kidneys went boom. It wasn't something she wanted to test to find out either, so she would have to assume that point was fast approaching – thus, finding a spot was imperative.

After walking a few more minutes, she settled for an area that was near the lake that had freaked her out earlier in order to keep a close eye on it in case something decided to climb out and try to drag her in. Claire looked around, saw three trees that seemed to stand apart from the rest, and decided for no reason other than really having to pee that near those trees was the perfect spot. She listened for her friends' voices and then, hearing nothing but the sounds of the woods, she went about her business.

She stopped, laid down her flashlight, and cleared off a proper area as best she could. She was ready for the sweet relief and kidney-saving to come, but her fear of the dark and the lake (and, oddly enough, the three trees behind her) short-circuited the entire system.

"Man," Claire said aloud. "Need a distraction." A twig broke in the woods. "Not that kind!" She picked up her flashlight and pointed to where she thought the sound had come from. "Who's there?" There was no response. "I said who's there? Is that you, Lindsey?" Claire said in the fakest brave voice she could muster.

She could only see the eyes. Two tiny beady eyes. She screamed and dropped her flashlight. The light caught the raccoon, who seemed not to be frightened by the light nor by the "not capable of peeing" screamer. She reached for a stick and threw it at the animal, though it was nowhere near its target. It couldn't have been farther away if she had thrown it backwards.

The raccoon seemed to mock her attempt at scaring it away, yet left anyway. Perhaps out of boredom. Or pity. Claire laughed. "Thank God no one was here to see that. Which proves yet again why I'm right never to use the bathroom around people. Or when I'm throwing sticks at raccoons." She could only imagine what Vanessa and Lindsey would say if they were here.

If anyone sought to define the perfect best friends, Vanessa and Lindsey would be nowhere near the top of anyone's list. Probably not even on anyone's list of "friend possibilities," besides each other's. As discussed earlier, Vanessa was a borderline sociopath and Lindsey . . . well, Lindsey was Lindsey. Not really what most people look for in a friend. Except for Claire, who saw what they showed the world and knew they both had slightly less scary sides that they hid from almost everyone else. Or at least that's the tale she told herself to justify her friendship with them. Besides, she was as messed up as they were. In a less scary and non-threatening way, of course. They were perfect for the girl who had always marched to the beat of a drum that didn't exist.

This had never really made any sense to Claire, but her mom had said it enough times that she had started to believe it. And she had thought everyone would be cool with the nonexistent drum she marched to until third grade, when she realized that they weren't.

Claire was at recess, along with everyone else, and as she walked around to see who she wanted to play with that day, she thought about why she never had a set group to play with. It seemed that almost everyone else had a group of friends they played with consistently. Every day, even. Claire, though, was more of a free agent. She played with different groups each day, so perhaps she was part of every group. Or none. Which was cool except for when it came to being invited to birthday parties. It seemed that belonging to no groups also meant that no one thought of you when telling their parents who they had to have at their party. The price you pay, Claire's dad always told her, for being a lone wolf. Lone wolf. Claire liked being called that. It always made her seem tougher than she was.

On that day, Claire didn't feel that any of the groups were quite right for her, so she went off alone and sat by a tree to tell herself stories. She did this at home, so why not at school, too? She started her story, playing the tough-minded scullery maid, her favorite character, as she saved the kingdom from the Norms. Norm wasn't short for "normal," as one might think. Instead, Anastasia (her scullery maid character) was defending the kingdom from a band of attacking people named Norm. All of them.

As Claire, now a teenager, thought back to that day, she remembered specifically the story she had told because it was amazing. The moment that happened in real life during that story . . . not so much.

She was in the middle of the climactic battle when, for the first time, she noticed all the eyes on her. She stopped telling the story and looked around at what seemed to be the entire school looking at her.

"Hey, guys!" Claire had said, with no sense of embarrassment.

"What are you doing?" Allison, the little girl who had never liked Claire, said.

"I'm telling myself a story and acting it out. You guys can play too, if you . . ."

She never got to finish that sentence before the laughter started. Every single kid laughed, which still amazed Claire to this day. Then there was the name calling as they all wandered off. They seemed to settle on "Dumb Claire," which disappointed and saddened Claire because it showed no creativity and didn't even relate to what she was doing. They were the dumb ones. As she watched them walk away, laughing while chanting their ridiculously unclever nickname, Claire was left alone and shattered.

Well, not shattered. She was cracked though and hurt and changed for good. She'd rather avoid being overly dramatic. After a moment, she continued her story. But a little more quietly this time. A lot more quietly.

And to be fair, it's not that the other kids were mean to her or that she didn't have any friends. Even though she didn't belong specifically to any group, she had friends. But, after that moment on the playground, she was aware that no one seemed to ever really get her. How she had never noticed that before was beyond her. That realization only hurt when she thought about it, so she packed it away and filled her mind with other things. The things most students found dorky or uncool, she loved. Including school. And that decision had served her well because it allowed her to still be the Claire that her parents, or pretty much the world, needed her to be.

Camp was a different story, though. Because she wasn't good at camp. And that's where having Vanessa and Lindsey made things better. Because even though they loved to make fun of her, they wouldn't let anyone else do it. Protecting Claire was one thing they could both agree on. She found this out when they first met.

It was the twenty-third day of camp. The first twenty-two days, Claire had tried to bond with her bunkmates and had failed miserably. Her bunkmates, who had all happened to be lifelong friends, had arranged to be in the same cabin for the fifth straight year, which wasn't supposed to happen, but their parents had connections. Their perfect summer, however, was ruined when one of the girls had gotten sick (arrested, per the rest of camp). And since they were one camper short and all cabins needed to be full at the most popular and now only camp within a 100-mile radius, someone, in all their brilliance, decided to put the awkward new girl with them. What could go wrong? Pretty much everything. Starting with the fact that Claire's plan to insert herself in this tribe was to use tips garnered from *How to be Hip and Make Friends Fast*, the definitive guide written in 1965. The only time that she went "off script" (and let's face it, being "on script" was by no means a good thing) was the time she decided to place decorative ivy on all their beds as a way to bring the beauty of nature into the cabin. The only problem was that this "decorative ivy" was decorative *poison* ivy which, of course, they were all allergic to. What were the odds?

From that day on, Claire could do no right with them. No matter what she did, it was a terrible decision. And they made fun of her constantly. But her dealings at school had built up a tolerance for this type of bullying, and besides, the rest of camp was going well. Until they started to turn the other campers against her as well, and for the first time that Claire could remember, she was not happy. In fact, she wanted to go home, but since her family motto was "Turks Never Quit," she trudged along, making the best of it.

Then came the Camp Olympics and Claire's almost death.

Every summer, the camp had the Camp Olympics, where all the cabins would compete in a variety of events to get the title of "Best Cabin." Most of the events were your traditional summer camp games, some academic games (which Claire was highly thankful for), and even some modified Olympic games thrown in as well. Turns out that Claire's bunkmates had won the last four years, and, after failing to get Claire removed from their team despite their best efforts (saying that she had "highly contagious rickets" was Claire's personal favorite), they decided to embrace their new teammate to win their fifth title in a row. Or so it seemed.

On the day of the Olympics, Claire was more than a little nervous, knowing that this was her last chance to make this summer not a total disaster. So for one day, Claire dismissed her "lone wolf drummer" self and was determined to help the cause and be normal. The day got off to a great start when her bunkmates invited her to breakfast, a first. There, you would've thought that Claire was part of their lifelong frienddom.

(Claire, in retrospect, noted that she should perhaps have seen their behavior as suspicious, but, ever the optimist, she had gleefully soaked up the newfound attention.)

After breakfast, the Olympic events started, and her cabin raced out to the lead, with Claire winning gold for her cabin in any event that required brains. In all the others, especially the ones involving running, the best that could be said was that at least she wasn't *always* last.

Then it was time for the team canoe race, the most important contest in the Camp Olympics. Her cabin was running slightly ahead of the second-place team, comprised of campers that all looked 25, except for Marissa, who was super tiny. There were rumors that she had brought in ringers so that she could finally win, but nothing was ever proven. Besides, it didn't matter because her bunkmates had told her that this was their event, and they would easily win it. During rest time, they made Claire sneak out to claim the best boat while they took naps. After almost getting caught five or so times and falling into the mud pit that had been used for the tug of war earlier, Claire made it to the dock and the boats and picked the green one, because, of course, after finding out that she was going to be on the team, she had done research on what makes a boat fast and then had tested out each boat the night before and had found the green one to be the best based on her criteria. Claire got in the boat and waited for the others, coming up with possible reasons why she was there so early. The best one she could come up with was "I'm not," which made her seriously hope that no one noticed.

After about 30 minutes, the other campers all headed to the dock, and Claire watched as the canoes quickly filled up. Then two girls got in the blue canoe next to her canoe and sat down. Claire turned to them.

"Waiting for the rest of your team too?"

"Nope. We are the rest of our team," said the smaller one. "We aren't good teammates."

"Oh."

The taller girl looked at Claire. Claire couldn't believe how perfect she was. She was beautiful, tall with long red hair where every strand seemed to know exactly where it belonged and blue eyes that she couldn't stop looking at. Plus, her outfit was the kind you see on the cover of a magazine. Just like her.

"You're the girl who gave all your bunkmates poison ivy, aren't you?"

"I . . . I guess," Claire managed to say. "It was an accident. I thought it was decorative ivy."

"Yeah. I think that grows in stores." The girls laughed as Claire, who wasn't sure of a proper retort, turned and faced the lake to wait for the rest of her team. They arrived a few minutes later, looking well-rested. Claire tried to start a cheer, but it fell rather flat.

The race was about to begin. There were markers floating in various spots of the lake that would guide the boats around the "track," which led to the middle of the lake. Once there, they were supposed to turn around. A huge chain tied between two buoys stretched across most of the middle of the lake, which held signs warning the boaters to go no further. Past the chain was the old camp's side of the lake. The water there was always mysteriously dark, almost black. And apparently, there was a reason it was called the "old camp," as in "the camp that's no longer there because something awful happened there." At first, the campers figured it was something made up, but years later, Claire would learn the awful truth from Vanessa.

Natalie, one of the counselors, blasted the air horn, and the race began. Claire's team started paddling, and they were out in front in a matter of seconds. Soon they were almost to the dark side of the lake.

"Hey, guys, we should start turning around now!" Claire yelled out.

"Oh, not yet," Caroline, the most annoying of her bunkmates, called back. "Just a little further!"

"But we're almost to the chain." Claire began paddling furiously in the opposite direction, but then Sally, the one built like a tank, grabbed Claire's oar and threw it in the water. "Hey, what are you doing?"

"Only this." Sally grabbed Claire, who started kicking as Sally picked her up. Claire was amazed by how strong this monster of a girl was. Sally ducked low enough for Claire's head to smack into the chain as they moved into the dark side of the lake.

The girls ignored the counselors yelling for them to turn back and focused only on Claire.

Then Sally ripped Claire's life vest off and threw her into the water.

"Have a nice swim, Claire!" Her bunkmates turned to head back but were quickly rammed by another canoe, causing theirs to flip over. The shocked and spluttering campers hung on to their overturned canoe and looked to see what had happened. It was two girls in a blue canoe.

"It seems your boat turned over. You should be more careful," said one of the girls.

"Also, try not to drown," said the other one. "Or do and reduce the jerk population of this camp, which seems incredibly high."

The girls paddled off and retrieved Claire's life jacket, then came back to where Claire was bobbing and screaming. They threw her the life jacket, which she grabbed. She continued screaming.

"You have a life jacket, and you can swim. Relax, you're not going to drown."

Claire stopped yelling for a moment and looked up. It was the two girls she had talked to earlier.

"Take my hand," said the smaller girl with the wind-blown dirty brown hair. Claire reached for her hand and was pulled in. "I told you they deserved it." She smiled. "I'm Lindsey, and this is Vanessa."

"I'm Claire."

And that's how their friendship started: with Claire being thrown out of a boat, and Vanessa and Lindsey rescuing her. The rest of the race was canceled, and all of Claire's bunkmates were sent home because their actions "reflected poorly on the camp." Claire changed cabins since no one was left in hers, and moved to Vanessa's and Lindsey's, whose cabin also happened to be less than full.

From that point on, the three girls were inseparable: Vanessa was the leader, Lindsey was the mean one, and Claire was the Claire of the group. At least, that was how Lindsey defined her one night last summer. The two of them were sitting outside the cabin after Vanessa had fallen asleep. Claire had no idea what she meant, and Lindsey, in a non-Lindsey moment, said that Claire made them better. Claire got emotional and hugged her, which ended their moment as Lindsey, who was now uncomfortable, pushed her off the steps. It was moments like that, though few, that made Claire closer to Lindsey than she was to Vanessa. She knew Lindsey liked her. She wasn't sure if Vanessa liked anyone. Or could like anyone. She could be super cold and unfeeling sometimes. And she would do things that, well, scared Claire. That's why, even though Vanessa often stood up for her, Claire was always uneasy around her, though she tried not to let it show.

- - - - - - - - - -

"So, what's your story, Dani?" Vanessa asked, moving a stick slowly through the fire.

"What do you mean? Like my ghost story? I told you, I . . ."

"Not the ghost story. *Your* story."

"Oh," Dani said, growing uncomfortable.

"I mean, we know you had a bad day or something and have an affection for your hood, but so far, we've gotten nothing else from the girl sitting alone in the woods. So?"

Dani sat there silently, watching the fire. Vanessa and Lindsey exchanged a glance. "When will Claire be back?" Dani asked, trying to change the subject.

"She'll be gone a while," Lindsey said. "She probably walked a mile. But don't worry, we'll fill her in on whatever you say."

"It's just, I . . . don't like talking about myself."

"Tell you what, I'll go first then," Vanessa said. "I'm an only child. Wasn't always though. My mom and dad are both "lifetime academics," whatever that means. My mom's the dean of a big university up north, and my dad is a professor of human studies or something made up like that. He also writes a ton of books that people apparently like. At some point, a well-defined point in time, they decided that they were no longer big on things such as feelings, emotions, or spending time with me, so my childhood was quite magical. I suppose they love me, but who knows. Or cares. I had one cat. When I was nine. A kitten that I found at a gas station. Named him Sammy after this boy I liked at school, who I thought would be impressed by my naming of a cat after him, but I misread that, and he didn't talk to me after that day. And about a week after that, Sammy was found dead. The cat, not the boy."

"And that was the last time she ever loved anything," Lindsey said dramatically.

"Maybe," Vanessa said, looking back to the fire.

"She also forgot to tell you that she goes to a prestigious boarding school, takes trips all over the world, lives in a mansion, and is always the hottest and smartest girl in the room," said Lindsey.

Vanessa turned to her indignantly. "Hey, it's not a mansion."

"At least you found something to disagree with, and it *is* a mansion. You know what? I'll finish your bio. Vanessa has the perfect life. Besides the cat thing. And the fact that it's Karla, her glorified nanny, that takes her on the trips, not her parents."

"They finance them, though."

"Shhhh! Bottom line: her parents are loaded, she's smart, she's pretty, she's good at like everything, everybody wants to be her, and she could have like a billion friends, but she only has Claire and me."

"Because you guys are the only ones I need."

Lindsey turned to her. "Oh, that's so sweet that my angry dead heart is . . . I don't know. Something." She turned back to Dani. "The question is . . . why? Why would someone who could have it all settle for someone like Claire, who though charming is quite tiresome, or me, who . . . God, I would be my own last pick to hang out with. But here's Vanessa, Ms. Everything, hanging with the equivalent of lame townies."

"First, Lindsey, I don't want to hang out with anyone but you guys, and second, you flatter me." Vanessa turned to Dani. "I am not what Lindsey makes me out to be. At all."

"It would be okay if you were."

"Well, I'm not. And Lindsey, since you shared some of my story, I'll share some of yours. Lindsey . . ."

Lindsey cut Vanessa a look, and Dani saw a moment of fear in Lindsey's eyes that was quickly suppressed. "That's not how this works. I get my story. I was born in a small farming village to a prostitute and a one-legged mime who was always trapped in a box."

"Not sure if you know this," Vanessa said to Dani, "but that's not true." Dani laughed. "So, as I was saying . . ."

Lindsey stood up. "Oh, would you look at the time. Better check on Claire. I'd hate for her to get lost and be gone forever."

And with that, Lindsey headed for the woods.

- - - - - - - - - -

Claire stood up after finishing and looked around. At that moment, she quickly realized that she had no idea how to get back.

"Crap."

She peeked around, hoping that her flashlight would provide a shining beacon that would illuminate the direction from whence she had come. Alas, her shining beacon of hope only illuminated trees and more trees and that scary, scary, lake.

"This is hopeless. Why do all these stupid trees have to look the same?"

To ward off her impending sense of dread, she began singing all the camp songs she could remember. Not remembering all the lyrics, she combined the ones that she did know into one big song that made little to no sense but accomplished the task of relaxing her.

Then she saw it. Off a little way to the right of the three trees. A broken wooden sign that was now almost completely covered by vines.

She walked over to the sign and knelt, placing her flashlight between her knees, and began clearing away the vines. As she did, she noticed that there was a picture of three girls with something written underneath it. The sign was so weathered that Claire could barely make out any of the words.

"In memory of . . . who died . . . may their spirits be forever . . . something." She studied the picture for a moment and thought about the story Vanessa had told her and Lindsey. "Three? I thought there was only one that . . ."

Then she heard footsteps approaching.

- - - - - - - - - -

"What's up with Lindsey?" Dani asked.

"She's Lindsey, that's what up with her," Vanessa said. "She doesn't talk about herself or her family or her feelings. Ever. And by ever . . . I do mean ever. We've been friends now for forever, and she's barely told me anything about her family except that they're super religious and don't get her. I think she's told Claire some things but not me. That's cool though. I know more about her than she thinks."

"Really?"

"Yeah, let's just say that Lindsey's not as badass as she acts. She's got some serious secrets, and some aren't as secret as she imagines they are." Dani nodded. "What about you, Dani? You got secrets?"

Dani shifted uncomfortably. "No."

"C'mon, I told you all about me. Even my dead cat. And to be honest, you are a big secret to us all. We're putting a lot of trust in a girl we only met tonight, who was sitting in the deep dark woods in the middle of the night, and whose face we can barely see because she refuses to take off her hoodie. I mean, you could be a ghost sent here to kill us or something."

Dani laughed. "You got me. But fine, what do you want to know?"

"Anything you want to tell me," Vanessa said, throwing some sticks into the fire.

"Well, it's only my dad and me. My mom died when I was eight. Car accident. She was . . . amazing. Her death messed up the family because she held everything together and made it work, you know?"

Vanessa nodded. "Yeah. What does your dad do?"

"He paints."

"Paints what?"

"Pictures and stuff."

"Any good?"

"I like them, but he doesn't make a lot of money from it or anything. And once Mom . . . you know, he . . . uh, I don't know. He blamed himself, and . . ."

Dani stopped talking and looked into the fire. Vanessa walked over and sat beside her.

"I'm sorry about your mom. And your dad."

"Yeah. He tries. He really does, but . . ."

Both girls sat in silence for a moment. Dani stared at the fire, and Vanessa stared at Dani as a doctor would a patient.

"Do you get picked on a lot?"

"Because of my mom's death? Or my dad's failure as a painter?" Dani asked, looking at her.

Vanessa laughed a little. "No, I mean in general. Do you get picked on a lot . . . in general?"

Dani stared at Vanessa for a moment, trying to hide the irritation she felt for that question. "Wow. That question came out of nowhere and seems a little insensitive since we were just talking about my dead mom, my failing family, and . . ."

A shocked look came over Vanessa's face. "Oh wow. I can see how you would take that question that way," she said. "Listen. My parents caused me some serious harm by basically raising me to be an emotionless monster, and I forget that most parents don't do that, so their kids feel stuff. I'm sorry. But, to be fair to me, I figured you would much rather talk about being picked on than your dead mom and failing family."

"You have a point, but why ask that question?"

"Well, you're out here, by yourself, and when Lindsey made one of her typical lame comments, you said something about being 'picked on enough.' And now with the knowledge that you have a dead mom and a probably distant dad who feels like he's failing you because he feels like he failed your mom, you're probably a little messed up socially."

"It could've been a one-time thing."

"I don't think so."

Dani shook her head and smiled. "Nice job, shrink. And yes, I guess I do get picked on a lot."

"Why? You seem okay to me."

"Thanks, that's what I shoot for, being okay in other people's eyes. To be honest, I don't think there's much wrong with me, but apparently, most other people disagree and find me . . . not okay. And if I knew why that was, I would change it, but I don't think I can. I guess it's me. I was born *off* in some undefinable way that everyone else can see. Take you, for instance. You choose not to be a part of anything, but if you ever decided that you wanted to be, you'd be welcomed in a heartbeat. Me? Not a chance. I used to always want to be part of something, anything, inside that magical circle, but there never seemed to be an empty spot."

"You said 'used to.'"

"I did. Because after . . . well, at some point, I didn't care anymore. I said, 'screw it.'"

Vanessa smiled. "It's probably better that way anyway."

"I guess." Dani looked at the fire and then back at Vanessa. "When do you think Lindsey and Claire are going to get back?"

Then they heard a scream.

"Pretty soon."

- - - - - - - - - -

"God! Why would you do that?"

"I got you! I finally got you!" said Claire, standing over Lindsey triumphantly, a smile stretching over her entire face. "You should have seen your face when I jumped out." Claire pointed the flashlight at her face and recreated "Lindsey's Terrified Look." And then she started laughing. That is, until Lindsey pulled one of Claire's legs out from under her, causing her to fall next to her.

They lay there a moment, and then both started laughing.

"I can't believe you got me," Lindsey said. "And to think, I was only coming to check on you."

"Really?" Claire said. "Is that why you came out of the woods running and screaming?"

"Yeah. I always do that when I'm checking on someone."

"I'm sure you do."

"Look at that," Lindsey said quietly, pointing up at the sky. Claire looked up. "There wasn't a single star out before, and now . . . they're everywhere."

"It probably has something to do with the clouds." They were silent for a moment. "Besides scaring me, why else did you come out here?"

"Do I need another reason?" Claire shrugged. Lindsey sighed. "Well, if I'm being honest, Vanessa was starting to make me uncomfortable."

"Oh, did she want you to open up and share stuff?"

"Yep. And I think we all know that's not something I do or plan on ever doing. Especially in front of someone we just met. Or anyone."

"You opened up a little bit to me before."

"You're different. And you promised to never speak about that, which you just did."

"Around Vanessa. And Vanessa's not here right now. Besides, we both know you're hiding something from us."

"Oh, do you?"

"Yeah." Claire poked her teasingly in the side. "We talk about it all the time. Your deep, dark secret."

"There's nothing deep and dark about me except my soul," Lindsey said, her body tensing up. She stood up and walked closer to the lake. Claire jumped up to follow her but stayed back, well clear of the lake.

"C'mon, you can tell me, Lindsey. You know you can. Keeping secrets isn't good for you. I won't tell Vanessa." Lindsey turned towards her, looking at the ground. Claire took a few steps closer until they were face-to-face. "Look, every time you and I talk when Vanessa's not around, it always seems like you want to tell me something, but then right before you do, you get uncomfortable and tell a stupid joke."

"You're stupid."

"See? You're uncomfortable now." Claire put her hands on Lindsey's shoulders. Lindsey looked at her oddly but didn't move. "You can tell me." Lindsey continued looking at Claire with that odd expression. Then a different look came over her face.

"You're right. I have been keeping something from you guys. And it involves you."

"Really?"

"Yeah. But you have to promise not to tell Vanessa."

"Of course."

"Okay . . . my secret . . . my deep, dark secret is that . . . I'm in love with you, Claire. I always have been. From the moment I pulled you out of the lake."

Claire stared at her. "Really?" A small but noticeable smile crept onto Claire's face, but it quickly disappeared when Lindsey started laughing. Claire pulled away. "You're a real jerk, you know that?"

"Get that all the time." Lindsey watched as Claire turned away and started walking back to the woods. "Hey, don't be mad. The two of us weren't meant to be, that's all. And what was that 'putting your hands on my shoulders' stuff?"

Claire turned back to her. "I was trying to be a comforting friend. I guess it was wasted on you. Like always."

"Whatever," Lindsey said. Claire walked off further from her, and she followed. "Look, it wasn't wasted, Claire." Claire turned back to see Lindsey standing in front of her. "I know I can talk to you. I . . . don't . . ." Lindsey sighed, wanting to say more but unable to. "God!"

Claire decided to bail her out. "So . . . do you know how to get back?"

"You don't remember, do you?"

"No."

Lindsey laughed. "I'll take you back, but you gotta promise me one thing."

"Which is?"

"I'll tell you on the way back." And with that, Lindsey took off running.

"Why must we always run?" Claire yelled, rushing to catch up.

- - - - - - - - - -

Vanessa and Dani heard Claire and Lindsey before they saw them.

"What do you think happened?" Dani asked Vanessa.

"Well," Vanessa said, pretending to ponder. "Lindsey snuck up on Claire, scaring her. Claire got mad but not too mad. Claire probably considered coming back here without her but couldn't because she didn't know the way. Lindsey, knowing this, raced off ahead of her, causing Claire to have to run in order not to be lost in the woods forever."

"Spot on, friend," Lindsey said as she burst into the clearing with Claire close behind. Lindsey turned to her, breathing heavily. "Right, Claire?"

Claire smiled. "Yep, that's exactly what happened." Lindsey smiled back at her, her normally harsh features softening for a moment in the firelight.

Then she flopped down on a log. "You are way faster than you used to be," Lindsey said, stretching her legs out in front of her. Claire rolled her eyes and sat down next to her. Lindsey nodded at the fire. "Way to keep the fire going, girls."

"It will last long enough," Vanessa said.

Dani turned to Claire. "So how was your pee time?" she asked.

"Uneventful," Claire said. Then she remembered the sign. "Though I did see this sign. Like one of those memorial things, you know? Had a picture of three girls that I guess all died. But that's not the story you told us, Vanessa. You said . . ."

"These camps have been around a long time. I'm sure tons of campers have died."

"That's a charming thought," Lindsey said.

"But . . ." Claire tried to continue. "Their clothes weren't that old-fashioned, and . . ."

"No one cares, Claire," Vanessa said, standing up. "Because I'm telling the next story."

"Please tell me it's not going to be one of the scary stories that's not only externally scary but internally scary as well," Lindsey said.

Vanessa laughed. "I have no idea what you're talking about."

"Yes, you do," Lindsey protested. "You're never satisfied with simply telling a scary story. You have to also tell one that is psychologically damaging to anyone who listens. Can't you ever settle for some good cheap scares? That one you told about 'The Forgotten Promise' is still giving me nightmares."

"And that's why I tell them," Vanessa said, walking away from them. She took a brief dramatic pause before continuing. "Now, this story is called 'The Way It Was Meant to Be,' the story of a girl who was granted three wishes from the thing that lived in her closet."

CHAPTER 7

Vanessa's Story

Cassie saw the creature for the first time when she was five. She had been sent to her room without supper again for an amazingly vicious tantrum. She couldn't remember exactly what caused it, but it didn't matter because it was only another in a long line of tantrums, the first one most likely coming when she exited the womb. With this one, she remembered hitting her mom as hard as she could and saying she wished she was dead. Or maybe yelling it. Probably yelling. Her parents, who were done with her by this point, banished her to her room, and she stormed upstairs and slammed her door moments after hearing her dad yell, "And don't you dare slam that door!" She flopped onto the bed and continued screaming her traditional hateful things about her family. Until realization hit about who she really hated, and she broke down in tears, following the typical formula of her tantrums.

At some point, she fell asleep, the kind of restless sleep where you constantly almost wake up but never fully get there. Well, until your closet door starts slowly opening with creaks it had never had before. When that happened, sleep would not come again.

She pulled her sheets around her head and peeked at her closet door. The moonlight provided a ghostly cascade of light around the door as Cassie became more and more afraid, goosebumps quickly covering her flesh. She pulled the sheet over her face, no longer able to deal with what she knew was the monster in the closet.

Then the footsteps started. Heavy footsteps that echoed loudly inside Cassie's head. Each moment drew them closer and closer. At some point, and that point was moments away, whatever it was would be by her bed. What was she going to do?

She came up with a plan: roll off the bed and under it in one swoop, hoping that the thing wouldn't see her. It was an awful plan, but she was five, so what do you expect? She took a deep breath, adjusted the covers, and tried to fall quietly. Instead she hit the floor loudly while knocking the wind out of herself. Somehow, she managed to roll under the bed.

The figure stopped at the foot of her bed. Cassie held her breath as best she could, but the lack of oxygen started to get to her. She didn't know how much longer she could hold out. Fortunately, or unfortunately, she didn't have to worry about it because her bed was thrown against the wall, and the creature quickly loomed above her. Its mouth opened wide, showing Cassie millions of sharp teeth. Cassie screamed out in terror, but when the creature raised one of its fingers, Cassie's screams quieted.

The creature, with reddish-brown flesh covered in boils

which seemed about to burst and the blackest eyes Cassie had ever seen, lowered itself closer to her face while pressing down on her, and smiled a horrible smile that would haunt Cassie every night of her life. The figure hovered over her for a moment and then whispered in her ear, "Three wishes are yours to do with as you please. Use them, or I shall never leave."

The next thing Cassie knew, she was back in bed, no sign of the creature or what it did. Like it had never happened. Like it was a dream. But it wasn't, and Cassie knew that it wasn't. She also never forgot where the creature lived.

That was 12 years ago, and the creature hadn't made its presence known as strongly as it had that first night, but once a month or so, Cassie would open her eyes in the middle of the night, awakened by a soft sound, and see it staring at her. Waiting. Wanting something: the first wish, a wish that Cassie would never make. Or that she never planned to make. She ended up making two wishes, but the first one didn't happen until the day her sister came home.

Cassie, now 17, sat in the living room on the red velvet couch that had been her great grandmother's, looking around at the walls covered in photographs of a different time. A time that, at this point, seemed worlds away. Almost as if it had never existed. The looks on their faces, that was the biggest difference. Cassie couldn't remember a time that her family had had those looks. And no, it wasn't simply happiness. It was something different. Something grander. Something Cassie couldn't quite define because she had never been able to bring out that feeling, whatever it was, in them. She imagined that even her birth was probably greeted by a response that was lacking. "Oh, look, it's a baby. She'll be fine, I suppose." Fortunately, her parents didn't have to settle for Cassie. Because along came Daphne, delivered by heaven's very own stork.

Daphne. Her sister. Correction: her now-dead sister.

Cassie, older by seven years, vividly remembered the day they brought her home. Nana had made her wear her only dress, a bright red number with sparkles that could not be more uncomfortable. Cassie had fought the idea because Cassie always fought doing things she didn't want to do, and wearing a dress was perhaps number one on her list of things she didn't want to do. She relented, however, after she could take no more of Nana's guilt-tripping. The bribe of ice cream helped as well. She remembered waiting by the door for her mother and father to bring her new baby sister home. And despite her natural inclinations, even at seven, Cassie was excited to meet her new sister. She would finally have a playmate.

The moment the door opened and Cassie first laid eyes on her, she was instantly smitten. Her new sister, Daphne Anne, was perfect. Her blue eyes seemed to glow, and her smile radiated from her as if she came from the stars in the sky. And when Daphne first saw Cassie, Cassie swore that she smiled at her. She had to hold her. She begged her parents, but they said maybe later. "Maybe later" wasn't good enough. Cassie didn't want to wait. She wanted to hold her now. Cassie kept persisting and started reaching for her. Her dad then grabbed her and told her to stop.

Everything that came next was a blur. Cassie, now in the midst of pulling a Cassie, tried to break free from her father's grasp, causing him to fall right into Nana, which in turn caused

Nana to fall, crashing her head into the coffee table. Looking back, it seemed to Cassie a ridiculous course of events.

Cassie at first laughed but stopped when she saw the blood coming from her nana's head. So, so much blood. Her father rushed to Nana as her mother tried to console Daphne who, frightened by all the commotion, had started crying. Wailing, more like it. Cassie was quite proud of the pipes on her little sister.

"Go get a towel, Cassie!"

Cassie ran to get a towel in the downstairs bathroom, and when she returned, she saw that Nana's eyes were still closed. She stood there staring, holding the towel.

"Is she dead?"

Her dad looked at her. "No, she's not. Now give me the towel!"

"You don't have to yell at me! It wasn't my fault!" Cassie said, throwing the towel at her dad.

"It was your fault, Cassie!"

And there it was. A common refrain that could've been her parents' motto, especially her dad's, when it came to talking about her. Her anger was replaced by something that would become her most common feeling. Shame. She fought to hold back tears.

"I wanted to hold Daphne."

"We know, Cassie," her mother said, battling not to raise her voice as she tried to console Daphne. "But it wasn't the right time."

"What about now? Maybe I can help by getting her to stop crying. I am her big sister, so . . ."

"You can help by going up to your room. We don't need you around right now. We have to take care of your nana."

"But . . ."

"Go to your room, Cassie!" her father yelled, not looking up. Cassie ran to her room without saying another word. On the way upstairs, she heard her dad tell her mom to call an ambulance because he couldn't stop the bleeding.

- - - - - - - - - -

He never could stop the bleeding. Neither could the doctors. And Nana never left the hospital.

An accident. Accidents can happen at any time. An inch or a couple of seconds can be the difference between life and death. In this case, those seconds or inches meant that Nana was dead. Cassie's mom had told her that it wasn't her fault and that she knew, for a fact, that Nana didn't blame her and that Nana loved her. Cassie asked her mom if her dad blamed her. She said of course not.

She was lying. One night, Cassie lay in bed after she had been sent to her room yet again for not wanting to eat what she was served. (It was mushrooms. Why would any kid eat mushrooms? Or anyone?) She was haunted by dreams of her nana coming back to seek revenge. In those dreams, her nana was not the Nana she remembered.

Her lovely white hair, which had always been perfect and which she had always let Cassie brush, was tangled and dirty, covered in blood and maggots. Her favorite dress, one that Cassie had helped her make, was tattered and torn. But what was worse was her face. It was hollow. Her eyes were bloodshot, and her teeth were black and razor sharp. She had climbed through Cassie's window and crawled into her bed. Cassie screamed and screamed, but no one came to help her.

Then she woke up with a start. Her nana was gone. She got up and ran to her parents' room. She was about to knock when she heard her father's words. The words that she could, would, never forget.

"She breaks everything. I only hope that Daphne is nothing like her."

Cassie didn't knock that night, or any night after that. She ran back to her room and thought she might cry, but the tears wouldn't come.

She breaks everything. I only hope that Daphne is nothing like her. Her father's words echoed in her head, over and over – until Cassie had an idea. She would fix things. Somehow.

Her closet door slowly began to open at that exact moment, and Cassie knew how she would do it.

"I wish Nana would come back."

- - - - - - - - - -

The funeral was surreal to Cassie, who had never been to one and didn't fully understand their purpose. There were people walking around everywhere before the service, shaking hands or hugging, most in tears with some even laughing. Cassie, her mom and dad, and Daphne were standing in a line, along with her cousins and other family members, as people lined up to say random things that involved either "So sorry for your loss," "She was such a good woman," or "My, aren't you growing up to be such a big girl?"

This entire ordeal creeped Cassie out, and she wanted nothing more than to run outside and play. She didn't though. She had already received a stiff lecture about being a good girl, and this time, that's exactly what she would be. A good girl. There was one point where she caught a glimpse of Nana's casket. She reached for her mom's hand, but she was too busy with Daphne, who was happily squirming and making everyone smile through their tears.

She looked up at her dad, who hadn't acknowledged her since they got to the funeral home. She reached for his hand, and he turned to look at her. She smiled at him sweetly, to which there was no response. He left his hand limply in hers until someone came by, and then he quickly dropped her hand to shake the guy's hand. Her hand fell gently back to her side, and she stared at the ground. Then she heard it.

"Cassie."

She looked at her mom, who was busy in conversation. She looked at her dad, but his back was to her.

"Cassie."

She continued hearing her name but couldn't find where it was coming from. She looked at the casket.

"Cassie."

Did it work already? She ran over to the casket and looked in. Nana lay there, looking a little like herself but also like a part of herself was missing. The guys at the funeral home had done their best to hide the wound on her head, but they had apparently done a bad job of closing the wound, because as Cassie stood there, blood started pouring from her grandmother's head. Cassie's eyes grew wide, terrified of what she was seeing. Then her grandmother's eyes shot open, only there were no longer eyes there, just empty sockets. She grabbed Cassie by the shoulders and pulled her close.

"Be home soon, little one."

Cassie shrieked and fell to the ground. She started sobbing, and her mother rushed to her.

"Cassie, are you okay?"

"It's Nana."

"I know, sweetie. It's hard that . . ."

"No, it's not that. Nana's coming back."

Then Cassie passed out.

And Nana did come back. Two days after her funeral, which Cassie didn't attend because she was still recovering from her "spell." Cassie was at the dinner table with their babysitter, Karen, who had made them macaroni and cheese and peas. Her parents were gone to Nana's house to, in her mother's words, "tidy up Nana's house."

Daphne was upstairs asleep in her crib while Cassie pushed her food around. She hadn't felt like eating since the funeral.

A loud knock at the front door woke them from their mindless grazing. They turned to the door as the knocking continued, louder and louder until it felt like the entire house was going to collapse under its wrath.

Karen jumped up from the table, a terrified look coming over her face.

"Hold on a second! I'm coming!"

"Maybe you shouldn't . . ." Cassie started to say, but then the door was blown off its hinges as something rushed into the house in a blur. Cassie watched in horror as Karen was violently torn into. Moments later, Karen's lifeless, ravaged body fell from the thing's grasp. The creature then looked at Cassie, who could do nothing more than stare at the sight before her eyes.

It was Nana. Still wearing her burial clothes.

Daphne started crying upstairs. Nana turned to the stairs and smiled, Karen's flesh still in her teeth. Nana slowly turned back to Cassie.

"Somebody needs her nana."

Nana began slowly walking to the stairs. Cassie looked around the room for a weapon of some sort, but nothing was there that seemed capable of killing a returning-from-the-dead-monster-Nana.

Then she remembered her mom's ax.

She ran as fast as she could out the kitchen door and to the shed. She crawled over the tools and equipment that no one ever bothered to put back in their proper places to reach the ax that was hanging on the back wall. She grabbed it and ran back to the house. The living room was empty when she got there. She then heard a menacing voice singing from upstairs.

"Hush little baby, don't you cry. Nana's gonna . . ."

"Daphne!"

Cassie ran up the stairs as fast she could, and when she arrived at the top of the stairs, she saw Nana's bloody hand reaching for Daphne's door.

"No!" Cassie screamed. She closed her eyes and ran towards Nana, holding the ax above her head.

What followed next would be her constant companion for the rest of her life. She had now been responsible for killing her nana twice. The image of Nana's head lying on the floor beside the door to her room with her dead eyes open and a smile across her lips would greet Cassie every time she closed her eyes.

Her mom and dad arrived home moments later, rushing upstairs after seeing Karen's body and the trail of blood going up the stairs. Upon seeing the carnage upstairs, her mother began crying as she snatched Daphne from the crib and ran downstairs, calling for Cassie to follow. Cassie, sitting quietly on the top of the stairs covered in her nana's blood, gradually stood up, turned, and watched as her dad, seeing his mother's decapitated body, collapsed to the floor. She slowly walked down the stairs.

- - - - - - - - - -

No one talked about what happened. With no actual explanation that anyone wanted to admit, the police covered everything up as best they could and called it a "burglary gone horribly wrong." No mention of Nana or Cassie's actions made it into the final report. Cassie was sent to a therapist, which didn't go well because opening up was key to a successful session, and Cassie refused. Her dad, after having to bury his mother yet again, went away for a few months to deal with things, and her mom had decided it was best to pretend that all that had happened hadn't happened. Denial, as for so many others it seemed, was their friend.

When her dad came back, the family moved, and everything returned to normal, or some semblance of normal. Cassie, trying to make up for a guilt that she could not get rid of, did her best to be the daughter they had always wanted her to be. Needed her to be. But she couldn't. No matter how hard she tried. At least they had Daphne.

- - - - - - - - - -

Daphne was wonderful. So adorable, so smart, so . . . everything. If there were ever a perfect child, Daphne was it. She charmed everyone that she met, and her parents never had to brag about her because everyone else already did.

Cassie would watch, happy that her parents were happy. She loved her family, even though, well, she couldn't make herself say it. Or think it. But it was there. And it didn't matter because as Cassie had gotten older, she had turned off whatever feelings she used to have, almost becoming robot-like.

Except when it came to Daphne. Cassie had no problem understanding why everyone was so smitten with her because she was too. Daphne always wanted Cassie to read to her, teach her things, play with her. And Cassie never said no, because finally, Cassie was someone's first choice. And something she didn't break.

The only time that Cassie would allow herself to be jealous was late at night, when sleep wouldn't come, and her mind ran rampant. Thinking about how perfect Daphne was. And how everyone looked at her. If only people could look at her that way. If only her parents could, but Cassie knew they never would. And the creature, who had stayed away after the first wish, started coming again. Telling her that it could help her with her little Daphne problem. Cassie would yell out at the creature not to touch Daphne, and the creature would remind her that it could do nothing unless she wished it to. And she would, the creature told her, in time. Cassie denied it, and her denial was greeted by the creature from the closet with laughter.

"Your words say one thing, but your heart says another."

But that wasn't true. It couldn't be. Because she loved Daphne, and if she couldn't make her parents happy, then at least Daphne could. Every painting needs something in the background to be complete, and maybe that's where Cassie belonged. In the background. There, but not there.

Somewhere, though, lurking way below the surface in that room that she had boarded up long ago, was that yearning for one time. One time that *she* was the one whom her parents loved the most. Just once.

And that need, buried so deeply, was the reason that the second wish happened. The one that would take Daphne away.

- - - - - - - - - -

And it was her fault. Of course it was.

On April 6th, the day before her fourteenth birthday, she had gotten into a fight at her school. It was with Tina, a girl who always ran her mouth and picked on people. This time, she'd finally gone too far. She was picking on Carolyn, a girl that Cassie liked, one of the few people who could say that. And Tina, a mouth breather who was also the biggest bully in the school, would not leave her alone. In the cafeteria. In front of everyone. Making fun of her lisp, the way she looked, everything. But when Tina knocked Carolyn's tray to the ground and shoved her, making her cry, that was it. Cassie ran up and punched Tina in the face. Tina fell to the ground, and Cassie jumped onto her and continued punching her until a group of teachers pulled her off. She had only planned on punching her once, but she lost control. That darkness that had always been within her came out again, and because she couldn't control it, she had almost sent Tina to the hospital.

The school suspended Cassie and sent her home early. Her parents couldn't, wouldn't, get her. Normally the school would keep the student there until someone could come and get them, but Cassie was out of control and stormed out of the school. No one moved to stop her. She walked the three miles home. She thought of boarding a bus and going somewhere, anywhere else, but she didn't have any money, so she clung to the hope that maybe her parents would take her side for once.

Sure, she had bloodied Tina, but she was defending a girl who couldn't defend herself. Some credit would have to be given for that, right? Maybe even feel a little pride because their daughter was helping the helpless?

Nope. As soon as she walked in, both of her parents started yelling at her. Telling her how disappointed they were in her, and how they had tried everything to help her, but maybe there was no help. She knew they were saying words that people say when they're angry, but it still stung. Because she had heard them so many times before. Then Daphne, after getting off the bus, walked through the door and proudly announced that she had gotten yet another big award at school.

Her parents instantly forgot about Cassie and started celebrating Daphne.

Now Cassie, no matter what anyone else thought, had never

been jealous of Daphne. Ever. She loved her more than she loved anything. Especially herself. But this time was different. Of all the times for Daphne to do yet another amazing thing. At Cassie's new lowest moment.

She stood there silently and watched as her parents gushed over her younger sister in a way that they had never done for her. And there had been times that they could have too, but they never had.

She was content to stand there silently, though. Anything to avoid being yelled at yet again. But then her dad turned around and looked her straight into her eyes, and Cassie did not see an ounce of affection there.

"Why can't you be more like your sister?"

And that was it. Cassie lit into all of them, saying all the things that she had thought but had never dared to speak. About all the times that she had tried to be the daughter they wanted, but nothing she did was ever good enough. About how she knew her dad had never forgiven her for what happened to Nana even though she was only seven, the same age Daphne was now. About how she knew that they would rather not have her around because she broke everything.

Daphne tried to give her a hug, and Cassie started to push her away but couldn't. She instead ran to her room, slammed the door, and threw herself onto the bed, her sobs uncontrolled.

Minutes later, a little knock came at the door.

"Cassie." It was Daphne's tiny voice.

"Go away, Daphne!"

Instead, the door opened, and Daphne walked in. "I wanted to say I'm sorry . . ."

The flower vase hit the wall right beside Daphne. "I told you to go away! This is all your fault!"

And she didn't say the next thing aloud. But she thought it. Daphne walked out of the room without saying a word, shutting Cassie's door quietly as she left.

Then Cassie heard the voice hiss from the closet. "You shall have your second wish."

The closet door swung open, and Cassie couldn't see anything leaving the closet, but she felt it sweep past her. Moments later, she heard screams coming from Daphne's room.

She leapt off her bed and ran to Daphne's room, only to watch helplessly as the creature swallowed Daphne whole. The creature turned and wiped its mouth.

"You are now the only one." And the creature disappeared.

- - - - - - - - - -

No one ever found out what happened to Daphne. The police were called and search parties were formed, but they would never find her. She had simply disappeared without a trace.

They had asked Cassie if she knew anything, but what was she going to tell them? That she had mentally wished for the creature in her closet to get rid of her sister, and it ate her? Yeah, that's a one-way ticket to the loony bin. So, she said she didn't know anything. And then she cried.

The demon was right, though. As the years passed, her parents did hold her more and perhaps, possibly, even start to love her. And Cassie tried to be the daughter that they had always craved. To be more like Daphne. She stopped getting in trouble, her grades improved, she started listening better, and she almost liked herself.

But she knew the truth. The truth of what was happening with her parents. Oh, they gave her kisses and hugs, told her they loved her, and acted like they were happy. She wanted to believe them, but something rang hollow in their words and actions. Because they were hollow. They tried to hide it, but she saw in their silent moments when they thought she wasn't around. She saw it when they were alone or when they sat together on the porch at night, where they spent most nights gazing out, seeing nothing. Daphne's disappearance had left a crater-sized hole, and now they weren't living anymore. They were existing. Going through the motions of a life they no longer cared to live because that's what they felt they had to do. And no matter how hard Cassie tried, she knew that she could never be their Daphne. And moment after moment, day after day, year after year, that only became clearer.

That's when Cassie, now 17 and getting ready for college, knew what her third wish would be. She got off that red velvet couch and headed up to her room.

- - - - - - - - - -

Ever since Cassie had made her second wish, the creature had not talked to her. But Cassie knew it was there. And that night, after kissing her parents goodnight in the bed where they had spent all day in a saddened, darkened, and drunken stupor, she walked back into her room and locked the door. She crawled into bed and stared at the closet.

"I'm ready for my third wish," Cassie said, pulling the covers around her.

For a moment, nothing happened. Cassie, knowing she had nothing to lose, got out of bed and walked to the closet door. She opened it and looked in.

"I said I'm ready for my third wish!"

At that moment, the moon went out. That's the only way that Cassie could explain it. It was complete and utter darkness. Her room began shaking as if she were trapped in the middle of an earthquake. The shaking was joined by a wind that whipped up out of nowhere. Cassie ran back to her bed and dove under the sheets, instantly regretting her decision.

She felt a force suddenly pick her up. Her fingers scraped desperately for the bed but to no avail. The force flung her across the room, only stopping when she crashed into a wall. She fell to the floor and screamed out in pain.

Then everything stopped. Cassie opened her eyes slowly, and there it was. The moon had returned and cast a pale glow on its red eyes.

"Hello, my dear," the creature said, smiling, showing the multitude of razor sharp teeth that filled its mouth. Cassie stared at it mutely. The creature laughed and sat down on Cassie's bed. It carelessly crossed its legs and looked at her. "So, you want your third wish?"

"Yes," Cassie said, making no effort to move.

"Excellent. Though, if I were you, I would put a little more thought into this one because your others did not seem to bring what you desired."

Cassie thought back to everything that had happened

because of her. Nana, Karen, and Daphne dead. And her parents were nothing more than living corpses. All because of her. The images flashed before her, causing her to wince while convincing her that she was doing the right thing.

"Are you going to sit there in a crumbled heap remembering your other wishes, or are you going to make your final wish?" the creature rasped.

Cassie shook off the past and pulled herself out of her now-broken dresser.

"No. I'm ready. And I'm going to get it right this time."

The creature smiled and stood up to its full height, towering over the teenage girl. "Do tell." Cassie leaned in and whispered in the thing's ear. A look of shock came over its face, and it pulled away slightly. "Are you sure that's what you want?"

Cassie stared at the thing with no hesitation or fear. "Yes. I'm tired of breaking things. For once I would like to fix something."

"But there will be no coming back. Your story will end. Or, to be exact, it will have never been told."

"I know. It's better this way. I know that now. Promise me you will keep the second part of the wish too."

The thing smiled. "Of course. Now if . . ."

"I am."

"Then it shall be so."

And Cassie was no more.

- - - - - - - - - -

The family's old house was decorated for a party. Balloons and streamers were everywhere. Family and friends filled the house, talking happily about things that were probably of no importance to most except to the people that were sharing them.

Nana came in with a big smile, looking beautiful and vibrant. She happily shushed everyone. Silence filled the house as all eyes turned towards the door, patiently awaiting the arrival of the special guest.

Anticipation grew quickly, and then her voice was heard outside the door.

"What's going on?"

"You'll see," her father said.

"I'm so excited!"

"I know you are, dear," her mother replied. "Now open the door."

Daphne opened the door and was greeted by a loud "Surprise!" The living room was full of her family and friends. Daphne was barely able to contain her glee.

And the singing of "Happy Birthday" began.

She then saw the giant cake in honor of her fourteenth birthday; her smile lit up the entire room.

As it always had.

Cassie smiled from outside the window. A smile with a hint of sadness for what, after her wish, never was.

As she began fading away, the second part of the wish now fulfilled, she looked to the mantel and saw the family picture, which once upon a time had included Cassie but now included her two parents and their only daughter, Daphne.

The way it was meant to be.

CHAPTER 8

"Goddammit, Vanessa!" Lindsey exclaimed.

"What?" Vanessa said innocently.

"Can't you, for once, tell a story that doesn't make me wish I had never been born? I swear you're going to get me sent away long before I'm meant to."

"At least it was shorter than yours," Vanessa said. "What did you think, Dani?"

"Disturbing. On so many levels," Dani responded. "I liked it though. Well, as much as one can like a story that's super dark throughout and had such a depressing ending."

Vanessa shrugged. "I see it as more of a happy ending. She made things the way they were meant to be. The way that made her family happy."

"By making herself disappear," Claire said. "Depressing."

"I guess."

"So where did you get this story?" Dani asked.

"Made it up."

"Based on what?"

"Somebody I know."

Lindsey piped in. "This is the point at which Vanessa says that the 'person she knows' is herself, which no one will believe."

Vanessa stood up and walked away from the group. "We've all got our things, Lindsey."

"So, you are saying it's you?"

"No," Vanessa said non-emotionally. "I'm saying we've all got our things."

Dani stared at her. "Even you?"

Vanessa turned to Dani. "Even me." She could see the doubt on Dani's face. "Look, Dani, I know you don't know me as well as these two, and all you do know is what Lindsey and I said earlier. Yes, I'm pretty, athletic, probably the smartest student in our school, and my parents are loaded. And I'm not even saying the story is about me. I'm simply saying that even when it seems like someone has everything, they may be missing something that they would give all that other shit up for to have." Vanessa noticed Claire moving towards her. "And Claire, if you try to give me a hug, I will kick you in the face."

Lindsey laughed. "That's my girl."

Claire stopped moving and smiled at Vanessa. "Then I will give you an air hug." Claire hugged herself tightly and then looked back at Vanessa. "That was for you."

"Thanks," said Vanessa, seemingly unaffected by sharing some apparent truth about herself. And to be honest, she was completely unaffected. Never being the emotional one, she could simply see that what was, was. Your feelings about it were completely irrelevant because feelings were affected by too many variables and thus pointless. At least that's what her dad had told her so many times that it became her truth. So screw it.

Lindsey stood up. "I can't believe I'm doing this, but," she turned to Claire. "Claire, you tell the next story."

"Wait, what?" Vanessa said incredulously.

"That's right. After your story, I need my palate cleansed, or the entire night will be ruined. Enough of this teen angst shit. Claire, please tell your what will clearly be awful story."

Claire jumped up. "Yes!"

"How could you, Lindsey?" Vanessa asked, throwing a stick at Lindsey.

"Your fault. The only way to fix it is for Claire to tell her story."

"That's highly doubtful."

"What's wrong with Claire's stories?" Dani asked.

"My stories tend to be inaccurate," Claire said matter-of-factly.

"In what way?"

Vanessa laughed. "All ways. You see, the very first story Claire told lasted for about, I don't know, days or something, and when she got to the end, the climax, she realized that the climax to the story she was telling actually belonged to a completely different story, which made her story make no sense whatsoever."

"And she hasn't gotten better since. She never quite knows any of her stories," Lindsey added.

"I'll have you know that I know this one. Mostly," Claire said proudly.

Vanessa turned to Lindsey. "Are you sure you want this to happen?"

"I do."

"Then God help your soul."

"Oh, it's much too late for that, my friend. Much too late."

"What's your story, Claire?" Dani asked.

Claire stood up on a log excitedly and cleared her throat. "It's called . . ." She looked off into the distance. "The Tale of the Golden Arm!" Vanessa and Lindsey started laughing but stopped when Claire dramatically pointed at them. "Go ahead, laugh, but soon you'll be crying. Crying in fear!" She then stepped down off the log and paced around as she began, "It was a dark and stormy night, the darkest and stormiest night since the last night that was really dark. And stormy!"

CHAPTER 9

Claire's Story

The fog was rolling through the woods like something really thick and air-like, but the kind of air that you can't see through. Like a thick fog.

If Sal had his choice, he wouldn't be out here. But he didn't. Because he was with Jamie, though not at this exact moment. If he left, she would kill him. Literally. Because that's the kind of person she was.

Jamie. They had met when they were six at a playground in a neighborhood where neither of them lived. Sal was there because his playground was full of kids who didn't make Sal's sandbox time gleeful, so Sal's parents took him to this old, rundown park that was stuck between a dump and some type of chemical company that had been fined over and over again for poisoning the water supply of the town. In some cases, they had literally been recorded pouring poison on the townsfolk. And Jamie was there because, well, she wanted to be. Even at age six, Jamie had made up the rules that she followed. Sal wasn't even sure she had parents.

And that's where they first met one overcast afternoon. Sal was sitting in the sandbox all alone except for his pal Franklin. Franklin was a fern and Sal's only friend. They were currently in the midst of a deep discussion on why people didn't like Sal. Sal always found Franklin's words firm but supportive. Today was no different.

"Sure, the fact that my best friend is a fern may be the cause of some of it, but . . ."

Sal never finished his statement as he was hit in the head by something. He looked down and found the object.

An acorn.

Then the chittering started. Sal looked around but saw nothing. He pulled Franklin close to him, leaning down and whispering, "Don't worry, buddy. I'll keep us safe." He covered where he imagined Franklin's eyes to be and closed his own.

The chittering grew louder, and was that the scurrying of thousands of tiny feet? The sounds grew louder still, and six-year-old Sal thought of running but decided it would be a better choice to make himself invisible. He and Franklin cowered.

It did not work. The noise stopped, but Sal, and probably Franklin as well, understood that it didn't mean they were safe. Whatever it was, Sal knew, was now in the sandbox. He slowly opened his eyes and saw a sight that made him instantly wet his pants.

Squirrels. Surrounding him and Franklin. They stared at the pair with their beady little eyes and what Sal knew was malice in their hearts. Sal muttered to Franklin something about not moving and then looked back at the squirrels. He tried to find their leader because maybe, just maybe, he could establish a dialogue with her and perhaps talk his and Franklin's way out of this. Though he had never quite mastered the prized ability of conversation. Maybe this time would be different.

He never got the chance. The squirrel that Sal had deduced was the leader gave a slight head nod, and all the squirrels pounced as one on Sal and Franklin. Sal tried to curl up in a fetal position, but it was no use. As the squirrels scratched at Sal, he swore he heard tiny squirrelly voices laughing and mocking him and his fern friend. He then felt some squirrels tugging on Franklin to get him out of Sal's grasp. Sal struggled to hold on to his best friend, but it was no use. The squirrels were way stronger than he was, and soon a group of them had Franklin the fern in their furry little paws. The violence around him ceased, and Sal looked at the squirrel bullies and his poor defenseless ferny friend.

"Please don't hurt him! Take me instead."

- - - - - - - - - -

"Seriously, what the hell is this?" Lindsey interrupted, shaking her head in disbelief. "I mean, your stories are normally appalling, but a best friend fern, ferns suck by the way, and squirrel bullies?"

"It's important for the story. Trust me. I have to tell this part to give meaning to everything that happens in the present time."

"Well, the only meaning I'm getting right now is that you should be banned from ever telling stories again," Vanessa added, and she and Lindsey started laughing. Claire turned to Dani.

"What about you, Dani? Do you have a more evolved opinion than those two about my storytelling prowess?"

"It's different. And I bet it . . . gets good," Dani said. Vanessa and Lindsey looked at her, identical incredulous expressions on their faces.

"Doubtful," said Vanessa.

"It's supposed to be scary. Not stupid," said Lindsey.

"Sometimes," Dani continued, "the scariest stories come when you least expect them."

"Exactly," Claire said, smiling. "Thank you, Dani. Finally, someone that appreciates quality, nonlinear storytelling." Lindsey and Vanessa snorted. "May I continue?" Dani nodded, Lindsey rolled her eyes with a reluctant smile, and Vanessa shrugged indifferently. "Good. As I was saying before I was so rudely interrupted . . ."

- - - - - - - - - -

The squirrels laughed at Sal's urgent plea. Then the ones holding Franklin threw him to the lead squirrel, which Sal decided looked like it was named Tia. He watched in horror as Tia lifted Franklin into the air and threw him down to the ground, shattering the vase that Sal had made for him in school. Franklin's body lay lifeless in the sandbox.

"Noooooooooooooooooooooooooooooooo!" Sal reached for Franklin from his knees, but a squirrel wearing a beret bit him on the hand. He screamed in anguish and pulled his hand back. Then three squirrels, the toughest and meanest-looking ones, stood in front of him as the rest of the awful beasts began pulling Franklin apart, leaf by trembling leaf.

Sal burst into tears and averted his eyes. He could no longer watch this.

"Hey, how about you pick on someone your own size?"

Sal looked up as someone dressed in a leather jacket punched Tia in the face, knocking the leader of the squirrels out of the sandbox onto the broken slide. She lay there, unconscious.

"Anybody else want some?"

The squirrels looked at each other and quickly ran off, stopping to retrieve their dazed leader on the way. Sal watched as the figure, a girl about his age, walked over to him.

"You okay?"

"I got attacked by squirrels."

"You did."

"And they killed Franklin."

"Franklin?" the girl asked, looking genuinely confused. Sal pointed to the mess of green scattered in the sandbox. "Oh. Sorry about your watermelon."

"He was a fern. And my only friend."

"Well, now I'll be your only friend," the girl said, extending her hand. "I'm Jamie, and I'm six."

"I'm Sal, and I'm six too," Sal said, taking her hand. Jamie looked down at his pants.

"You peed yourself."

Sal looked down and nodded. "I did."

- - - - - - - - - -

Ever since then, 18 years to the day, they had been best friends. And now partners in their new career: grave robbing.

Which was why Sal was now out in the middle of a dark forest with trees so tall that you couldn't even see the tops of them, if they even had tops. Might have something to do with the fog as well. And the fact that it was night. He was waiting for Jamie, who wasn't there yet, but he knew he wasn't alone. Not by a long shot.

Because *they* were watching him. They were always watching him. Ever since Franklin went to fern heaven. He could now feel their beady little eyes staring holes through his heart. Sal was sweating profusely, something he always did when he was scared.

"Come on, Jamie. What's taking you so long?" he muttered. "You know I hate being in the woods at night. Everything gets crazy. Especially those tree-climbing, nut-eating freaks." Sal looked up in the trees and yelled, "I know you're watching me! I know you're . . ." He turned around, screamed, and collapsed to the ground. This was greeted by laughter.

"Nice move, Salazar."

Sal jumped up and tried to dust the dirt and shame off himself.

"Did I scare you?" Jamie asked with a smirk.

"Yes," Sal said, rather irritated with the question. "But the squirrels did it first."

"So that's who you were yelling at."

"Yes."

Jamie started laughing. "You're losing it, man."

"Of course I'm losing it. You left me out in the woods by myself for like forever. What took you so long?"

Jamie set down the sack she was holding and knelt beside it. "Digging up graves takes a long time. I had to dig up 13 of them before I found the right one."

"Why didn't you look at the name on the tombstone?" Sal

asked, kneeling beside her. Jamie looked at him as if his question made her reconsider all the work that she had done. She thought of giving him credit for realizing something she'd missed but decided to pass on that opportunity.

"I thought about that, but you know what they say: digging up graves is a lot of fun."

"No one ever says that, Jamie."

"Well, not aloud," Jamie admitted. "But I am what I am and proud of it. Besides, I found a lot of great stuff." She reached into the bag and began pulling things out. "See? A gold locket, several watches, a couple of scarfs, and this!" Jamie whipped out a skull. Sal jumped back and fell.

"Is that a human skull?"

"You bet it is. Look, there's even a little bit of an eye left. Want it?"

"No!"

"Okay, fine. I'll give it to you for Christmas," Jamie said as she threw it back in the sack and stood up.

Sal, once again having to dust himself off from falling, got up and stood beside her.

"Did you at least find what we came here for?"

"Oh, the golden arm? Yeah, I got it right . . ." Sal put his hand over Jamie's mouth.

"Shhhh! Not so loud. They could be listening."

"Other grave robbers?" Jamie asked. "I'd like to see them . . ."

"No, much worse," Sal said, removing his hand. "Squirrels."

"Have you seen any?"

"No . . ." Here, he lowered his voice to a whisper. "But that's how you know they're there."

Jamie laughed and shook her head. "Well, then I suppose we should hurry." She reached back into the bag. "You can't imagine how tough bones are to cut through. She held up surprisingly well for being dead 200 years. Ah, there it is!" Jamie pulled out a sandwich. "My sandwich." She took a big bite.

"Why would your sandwich be in that bag?"

"I didn't have another place to keep it," she said through a mouthful of sandwich as she continued rummaging through the bag. But then she found what she was supposed to be looking for and pulled out the arm. The golden arm.

Sal's eyes grew wide. Jamie handed the arm to him, and he looked at it from every possible angle, knocked on it, and then looked at Jamie.

"You sure it's the right one?"

"Doubt there're many golden arms lying about," Jamie said.

"Don't be so sure," Sal said. "My mother harvested golden arms when I was little."

"Really?"

"No," Sal admitted. "Although I always wished she had. Harvesting golden arms was the key to popularity where I was from." Sal paused and looked out. "Michigan."

"I know. We're from the same state, dumbass."

"But it doesn't matter," Sal said, a big smile crossing his face. "Because with this . . ." he held out the arm, "we'll be set for life. Live where we want, eat what we want, and never dig up any more graves."

"Well, we still will, but now we'll do it for fun," Jamie said. "But I wouldn't get too far ahead of yourself there, Salmon. We might have the golden arm, but to enjoy it, we gotta survive."

"Right." Sal nodded. "The squirrels."

"No, not the damn squirrels!" Jamie said. "Something far worse."

"What could be worse than squirrels?" Sal asked, growing nervous.

Jamie smiled dangerously and walked closer to him. She stopped inches from his face. "Oh, nothing but . . . the curse."

"The . . . the . . . curse?" Sal stuttered. "What curse?"

"Wait, you haven't heard of The Curse of the Golden Arm?"

"No," Sal said, shaking his head. Then it was as if a light clicked on. He looked at the golden arm in his hand and then back at Jamie. "*This* golden arm?" he stammered. Jamie nodded. Sal threw the arm to the ground.

"Hey," Jamie said, picking the golden arm back up and cradling it lovingly. "I worked hard to find this."

"What's the curse, Jamie?"

Jamie, always good at telling stories and scaring Sal, strolled away from him slowly. "Well, legend has it that the woman this arm belonged to was given it by her husband after she had lost her arm in an accident. Then the husband died at sea, and the arm became her most treasured possession because it reminded her of her beloved. When she died, she was buried with it, but people knew – the wrong people – and they kept trying to steal it. But each time someone did steal it, days later they would end up dead, and the arm would be found back in her grave. And now it's in our hands."

"Do you think it's true?" Sal asked, backing away from Jamie and the arm.

They turned when they heard moaning from somewhere

146

deep in the woods coming towards them. Jamie turned back to Sal and smiled.

"Well, I guess we're about to find out." The moaning grew louder. "Quick, Sal, you need to cower behind me!"

Sal and Jamie (who quickly stashed the golden arm in her bag and grabbed the sandwich she'd dropped on the ground) cowered together. They hid as they always did when they needed to cower: Sal behind Jamie, making himself as tiny as he could, and Jamie standing in front of him, her arms stretched out behind her like an umbrella protecting a small child who was allergic to rain. Sal had always been amazed by her flexibility. They cowered silently as the moaning grew louder and louder and closer and closer. They then heard footsteps, and the moaning stopped. The footsteps continued for a brief moment, and then all that could be heard was the tapping of a foot on leaves. Like someone, or something, waiting impatiently. Sal, clearly protected by the standing Jamie, looked through her legs and saw the figure.

It was a woman with wild-looking black hair and what looked to be blood dripping from her eyes. She was terrifying. Her dress, also covered in blood, was torn in many places. Sal thought that it certainly wasn't a flattering look, but he decided to let that thought train chug on without him when he noticed something else. He leaned up and whispered to Jamie.

"Jamie?"

"Yes."

"It's a woman – a super scary woman – and she has both of her arms."

"I can see that because I'm facing her."

"Who summoned me?" the figure demanded.

Jamie looked the woman over. "You're not the woman with the golden arm, are you?"

"Do I look like I'm missing an arm?"

"No."

"Then I suppose I'm not," the lady said with a huge hint of condescension. Jamie had never liked people who spoke to her with a huge hint of condescension, and this time was no different.

"You don't have a reason to be rude, lady," Jamie said, moving closer to her, ready to go at it with this thing. Sal, knowing exactly what Jamie's next move was and thinking that this time Jamie might have met her match, ran over to her but tripped over Jamie's bag and fell to the ground yet again. The woman and Jamie both looked down at him.

Sal spit some dirt out of his mouth and looked up at the woman.

"Who are you?"

"I think you know who I am," the figure said, growing more and more irritated as time went on.

"Look, lady . . ."

With a swipe of her hand, the figure sent both Jamie and Sal crashing into trees. They lay there stunned for a moment, unable to speak, as the figure walked over to them.

"My name is Bloody Mary!"

- - - - - - - - - -

"'And what the hell am I doing here?' said Bloody Mary," Lindsey said. "'Oh wait, is Claire telling this story?'"

Claire stared at Lindsey. "What are you doing?"

"Bloody Mary isn't in the story about the golden arm, Claire," Vanessa said, laughing.

"Duh. I know that." Claire hoped the bravado with which she responded would cover up the fact that she did not, in fact, know that. "That's why it's a new story. Kind of like a mash-up or something."

"Seriously?" Lindsey asked. Claire nodded (over-nodded). "Even though I doubt you're telling the truth, I'm willing to hear it out because it could be cool. Maybe."

"Great," Claire said, trying to figure out where to go now that she had screwed up her story. But then, it was as if the storytelling gods, who had never brightened Claire's doorstep before, stepped in and provided a story. A story that was unfolding before her very eyes as she stared at the other girls.

"So are you going to tell us or keep staring at us all weird?" Vanessa said.

"Oh, I am. And it's funny that you mentioned Bloody Mary mentioning who's telling the story."

"Why?"

"You're about to find out," Claire said with a gleeful laugh.

- - - - - - - - - -

"My name is Bloody Mary. And you called my name three times while looking in a bathroom mirror that . . ." She stopped and looked around. "That is not here because we are in the middle of the damn woods, which makes no sense. Unless Claire is telling this story."

"Who's Claire?" Jamie asked.

"Shut up! I wasn't talking to you," snapped Bloody Mary.

Jamie, now pissed, shoved off Sal, who had at some point climbed on her back for protection, causing him to fall into the mud. Sal tried to reach for her to stop her from making an obviously bad decision but failed miserably as he fell face-first into the mud. Again. Jamie walked angrily over to Bloody Mary and stared at her.

Bloody Mary, nonplussed, stared back at her. "What?"

Jamie's features softened a little. "I like someone who has the spunk to tell me to shut up. But I want to know who you are and who this Claire character is. And, let's be clear, since you're not missing an arm, this arm is ours."

"I don't care about a golden arm, because that's not my story. I, like the Lady with the Golden Arm, am an urban legend, with mine clearly being the better of the two. And as I said before, I show up when someone calls my name three times while looking in a bathroom mirror."

"To like talk or something?" Sal asked, wiping the mud off his face.

"No. To kill them."

"Then why would someone call you?" Jamie asked.

"People like to be scared, and they don't think I'm real. Until I leave them dead."

"And you're here why?"

"Because of Claire, who is clearly telling a story that once again includes me for absolutely no reason." Bloody Mary walked around and looked at her surroundings, an old graveyard that no longer drew any mourners except those with extreme guilt. All the graves were either surrounded by weeds or were falling apart. Bloody Mary looked to the sky and was greeted by a starless night with a faint hint of a full moon. Then she looked at Jamie and Sal, and a brilliantly amazing idea came to her. One that would provide her a purpose for coming here, and one that would bring closure. A smile crossed her face. Sal, who was now standing behind Jamie and not climbing on her back, was taken aback.

"Why are you smiling like that?"

"Because I had a thought. A new story idea, if you will." Jamie and Sal were both about to ask what story it was, but with a flick of her hand, both of their mouths disappeared. Bloody Mary laughed as she watched them struggle with what to do. Sal began crying, and Jamie started to charge at her, but this time was tackled by Sal, who tried to pantomime why her choice was a bad one. "He's right, you know. If I can make your mouths disappear, what else do you think I could do? Now you two sit quietly while I bring in a most important guest."

Bloody Mary moved away from Sal and Jamie and, with another flick of her hand, cleared the brush from around her, leaving a perfect circle in its place. Sal and Jamie watched as she closed her eyes and began chanting in a language that neither of them had ever heard. The wind began blowing intensely around them, causing them to hold on tightly to one another, which in turn made Sal smile and made Jamie groan and roll her eyes. The wind became so furious that flying debris made it impossible to see Bloody Mary.

Then it was over. And a teenage girl was standing there.

"Hello . . . Claire."

Claire looked around in shock. Moments ago, she was telling

the greatest story in the world, and now, she somehow was in the story. She looked and saw Bloody Mary staring at her with eyes seemingly filled with blood. This was not good.

"Oh, crap."

- - - - - - - - - -

"You put yourself in your own story?" Vanessa asked. Claire nodded and smiled. "Cool. Very meta."

"Wow," Dani said, impressed. "If all your stories . . ."

"They're not," Lindsey said. "Now let her keep going before she remembers she has no storytelling ability."

"Not a chance," Claire said, smiling. Then she realized what she'd said and decided to forge ahead with her story.

- - - - - - - - - -

Before Claire could move a muscle, Bloody Mary was inches from her face. Claire swallowed hard at the sight of Bloody Mary, unable to speak or move away. "Really, Claire, again?"

"Aw, man," Claire muttered.

"Do you ever get a story right? Ever? And why do I have to be in every one that you screw up?" Bloody Mary lifted her hand and the golden arm suddenly appeared in it. "See, *this* is a golden arm. It belongs to someone who *doesn't* have two arms anymore. Unlike me. Since I have two arms. Now, what was *supposed* to happen is that the ghost to whom this arm belongs, the one with one arm, comes shambling out moaning, 'Who has my golden arm?' Then she would kill both of these morons."

Jamie, noticing that her mouth had reappeared, turned around and punched Sal on the arm. "That's what I was about to tell you, Sal!"

"That would've been super scary," Sal agreed, whose happiness at having his mouth back had quickly been eclipsed by his now bruising arm. "And you probably could've told me that without punching me in the arm."

"No, I couldn't have, and wouldn't it? It'd be worth the dying part for the thrills."

"Highly doubtful."

"Well, it doesn't matter because it didn't happen. However..." Bloody Mary said, looking back.

"You're still going to die tonight." She turned back to Claire. "And so are you."

"Wait, what?" Claire asked, fear rising in her voice.

"That's right, Claire," Bloody Mary said, walking a short distance away and kicking a gravestone over. "It's nothing personal." She took a moment to reconsider. "Correction, it's very personal. I'm tired of showing up in every single story that you mess up. Why me? Why do you always go with Bloody Mary? There are thousands of urban legends. Yet it's always me."

"Are you sure you're not in this story?" Claire asked.

Bloody Mary turned back to Claire. "You have to be freaking kidding me! Idiot!"

Sal, either finding the courage he never knew he had or trying to impress someone, stepped in front of Jamie and looked at Bloody Mary somewhat bravely. "Hey, ease off the girl, will you? She can't help it if she can't tell a story."

Bloody Mary turned to Sal and began slowly walking – no,

gliding – over to him. "Were you addressing me?" she asked with a cold fury.

Sal looked at her and then at his feet, actively resisting the urge to collapse in a heap again. "Um, no, ma'am."

"Good, because if you were, I would kill you where you stand now instead of moments from now." Jamie pulled Sal back behind her. Bloody Mary turned back to Claire. "But see, Claire, tonight it all ends. Because I've decided to bring you into your own story and get rid of you for good."

"I would rather you not."

"Well, I am. Right now." She raised her hand and flicked her wrist. Claire's neck was broken instantly. Sal screamed out and buried his eyes into Jamie's back. Jamie could only stare at Claire's body as it now lay lifeless on the ground.

"Did not see that coming."

"What about this?" Bloody Mary said, snapping her fingers. Both Jamie and Sal were dead before they hit the ground.

- - - - - - - - - -

"What the shit, Claire?"

Claire turned to Lindsey. "Yes?"

Lindsey realized that everyone was staring at her, Vanessa smiling slightly, clearly enjoying how uncomfortable Lindsey was becoming. "Um . . . nothing."

"Come on, tell us, Lindsey. You know you want to," Vanessa urged with that infuriating smirk.

"I do not." That response was greeted by silence. "Fine, if you must know, I find broken necks to be a weak literary choice."

Claire smiled. "That's sweet."

"I don't know why you would say that. Also, I don't like abrupt endings."

"Good," Claire said, smiling rather innocently at Lindsey. "Because it's not over yet."

- - - - - - - - - -

Bloody Mary looked around at her work. It had gone much better, and more quickly, than she had imagined. The two grave-robbing idiots had managed to fall on top of each other like a modern-day Romeo and Juliet, if Romeo and Juliet's heads were both facing the wrong way. She laughed. She turned to her story nemesis, Claire, and walked over to her. The girl was oddly still quite beautiful even in death, with her intelligence radiating through.

Then Bloody Mary noticed that Claire's striking green eyes were still open and saw something in them that gave her pause. It was disconcerting. She had seen many people die with their eyes open, usually by her hand. But this was different. Because these eyes were moving.

"Do eyes do that when someone dies?" Bloody Mary wondered aloud.

"Nope," Claire said, now magically standing back up and smiling.

A look of disgust came over Bloody Mary's face. "Damn it."

"Right?" said Claire with a smirk. She then twitched her nose once, and both Jamie and Sal stood up, stretching a little as if they were sore.

"What happened?" Jamie asked. Sal screamed. "What, Sal?"

"Your head's on backwards!"

"No, it's not." Then Jamie looked down and then back up at Sal. "My head is on backwards." Then she started laughing. "And so is yours."

Sal looked down and screamed again.

"Sorry," Claire said as she twitched her nose again. Sal and Jamie's heads returned to the normal facing way.

"Okay, Bewitched, how did you do that?"

"Well, Ms. Bloody Mary, even though this might not be the correct story, it's still my story, and I didn't like your ending."

Bloody Mary grew angry, and her face visibly reddened, even beneath its usual coating of blood. "I will kill you again."

Claire smiled. "Only if I let you. And then I'll come back again."

Bloody Mary broke Claire's neck again. Claire collapsed to the ground, then popped back up again. "See?"

"I seem to not have as much power as I thought."

Claire shook her head. "You don't. You're a character in my story and only have the power I give you, so you have to do what I tell you. By the way, I brought myself here. Not you."

Bloody Mary could do nothing more than look at Claire as all that she had believed about herself crumbled in front of her eyes. "This sucks."

"For someone who imagined they had all the power and now finds out that they're nothing more than a puppet? I imagine it would." Claire walked over and clapped a hand companionably on Bloody Mary's shoulder. "I have an idea that will make you feel a little better and make this story make more sense. If you're okay with that, I mean."

Bloody Mary mused. "Don't pretend I have a choice." Claire smiled at Bloody Mary, who looked back at her and then, with feelings that seemingly came out of nowhere, said happily, "Yes!"

"I made you do that."

Bloody Mary glared at Claire, who was happily smiling back at her.

"I'm good with it as well," said Jamie.

"Me too," Sal agreed.

"Of course you two would be," Bloody Mary said, not taking her eyes off Claire. "You're both random characters that could be played by any ignorant jackasses."

"Hey!" Jamie said.

"No one cares," Bloody Mary said, quickly ending the discussion. "So, Claire, can we get on with this since I have been neutered and have no choice because we both know that characters are beholden to their storytellers? But for the love of all things unholy, please make it not suck."

"Oh, it won't suck," Claire said. She walked off a little and turned back to the motley group of characters that she had assembled. "I have to go now."

"Why?"

"Because my character part of the story is done. Enjoy my horrific ghost love story."

"Horrific ghost love story?" Bloody Mary, Sal, and Jamie said at the same time.

But there was no answer because Claire was gone. The three remaining characters looked at one another. Jamie eyed the golden arm, which now lay out in the clearing under a small tree. She looked at Sal and motioned to him to get it. He stared at her, confused as to what her head jerk meant. She did it again, this time more forcefully.

Suddenly Sal got it. Or at least he thought he did. He rushed Jamie and tried to tackle her. She, always expecting an attack of this nature from everyone and everything, stepped aside, grabbing Sal in the process, flipped him over, and threw him to the ground, causing Sal to scream out in pain.

"What the hell were you doing, Sal? You working for Buddy Mary over there?"

Bloody Mary turned to her. "My name is not Buddy Mary, you hick. It's Bloody Mary."

"Whatever," Jamie said. She turned back to Sal. "You aren't working for her, are you?"

"No," Sal managed to say through sighs of pain. "You were moving all weird. I thought you were having a fit or something."

"So you ran at me?"

"I was going to tackle you and hold you tight so that you wouldn't hurt yourself."

Jamie was oddly touched by this. "Well, that's sweet in a strange way. But I wasn't having a fit. I was trying to get you to go over and get the golden arm while she was feeling sorry for herself."

"I was not feeling sorry for myself!" Bloody Mary said, rushing over to them. "Well, I was a little. I exist to kill people, and now I can't."

"Why?"

"Because my, and I use the term loosely, 'God' won't let me," Bloody Mary said with a sigh. "Though if someone does say my name three times, I should be able to." She turned to them hopefully. "Any takers?"

"Nope."

"Cowards," Bloody Mary said, slumping to the ground. Silence filled the woods as none of the three seemed to know what to do. Then Jamie started packing up her bag and turned to Sal.

"Suppose we should be going, Sal. Got what we were going after anyway. Pick up the golden arm and throw it to me."

Sal looked at Jamie and then at Bloody Mary, not trusting that she wouldn't kill him. Bloody Mary looked back at him.

"What? I said I can't do anything to you." Sal took another moment, looked at the ground, picked up a rock, and threw it at her, hitting her squarely in the head. "Ow! Why did you do that?"

"To see if you could kill me."

"Oh, believe me, if I could, I would."

Sal smiled and ran for the golden arm. He reached down and picked it up. At that moment, the woods filled with a strong wind. Sal and Jamie stood close together, Jamie shielding Sal behind her as usual. Bloody Mary, now intrigued, stood up and looked around. Then they heard the ghostly whisper that seemed to come from everywhere and nowhere all at once.

"Who has my golden arm? Who has my golden arm? Who has my golden arm?"

Sal and Jamie looked at each other.

"Oh, shit."

Jamie turned to Sal. "Give it to me."

Sal started to hand it to her and then stopped. "No! If I do, she'll kill you."

"Better me than you. Now give it!" They started battling for the golden arm, unaware that another figure had appeared in the woods. A figure of glowing white, missing an arm. Bloody Mary, who did not miss the arrival, laughed.

"It doesn't appear to matter, you two."

Sal and Jamie stopped fighting over the golden arm and looked over their shoulders at the new figure, who smiled at them.

"Do you have my golden arm?"

Jamie snatched the arm away from Sal, who tried to get it back, but to no avail. Jamie looked at Sal and winked at him. She then turned back and walked over to the figure.

"Are you the Lady with the Golden Arm?"

"Not now. Because you're holding it."

Bloody Mary moved closer to the scene, determined to see the grisly end of the tall girl.

"Right," Jamie said, nervously shuffling her feet. "Do you want it back?"

"Of course. If you don't mind."

"Nope, here you go." Jamie handed the arm to the woman, who took it and gazed at Jamie happily. She then placed it near the spot where the missing part of her arm was, and the golden arm magically reattached. She shook it around a little to get the kinks out and then looked at Jamie in a way that said to Jamie that she needed some affirmation. "It looks good on you. Some nice bling."

The figure smiled. "I don't know what that means, but I'll take it as a compliment. And thank you for returning it. I find it so tiresome to always be searching for it and only being able to say one line. Repeatedly. Not to mention that when I am not in possession of my arm, my name is nothing more than a lie. But no more. Because of you, I again call myself 'the Lady with the Golden Arm.' Goodnight to you all."

Bloody Mary shoved Jamie out of the way. "Hold on a damn minute. This is not the way it should go."

The Lady with the Golden Arm looked at her, confused. "And you are?"

"Bloody Mary." The woman looked as if she were about to ask a question, but Bloody Mary cut her off. "Don't ask, you wouldn't understand, and it won't matter anyway. Because you are supposed to kill one of them. Both would work even better for me, actually, but at least kill the one who had your golden arm."

"Why would I do that?"

"Because she had your golden arm."

"But she gave it back."

Bloody Mary was beginning to grow angrier again. "It doesn't matter because you're supposed to kill the one who had your golden arm. That's the legend, and that's the way this story goes!"

"Must I remind you that Claire is telling this story, and in her story, I would never kill the one who gave me what I wanted. But she did want me to tell you that you'll be getting your happily ever after very soon."

It was Bloody Mary's turn to be baffled now. "But there's only one thing that would give me that."

"She knows." And with that, the Lady with the Golden Arm was gone, now able to enjoy her eternal rest after being reunited with her most treasured possession.

Once again, the three of them were left staring at one another. This time, however, there was a sense of foreboding on the part of Sal and Jamie because of what the Lady with the Golden Arm had said about Bloody Mary's happily ever after.

"What . . . what . . . is your happily ever after, Bloody Mary?" Sal stammered.

Bloody Mary floated over to them, inches from both of their faces. "I think we all know."

At that moment, a loud noise was heard in the distance. Someone was coming. Someone new. Someone unexpected. Sal and Jamie looked to the noise, thankful that they had been spared at least temporarily. Bloody Mary slowly turned towards the sound as out from the woods burst a huge lumberjack-looking man. "And that is not it."

"Ahhhhhh!" the lumberjack-looking man yelled. Then he stopped, looking confused. "Where's the car?"

"There is no car," Bloody Mary said, shaking her head.

"But there must be a car. I'm Hook Hand, and I have to get my hook stuck in a car to let two teens in lust know that I almost got them. See, I need the car because we got the two lovers right here," Hook Hand pointed to Sal and Jamie, who looked at each other, puzzled. "And I have my hook. See?" Hook Hand held out his hook.

"That's not a hook," said Jamie. "That's a spatula."

"It's not a spatula," Hook Hand said. "It's a . . ." He stopped abruptly when he saw what was actually at the end of his hand. It was indeed a spatula. "It *is* a spatula. Used to make delightful scrambled eggs." He paused after considering the words that had come from his mouth. "Ah, Claire must be telling this story."

- - - - - - - - - -

"Why a spatula?" Dani asked. "How would he even kill people with a spatula?"

"He doesn't," Claire said with a confidence that she had never shown before while telling a story. "Like he said, he uses it to make eggs! The best scrambled eggs in all the woods!"

"What?" the girls said collectively.

"And now the old Claire has come back," Lindsey said, smiling. Claire returned the smile confidently.

"Nope."

- - - - - - - - - -

Before Spatula Hand could say anything else, a roar erupted from Bloody Mary. Jamie, Sal, and Spatula Hand covered their ears and crumpled to the ground. They screamed out in agony as blood started pouring from their eyes.

Bloody Mary was done. Done with it all. She would no longer be a part of this stupid story. Or any story again. She was supposed to be feared and not controlled. And certainly not part of a story that made no sense. As she thought of all the times Claire had ruined her story, she became angrier and angrier, her roar growing louder and louder. She might not be able to get Claire, but she could make her characters suffer. She looked over at them, and they were suffering. The time for their heads to explode was drawing nigh, and this thought brought her such murderous glee.

Jamie lay there, trying desperately to think of something before it was too late. She had to protect Sal because that was her role. And as she looked at him lying there in pain, she realized something. Despite his bumbling ways and his many unlikable qualities, she liked him. Liked him a lot.

And now she had to save him one last time. With everything that was in her, she willed herself apart from Sal and started crawling over to where Bloody Mary stood screeching. Sal looked up for a moment and watched Jamie moving away from him.

Jamie slowly made her way over to Bloody Mary, still searching for a plan. The closer she came, the more the pressure built inside her head. She didn't have much longer. She had to think of something or they would all be dead. Then she remembered, and she knew exactly what to do.

She reached out for Bloody Mary's dress and grabbed it. She tried to speak, but the words wouldn't come out. Then she thought of the first time she and Sal had met, with him whimpering in a sandbox as his best friend lay beside him torn to pieces. Jamie suddenly found her voice.

"Bloody Mary," she began, barely above a whisper. She took a deep breath. "Bloody Mary." This time it was louder and clearer.

Bloody Mary suddenly stopped screeching. She looked down at the bleeding Jamie and smiled triumphantly. "That's two."

"I know." Jamie looked back at Sal and smiled. Sal stared back at her and finally realized what she was doing.

"Don't, Jamie!"

He started to crawl over to her, but it was too late.

Jamie turned back to the woman who would soon claim her life. "Bloody Mary!"

With a great roar, Bloody Mary, her eyes now a vibrant red, smiled at Jamie as she tried to scramble away.

"Come on, Sal!" But escape was not to be. Bloody Mary

extended her hand, and Jamie was unable to move. As Bloody Mary slowly walked over to where Jamie was now frozen, she twisted her extended hand slowly while Jamie turned to face her.

"I am so going to enjoy ripping out your heart." She laughed, thrust her left hand into Jamie's chest, and withdrew it, holding a still-beating heart.

A heart that did not belong to Jamie.

It was Sal's, who at the last moment had put himself between Bloody Mary and Jamie, who now lay a few feet away from her fallen friend.

"Sal!" Jamie rushed to him and sat down, cradling his head in her lap as gently as Jamie did anything. "You stupid, stupid bastard!" She noticed water on her face. "What the hell is this?"

"It's tears. For your fallen friend," Spatula Hand said, standing behind them with a look of sadness on his face.

Jamie continued to hold Sal. "Don't be dead, Sal. Please. I have something I need to tell you. Please don't be dead."

"Oh, he is dead," Bloody Mary said, smiling. "I have his heart in my hand to prove it." Jamie looked up, hate in her eyes. "You can have it if you want. It will give a completely different meaning to 'You have my heart.' Because you will physically have it." Jamie jumped up and ran at Bloody Mary, who laughed. "Sorry, sweetie. No revenge tonight!" With a snap of her fingers, she was gone. Jamie crashed into some bushes and lay in a heap. She didn't try to get up. Tears began falling, a fact that made her quite angry. Which caused even more tears.

Spatula Hand, who had always been moved by tragic love stories, walked over to Jamie and gently patted her on her back with his spatula hand.

"There, there, you. Would you like some eggs?"

"Screw off!" Spatula Hand backed away but continued watching her silently.

"Jamie, are you okay? Are you crying? I didn't think you could."

Jamie turned and saw Sal standing behind her. When she looked through him, she also saw him lying on the ground, dead. She slowly pulled herself up and walked over to where Sal was standing, and for the first time in her life, she didn't know what to say.

"What happened?"

Jamie took a deep breath. "You have a hole in your chest."

Sal started laughing. "No, I don't. I would . . ." Then he looked down and saw the giant hole that went clean through him. He stuck his hand in and began screaming, then turned around and saw his body on the ground and started screaming even louder. Spatula Hand could tolerate no more. He walked over and placed his spatula over Sal's mouth. Sal stopped screaming instantly.

"You're dead, buddy," Spatula Hand said calmly. "That is your body down there. And before you ask, the you standing here is the ghost you. You are a ghost." Sal looked like he wanted to say something, so Spatula Hand looked at him seriously and said, "I'll move this spatula, but if I do and you scream, I will never make you eggs. Understand?" Sal nodded, and Spatula Hand removed his spatula.

"I'm dead?" Spatula Hand nodded. "How?"

Jamie shoved Spatula Hand out of the way. "You kept me from having my heart ripped out by jumping in the way and letting Bloody Mary rip your heart out instead. Which was stupid. You should have let me die, Sal."

"I couldn't. Don't you understand?"

"No!" And before she could stop herself, honesty spewed out of her. "What I do understand is that people like me are the ones who do the saving."

"Why?"

"Because we're not worth saving."

"You've always been worth saving to me, Jamie. Always. And if I had to get my heart ripped out by Bloody Mary over and over again for the rest of eternity to save you, I would . . . try to convince her to kill me in some other way first because it really hurt. But if not, I would let her rip my heart out again and again."

"Why?"

"Because I love you. I have since the moment you saved me from those mean old squirrels."

"Wait," Spatula Hand interrupted. "Did you say, 'mean old squirrels'?" Jamie turned to him.

"Don't judge. You have a spatula for a hand."

"You bet I do!"

"Go sit over there," Jamie said, pointing to the rock where Bloody Mary had sat earlier. He did so without complaint. Jamie turned to Sal.

"Did you say you loved me?" Sal nodded and smiled. "No one has ever said that to me before. I didn't think . . ."

CHAPTER 10

"I don't think I can take this anymore," Vanessa said, bringing Claire's story to an abrupt end. "You had such a great story, and then your targeted audience became 40-year-old women who read romance novels in bed while eating chocolate chip cookie dough ice cream with curlers in their hair."

"That was specific," Dani said, laughing. She turned to Claire. "How does it end?"

"It ends with Jamie and Sal living happily ever after. Well, Jamie living happily ever after and Sal ghosting happily ever after with Spatula Hand making them some of his world-famous scrambled eggs."

"Oh."

Claire looked at Dani, confused. "That 'oh' didn't sound like you fully understand how good those eggs are. But really, how could you?" She turned towards Lindsey. "Okay, Lindsey, go ahead. Mock away."

Lindsey looked at Claire and could see that she was gearing

up for Lindsey's mocking wrath, but none was forthcoming. "It was the best story you've ever told. I thought it was nice that Sal broke through Jamie's cold dead heart by having his ripped out and showing her that even someone like her deserved . . . you know."

Claire was not prepared for a straight-up compliment from Lindsey. She blushed as a big smile broke out on her face, but before saying something weird that would ruin the moment, she stopped herself and said something not weird. "Thanks."

Vanessa looked at the blushing, giddy Claire and the uncomfortable Lindsey digging a hole with her toe. She smiled and then turned to Dani. "It's getting late. Dani, want to tell your story?"

Dani turned to Vanessa. "What?"

"You want to tell the next story?"

"I don't have one."

"I'm sure you do," Claire said. "Everyone's got a story. What's yours?"

"I said I didn't have one."

"You have to. Didn't your mom ever tell you one?" Lindsey asked.

"Not recently. No."

"Because she's dead?" Lindsey asked. Vanessa shot her a look. "Why are you looking at me that way? Oh." She turned back to Dani. "Your mom is dead, isn't she?"

"Yeah."

Claire ran over beside Dani and put her arm around her, causing Dani to pull away some. "I'm so sorry."

"It's okay," Dani said quietly as Claire returned to her spot by Lindsey. "And I just remembered, I do have one. A story. One I wrote for my dad based on stories he used to tell me when I was younger before things went to hell. It's not scary, though. It's funny at times but mostly just depressing."

"Of course it is," Lindsey scoffed.

"Does it have a ghost?" Vanessa asked, being sure to stop Lindsey from speaking more.

"Yeah."

"Is it at least good?" Lindsey asked.

"I like it."

"Then tell us," Claire said.

Dani looked at the three girls. This story was meant for her dad, but since he couldn't . . . she wasn't sure if she wanted to share it. But something about tonight had been different. Tonight had been something that she hadn't experienced in a long, long time, so she decided to tell it. "Okay, I will. But first let me say that my dad and I loved old movies, especially film noir."

"Film new what?" Lindsey asked.

"It's a type of story. Like mysterious, black and white. Very stylized. Well, my dad started telling me stories about a private investigator, Sullen Summers, who I think was based on him, and his adventures trying to solve crimes. Anyway, he stopped telling them after my mom died, so the story was never finished. A couple of years ago, I decided to finish it. For him. I wrote it at camp and buried it behind the cabin I was staying in."

"Like a dog?" Lindsey asked.

Claire gasped. "Why would you bury a dog?"

Before Lindsey or Dani could reply, Vanessa jumped in. "I think what she meant to ask was why did you bury the story?"

"Because I didn't want something to happen to it before I could give it to him."

"Oh. What's it called?"

"It's called 'Sullen Summers and the Case of the Dead Dame.'"

"Sounds promising. I'm in," Lindsey said, sliding down to the ground and leaning on the log.

"Once upon a time," Dani began, "in a city that had seen better days, there was a detective who had also seen better days. What he didn't know was that his life, somehow, was about to get so much worse."

CHAPTER 11

Dani's Story

"12:34," said Sullen Summers to himself. "That's odd. It was 12:34 when I woke up this morning. And 12:34 when I ate breakfast. And yesterday when I checked, it was also 12:34. Come to think of it, every time I've checked my watch for the past month or so, it's been 12:34. How strange."

"I'm thinking you have a broken watch there, Mr. Summers."

Sullen turned around and saw Carl in his usual spot beside the entrance to McPhee's Diner.

"Oh hey, Carl. Haven't seen you, well, since the last time I saw you."

Carl smiled. Sullen looked down at his watch. "Broken, huh?"

"How did you not know?" Carl asked.

"I don't know. Never noticed, I guess."

Carl nodded. "You mean you chose not to notice?" Sullen looked at him for a moment and shrugged. "I think there's a deeper message to that."

Sullen shook his head. "I don't think so, and I would know. You know, being a private eye who specializes in such things."

"Is that so?" Carl took off his blanket and tried to stand up. Before he fell back down, Sullen's hand caught him and pulled him to his feet. "Thank you, my friend. Now about this deeper message, I notice a lot living here on the street since I, as we are both aware, live on the street. People coming and going, hustling and bustling, like they have control over where they're going. Letting each day pass by while the things that matter, the people, the relationships, the moments, the watches, go unnoticed, becoming simply props. Props that are slowly going down the endless drain of life while resting in plain sight, broken." Carl placed his hand gently on Sullen's shoulder. "Do you understand?"

Sullen stared blankly at him. "No, I don't."

"Read between the lines."

"I don't know what that means."

"Probably should, though, right?" Carl smiled. "Or do you not specialize in that?"

Sullen sighed. He liked Carl, but sometimes he bothered him with his words. His big, big words and big, big thoughts on life. Mostly Sullen's life. He knew he was trying to help, but Sullen didn't need any help. He was an ace private eye with a beautiful dame on his arm. Well, not right now. But soon. A thought smacked him in the face. Damn. He looked at Carl. "What time is it? Because I'm assuming it's not 12:34." Carl looked up at the sky.

"It is not 12:34." He squinted. "According to the giant fireball in the sky, it's a little past four." A worried look crossed Sullen's face. "What's wrong? Supposed to meet your lady friend?"

"Yeah. An hour ago. I got to go, Carl. Nice talking to you." Sullen dug into his pocket and pulled out some bills. "Here you go. Get some lunch. Or dinner."

Carl looked at the money. "I'm not sure anyone would take this since it's covered in blood. Like your jacket."

Sullen looked down at his jacket. It was, in fact, covered in blood. "Yeah, I found these two bodies at a mansion, totally torn apart. I got their blood on me when I dug around their corpses to find some stuff. I also fell in a puddle of blood while there. Then I fell into the traditional puddle of water on the way here."

Carl stared at him for a moment. "Oh. See you, Sullen."

"You too, Carl!"

Carl watched Sullen go and then a vision, something he had grown accustomed to, filled his head. He saw images of the rest of Sullen's day, images that filled his heart with grief. "Poor Sullen." The next image, of a pineapple in a bikini, merely confused him. The vision now over, there was nothing left to be done because what fate had decided would be, would be and could not and should not be altered. Carl slowly sank back down and watched the people come and go, most of them completely unaware of all that they were missing.

- - - - - - - - - -

Sullen couldn't believe it. Late again. Because of a broken watch. That had been broken for how long? Maybe there was something wrong with him. He had always honestly thought something was off, perhaps by just a little bit, but enough to make sure that he was always close, but not close enough. When those feelings had come up in the past, he'd always pushed them aside because what would facing the reality of who he was do? Pretending that everything was okay and that it was going to stay okay was the way to live one's life. It had worked with Torchy even though . . . he pushed that thought down. Goal accomplished again. And if you forgot the broken watch, he had a decent reason for being late. An actual case. One he might be able to solve, which would be his first one in . . . well, it would be his first one ever. The Case of the Purloined Pineapple. Sullen had come up with the name himself. He liked coming up with clever names for cases, and this one practically wrote itself. A pineapple had been stolen, and "purloined pineapple" was an alliteration he could get behind.

He stopped walking and looked around, hoping that getting lost in his thoughts hadn't gotten him lost again. It hadn't.

There she was. Torchy, his love, his one and only. His "why." She was on the other side of the street, hurriedly walking somewhere. Probably to rehearsal. He yelled out her name, but she couldn't hear him. He took off across the street, and after getting hit by a taxi, landed in yet another puddle. Keep this up and the blood will be gone from my suit, Sullen thought. He got up, and after almost getting hit again, he crossed the street and looked for Torchy. She wasn't there.

"Was she a figment of my imagination?" Sullen wondered aloud.

"No." Sullen turned and saw her standing there. "Hi, Sullen." Torchy looked beautiful as always, but her expression was blank. Sullen was hoping for angry. Blank was bad. "You're a little late.

Like an hour. I would've left, but there was a bird exhibition at the museum focusing on crows."

"Your favorite." Torchy smiled. "Look, my watch was . . ." Sullen realized what an awful excuse it was. "I'm sorry."

"You always are." Torchy looked Sullen over and noticed that he was soaked. "You look awful."

"I got hit by a taxi and got knocked into a puddle."

Torchy gasped. "Oh my god, are you okay?" Then she noticed the blood. "It that blood?"

Sullen looked at the blood still covering him. So much for the puddles. He then looked back at Torchy. "Oh, it is. A lot of blood." Torchy gasped again. "But don't worry. It's not mine. I found these two people, torn and mangled by wild dogs, I think. I went through their belongings and got disgusted when I got blood on my hands, so I tried to get it off, but then I slipped on a huge puddle of more blood that I hadn't noticed and then fell face-first in said puddle of blood and . . ."

Torchy raised up her hand to stop him. "I'm about to vomit, Sullen. Please stop."

"Speaking of vomit, there was some of that . . ." Torchy's face went ashen. Sullen nodded. "Right, right. I'm sorry I'm late. Do you want to go somewhere and talk?"

"No," Torchy said. "I don't. And I don't want us anymore, either."

Sullen stared at her, unsure of what to say. Torchy had threatened this before, many times, and each one was deserved. But there was something about the way she said it and the way she looked that told Sullen that this time was different.

"I . . ."

"Look, you two, if you're gonna stage a breakup scene, at least do it somewhere where people aren't trying to walk. Geez!" Torchy and Sullen looked at the man, whose annoyance shone through brightly.

"Look, we're not breaking up."

The man laughed. "She's breaking up with you, man. It's in her eyes. You should see it. Thank God you're not a private eye or anything."

"I am a private eye," Sullen stuttered.

The shocked expression on the man's face told what he thought of this reveal. "Really? You?" Sullen nodded. The man laughed again. "And you couldn't see that she was breaking up with you?"

Sullen grew angry. "We are not breaking up!"

"Yes, we are." Sullen and the man both looked at Torchy. Sullen now noticed the look in her eyes.

"Oh. I see it now," Sullen said sadly. He felt a hand on his shoulder and turned to see the man looking sympathetically at him.

"Well, this has clearly gotten awkward, so I think I'll be on my way, but before I do, maybe this will help a little. She was way out of your league to begin with."

"That . . . doesn't help me at all." The man shrugged and walked away. Sullen looked around for Torchy, who was not there anymore.

"Not again!"

"I'm over here."

Sullen looked in the direction of the voice and saw Torchy sitting on a bench near the entrance to Willow Parks. He walked over and sat beside her. They sat in silence for several moments, Torchy playing nervously with her purse while Sullen stared at the ground. Sullen had never known that silence could be this loud and agonizing. He valiantly fought to come up with something to say. Something good. Something that could fix this.

"You're kicking me to the curb?"

Sullen shook his head, clearly understanding that his question failed to meet the standards of "something good." Torchy looked at him, tears building in her eyes.

"I don't want to, but I'm tired, Sullen."

Sullen saw an opportunity. He attacked with the enthusiasm of someone who saw a glimmer of hope after they thought all was lost. He smiled at her. "Well, maybe you need more sleep. You have been performing a lot, and . . ."

"I'm tired of you!" Torchy said, getting up and walking to a light post near the bench. She looked back at him. "I'm tired of you always being late and having something else to do. I'm tired of you making promises to me and not keeping them. I'm tired of you not having time for me."

"Wait, what? I have time for you," Sullen said, walking over to her.

Torchy turned to him. "Oh? When was the last time that we had an honest-to-God date? And no, crackers on a bench doesn't count." After losing his only option for a response, all Sullen could do was sit quietly. "Maybe this will help. Do you remember the last time you saw me perform?" Sullen still didn't have any idea. "Both were four months ago today."

"Was that a Wednesday?"

Torchy shook her head, exasperated. "I don't know!"

"I think it was. It wasn't me then. I had a poker game that night. I told you about it. It's been more like six months. Or more." As soon as those words came out of his mouth, Sullen realized that they shouldn't have. "But there are other reasons, too."

"Like what, Sullen?"

"I . . . I . . . ." He couldn't. This was getting too real. He had to find a way, another way, to save it.

He reached for her. She pulled away.

"No! And if it's not a poker game, it's one of your cases."

"Torchy, I'm Sullen Summers, Ace Private Eye. Solving cases is what I do."

"You haven't solved a case in years!"

If anyone else had said it, Sullen would've been able to laugh it off, but coming from Torchy, his girl, it hurt. A lot. He turned away and kicked a tiny pebble that wasn't there. Torchy, sensing that she'd hit him a little harder than she intended, tried to apologize.

"I'm sorry. I shouldn't have said that."

"No, you're right," Sullen said, not turning around or looking up. "I've never actually solved a case. I lied about the ones I said I solved. I . . . um . . . wanted to feel like I . . . deserved you because you're so . . . you. But I don't. And I know I don't. I've always known, by the way." Sullen turned around suddenly, an excited look on his face. "Though I got this new case about a stolen pineapple. You know what I call it?"

"The Case of the Purloined Pineapple?"

Sullen smiled. Of course she would know what he called it. He was going to continue, but then he looked at Torchy's face, which didn't have that "please continue this fascinating story" look. It was more of a "you're talking about a case right now that is proving my point" look. "Look, I'm sorry. But solving, I mean, trying to solve cases is what I do. It's my life, you know?"

"I do. But there was a time, Sullen, that I was a part of that life, too." Torchy turned away again. "I'm not anymore." Sullen tried to say that that wasn't true, because it wasn't. She would never know how untrue that was because Sullen wasn't good with words. He tried to say something nonetheless, but Torchy wouldn't let him. She turned and placed one of her fingers on his lips. "No. You know I'm right, and there are no words you know that could make it not true."

Now she was reading his mind? If only it weren't true. If he were Simon, he'd know what to say. Simon was so smooth. But he wasn't Simon because Simon would never find himself in this situation. Sullen watched Torchy slowly walk away from him and then stop. She looked up at the sky, and he thought what a beautiful picture it was. Even in sadness, Torchy was the most beautiful thing he had ever seen. And the smartest. And the most talented. She had always been on a pedestal that he could never reach. Not because he put her there, though he would have. It was just where she was. And she had always been out of his league, like that guy pointed out earlier, and it was never clearer than at this moment. If only he could say something, anything before she spoke again.

"I need . . ."

Sullen had to act fast. "Don't say another man. I don't think I could handle that."

"I was going to say that I think I need to leave."

"Thank God!" Sullen said, relieved. Torchy stared at him a moment and shook her head. Sullen realized why. "Oh no, I didn't mean that I wanted you to leave. I want you to stay forever. I meant that I . . . never mind." He quickly walked after her and gently took her by the shoulders. "Do you still love me?"

Torchy stared at him for a long moment. Sullen thought of rephrasing the question but, thankfully for him, Torchy spoke first.

"Sullen, I think I'll always love you, but . . ." She stopped talking when she noticed who was behind him, stomping her feet and smacking her gum in that annoying way she always had.

"Torchy, I promise I'm listening." Sullen saw Torchy motion behind him, so he turned and saw her. Carissa Cranberry, his secretary. She was dressed in what looked to be multi-colored lizard skin. Of all the times for her to show up. "What, Carissa?"

Still smacking her gum, she moved extremely close to Sullen's face.

"You would think that after breaking my heart, you could at least speak to me in a nicer tone." Sullen reached to push her away, and Carissa grabbed his hands and tried to put them around her in a hug. "Oh, Sullen."

Sullen pulled his hands away from her and backed up. "What? Stop! Why are you like this? I'm right in the middle of something."

"Talking to your hussy, I see," Carissa said, eyeing Torchy over Sullen's shoulder while awkwardly rubbing up against him. "Well, I need you to come back to the office. Now!"

"Why?"

"Two reasons. One, you have an appointment with Simon

Silvershoes that you can't miss, and two, I found some pictures that you and I need to talk about!"

"Pictures?" Torchy said, a questioning look coming over her face. Carissa looked at Torchy, sensing what she was thinking, and smiled.

"That's right. Pictures."

"What pictures, Carissa?" Sullen asked, growing tired of talking to her.

"You'll have to come back to the office and find out."

Sullen was about to say something, perhaps something clever and rude to Carissa, who phrased everything in a way that made him regret ever hiring her in the first place. But he didn't feel very clever now, with the whole "Torchy breaking up with him" thing and all. So, he decided to just go with rude.

"I'll be there when I want to because you're not the boss of me."

"She's gone, Sullen."

She was indeed gone. "I should have said it faster." Sullen turned back to Torchy as rain started to lightly fall.

"Why did you hire her in the first place?" Torchy asked.

"I don't know," Sullen said awkwardly. He took note of how well he did "awkwardly." "I guess I felt like I owed her something. Plus, she was always there anyway. Staring into the office through the window."

"Aren't you on the fourth floor?"

"Fifth." The rain began falling harder.

"Well, the rain's getting pretty bad. Maybe we could finish this later?"

"No," Sullen said, reaching into his coat and pulling out his umbrella. "I have this, see?"

"A stick?" Torchy asked, looking at him, slightly bewildered (but not really). Sullen looked down at his hand. It wasn't his umbrella.

"I guess I grabbed my stick instead of my umbrella." He realized how weird that sounded. "I, uh, collected sticks as a kid and never stopped, I guess." He threw the stick away without looking and hit a man who was jogging, knocking the man down. "Um, sorry. Total accident!" The man pulled himself up, made an obscene gesture at Sullen, and continued running. Sullen started to reach for Torchy's hand, but then a sudden jolt of pain in his mouth caused him to scream out rather loudly. He reached a hand to his mouth as if that would soothe the pain. It did not. Torchy started to reach out to him, then stopped herself.

"Is your tooth still hurting?" Sullen nodded through the pain. He had never been good with pain. Of any kind. "You need to get that looked at."

"I will. Once I get money. Or a dentist who needs a crime solved. Or at least an attempt made," Sullen said, noticing that other people, who were running to get out of the now massive downpour, were still taking the time to stare at the two people standing and talking in the middle of the park.

"Sullen?" He looked at Torchy. "You're in your head again."

"Right, sorry. Anyway, you want to get coffee or something? I don't want to let this go until everything is okay."

"I can't. I have to get to the club. Well, now I have to go home, change clothes, and then go to the club. I'm performing tonight."

Sullen smiled. "That's terrific. Simon told me you were performing at his joint. I'll be there. I have to stop by the office and see what Carissa's talking about and then I'll be there."

"The show starts in an hour and a half. You'll never make it. I might not make it."

Sullen put his hands on Torchy's shoulders. "You'll make it, and I will too. I'll be a little late, but I'll be there. I promise. No matter what. And after the show, we'll meet at our spot. Then I'll fix things, okay? Let me get you a taxi."

He ran to the road and hailed the first cab he saw. He leaned and talked to the driver for a moment, then reached into his wallet. Coming up empty, he told the driver to hold on and ran back to Torchy.

"You'll have to pay because I don't have any more money. I gave it to Carl."

"It's okay," Torchy said, looking at him with an unreadable (at least to Sullen) expression. The driver honked, and Torchy turned to him. "Hold on, will you! We'll be done in a second." The driver shook his head angrily but didn't leave. Torchy turned back to Sullen. "I hope you'll be there tonight. I need you to keep your word. For me. For us. I don't want to say goodbye, but . . ."

"Then don't." Torchy smiled and gave him a gentle kiss on the cheek. Sullen watched as she got in the taxi. The taxi shot off, and as he watched her leave, he had a feeling that it would be the last time he would see her. He pushed that thought aside, though. None of those feelings had been right before. Intuition was something in short supply for Sullen, which probably explained his lack of success in his chosen career. He looked to hail a taxi, then remembered his lack of money.

"Guess I'll walk back then." He took a moment and looked around. "Where the hell am I?"

He started walking in what he hoped was the direction of his office.

- - - - - - - - - -

"We're not taking cases right now," Carissa said, hanging up the phone as she sat on Sullen's desk. That was the twelfth case that Carissa had turned down today, but what of it? She and Sullen needed to talk, and nothing could get in the way of a conversation that was going to be difficult. For Sullen. Because they were going to talk about the pictures. Those filthy pictures. She looked at the clock. What was taking him so long? That floozy with the stupid name couldn't be that interesting.

Torchy Blaze. Clearly a fake name, which meant she couldn't even pick a good one. Why would Sullen choose to be with a woman with a name like that when he could be with someone who had such a beautiful name?

Carissa Cranberry. Elegant and beautiful. Sometimes the name fits perfectly.

They had been together for one entire week. She had stalked him for months, and it had finally paid off. Wait, not stalked. Loved. At first, Sullen didn't seem interested. Even accidentally filed a restraining order, but Carissa knew she'd eventually wear him down. And she did.

Their first date was at the office. As were all of the other ones. He had called her in for a "job interview" from the window where she was staring at him, but she knew what it really was. "Job interview," Carissa knew, was private eye for "love session," and it was magical. Sullen had asked her so many questions, dying to find out all he could about her. She was flattered. After about five minutes or so, he told Carissa she could go, but she knew what he really meant. She got up and walked seductively to the window, looked back, and blew him a kiss. A French one. She climbed out the window, closed it, and then turned back so they could continue their date, her Sullen working on the inside as Carissa sent him love glances from the outside.

Things went beautifully for a week after that. Carissa remembered him opening the window and hiring her to be his girlfriend. He had said "secretary," which she figured was European for "girlfriend." And everything was great until that hussy arrived.

Torchy Blaze.

"What are you doing in my office? You have your own."

Carissa turned and saw Sullen standing there, soaking wet and still covered in blood.

"Did you have an accident?" she said, ignoring the question.

"It's raining. Hard. And no, the blood isn't mine."

"It should be," Carissa said. "Glad you're finally done talking to your hussy."

"She's not a hussy. And you still haven't told me why you're in my office."

"And you still haven't told me what you're doing with these pictures!" Carissa threw the pictures at him, missing him completely and scattering them all over the floor. They looked at each other for a moment. Then Carissa knocked everything off his desk and lay there on top of it.

"If I weren't staring at the ceiling, I would be staring at you," she said, staring at the ceiling.

Sullen was too tired for this.

He reached down and picked up a few of the pictures and looked at them.

"These pictures are from a case I'm working on." Sullen stopped, stood up, and looked off dramatically. "The Case of the Purloined Pineapple." He turned back to Carissa, less dramatically. "So those pictures are evidence."

"Oh really?" Carissa asked. Sullen nodded. "Even this one?" Carissa jumped down, reached for a picture on the floor, then held it up to Sullen's face. "She's wearing a bikini!"

"Can't a dame pineapple wear a bikini? Give me the picture and get the hell out of my office."

Carissa put the picture behind her back and leaned seductively on Sullen. "Do you find her prettier than me?"

"It's a pineapple," Sullen said, turning away from Carissa's lips that were way too close to his.

Carissa grabbed his face and turned it towards her. "Answer the question, Sullen!" she yelled.

"You know what, Carissa? I do. I do find the pineapple prettier than you. And you know what else? I find this . . ." He pulled away from Carissa's grasp, searching his floor, and picked up a pen, the multi-colored kind. "I find this pen and all its colors prettier than you too."

Carissa snatched the pen out of his hand. "Oh? This pen? Well, let me tell you something. I pull off green, blue, red, and black better than this tramp any day."

Sullen stared at her, unable to speak and unsure how this bit of Carissa ridiculousness would end up. He found out shortly.

Carissa put the pen in his face and smiled in that way that

had always creeped Sullen out. "You better stare at her real good right now. Because you'll never see her again!" Then, as hard as she could, she threw the pen at the window.

It bounced off, barely making a sound, and hit the floor. Carissa looked at the pen, then to the window, then to Sullen, then back to the pen, then to the window, then to Sullen. She started breathing heavily as her mind attempted to process what to do next. It didn't take long.

She rushed to Sullen's chair and picked it up.

"What are you doing?" Sullen asked, his eyes growing wide.

"What I should have done the first time." With that, Carissa heaved the chair at the window, shattering the glass and sending the chair crashing to the street below. She then picked up the pen and threw it out the window. Rushing to the window, she screamed, "Enjoy the ride, whore!"

She turned back to Sullen with that creepy smile again, breathing heavily.

"We don't have money for you to throw chairs out the window. What is wrong with you?"

Carissa walked to Sullen's desk and sat on it. "Oh, many things, Sullen Summers. Many things. And every last one of them caused by you!"

"Get off my desk, Carissa."

"I am never getting off this desk again!"

The lights suddenly cut out, followed by a loud crashing sound. The office was in darkness except for the quickly fading daylight coming from the now broken window.

"Carissa?" Sullen asked in the semi-darkness. "Why did the lights go off?"

"Because I cut them off. For dramatic effect," said a voice near the door. Sullen turned to the door. He recognized that voice.

"Simon Silvershoes, the bookie with the heart of gold. Good to see you. Or not see you. I mean, I can kind of make out your . . ."

"Yeah, the 'turning the lights out' effect wasn't as dramatic as I imagined," Simon said, turning the lights back on.

"Probably had something to do with the light from the broken window."

"Yep. What happened?"

"Carissa threw my chair through it."

"Of course she did," Simon said. "Where is she?"

"I don't know," Sullen said, not bothering to look for her. "She was on the desk and then she wasn't."

"Oh, there she is. Behind the desk. On the floor. I can see her foot. She must have fallen off." Sullen turned.

"Ah, that's what that loud 'body falling off a desk' sound was," Sullen said as he walked around the desk, followed by Simon. "Are you all right, Carissa?"

Carissa popped up suddenly, causing both Sullen and Simon to jump back. "I am. No thanks to you!"

"Sorry," Sullen said. "Didn't know you were planning on falling off the desk."

"You would have known – if we were still dating." Sullen started to speak, but his words were stopped by Carissa's hand, which completely covered his face. He had no idea Carissa had such gorilla hands. Minus the hair. Or some of the hair. "Don't speak, Sullen. Because all that will come out will be lies. Lies covered in lies and more lies."

Sullen removed Carissa's paw from his face. "Your hand smells like a burger. Can I speak to Simon? Alone?"

"Sure. Fine. Whatever. I don't care." Carissa turned briskly and started to leave. She stopped in front of Simon. "Don't even think about stealing my man." She knocked into him as she left, slamming the door. Simon, after watching her go, turned back to Sullen.

"What did she mean by stealing her man?"

"Don't worry about it."

"She's one crazy broad."

Sullen laughed. "You can't even imagine."

Simon removed his hat and coat and hung them up. "So why did you hire her again?"

"Figured it'd be best to know where she was at all times instead of having her attack me when I wasn't expecting it."

"Guess that makes sense," Simon said, sitting down and making himself comfortable. He looked at Sullen's still-wet suit. "Fall in a puddle of water again? And then a puddle of . . . blood?"

"Slipped in the puddle of blood, then fell in the puddle of water later. Then got knocked into another puddle of water. By a cab. The blood, not mine by the way, is a completely different story. One that involves me almost getting arrested." Sullen went to sit down in his chair and fell to the ground. "Dang it. Forgot she threw it out the window." He stood up and leaned on his desk, trying to look professional in blood and water-soaked clothes and after sitting in a chair that wasn't there. "Look, we can make this quick, Simon. I don't have the money."

"Sullen. You said you would," Simon said, gently shaking his head. "I thought you had some cases."

"I have tons of cases, but I have to solve them to get paid, and I'm finding that part far more difficult. As always."

"Did you ever think about doing something different?"

"You mean like pottery?" Sullen asked.

Simon stared at him. Sullen had been, and still was, one of his best friends. They had met in the first grade, when Sullen asked Simon to lend him some money after Sullen had made a bet with some other kid about who was the fastest. (He had lost.) That was the beginning of both Simon's business and their friendship. And now Sullen owed him a lot of money. A whole lot. Starting with the loan in first grade.

"You have nothing on the docket?"

"Well, that's not exactly true," Sullen said, reaching for the pictures of the pineapple. "There is this one. It's a case that I have a couple of leads on, so I might be able to actually solve it."

"What's the case?"

Sullen looked off. "The Case of the Purloined Pineapple." He looked back at Simon. "There was another detective on it. Some dame. Not anymore, though. She and a friend were found tied up to chairs at this mansion in the middle of nowhere, and apparently, they'd been eaten by wild dogs. This is their blood, by the way. And a few other people's blood at the mansion."

"That sounds disturbing," Simon noted.

"Little bit."

"You have something to do with it?"

"What? Why would you . . . ow!" Sullen grabbed his mouth. Simon stood up.

"What's wrong? Is it a mouth thing?" Simon asked, rather gleefully.

"Yeah," Sullen said. "I got this tooth that's been killing me. Why did you ask it so gleefully?"

"You may recall that before I got into the bookie business at age six, I had always dreamed of being a dentist. So I'm always looking for opportunities to dig around in someone's mouth."

"Disgusting."

Simon shrugged. "What I can say? Childhood dreams die hard. Let me take a look." Simon walked over to Sullen, who held up a hand to stop him, looking sad. Simon smiled. "It's on the house. Now open up." Sullen opened his mouth, and Simon leaned in. The two men stood there, with Sullen's mouth open and Simon looking as if he was trying to stick his face in Sullen's mouth while making some worried sounds. "Ah, I see it. There's this thing called brushing your teeth. You should consider it." Sullen was about to offer a retort, but Simon stopped him by reaching his hand deep into Sullen's mouth, causing him to gag. At that moment, the door opened, and a gasp was heard. Then the door slammed shut, causing both Sullen and Simon to jump and Sullen to bite Simon's hand.

"Ow!"

"What is going on here?" Carissa asked, her face showing an extreme level of shock and anger that one wouldn't think was possible.

Sullen looked at Simon. "Sorry about biting your hand." He then turned to Carissa. "Do you need something?"

Carissa ran dramatically to Sullen, knocking Simon out of the way in the process. She grabbed Sullen's shoulders and slapped him. "I need to be able to trust you, Sullen. Which clearly I cannot."

"We're not dating, Carissa!"

Carissa removed her hands from Sullen and adjusted her dress. She then moved close to Sullen's face and stared deep into his eyes. "You wouldn't say that if we were dating."

"Got you there," Simon said, obnoxiously straight-faced.

"Don't help," Sullen said, looking over Carissa's shoulder to Simon. Carissa abruptly moved over to Sullen's desk and sat on the corner of it. "What are you doing?"

"Staying here because obviously I can't trust the two of you alone."

Sullen sighed. "Fine." He turned to Simon. "So, where were we?"

"Wait, does she think we're dating or something? Because you're not my type."

"That hurts. And if it helps, she thought I had a thing for a pen earlier."

"And I still do!"

Sullen and Simon both looked at Carissa, who laughed at them mockingly. They realized that they had no interest in continuing to converse with her and turned back to each other.

"So, how much you gonna get paid for this purloined pineapple case if you solve it?"

"Enough to pay you back and get me and Torch a cheeseburger. And maybe some fries. Probably not drinks, so I might need to borrow a couple of bucks." Sullen stopped as a worried look came over his face. "Crap. I've gotta go," he said, hurrying over to get his jacket and hat. "I told Torchy I'd be at her show."

"You'll never make it. It started an hour ago. By the time you get there, it'll be over. There's one tomorrow. Catch that one."

"No. I promised her I'd catch this one. I can't fail her again."

The phone rang. Sullen went to get it but Carissa got there first, largely because she was already sitting on the desk where the phone was.

"Office of Sullen Summers, ace private . . . LIAR!" Sullen tried to wrench the phone from her, but Carissa turned away. "Oh." She turned to Simon. "It's for you, office wrecker!"

Simon took the phone. "This is Silvershoes." As Simon talked on the phone, Carissa lashed out, somewhat subdued this time, about Sullen's relationship with Torchy, Simon, the pineapple, and the now perhaps deceased pen. She stopped when the tone of Simon's voice changed.

"Are you serious? The whole place? Why didn't you call me sooner? Were there any . . ." Simon's face turned ashen. "Oh my god. Who was it? No. Torchy?"

Sullen crossed to Simon. "Torchy? What about Torchy? What happened to her?" Simon held up his hand to silence Sullen so that he could finish the conversation. "I'll be there as soon as I can. Thanks." Simon handed the phone back to Carissa and took a moment to square his shoulders before he turned to Sullen.

"There was a fire, Sullen."

"At Silvershoes?"

"Yeah. The whole place went up. Everything."

"You mentioned Torchy. Is she okay?"

"No. She was the only one onstage when it happened. The ceiling above the stage collapsed, and there was nothing anyone could do."

Sullen sank into a chair and put his head in his hands. "No."

"I'm so sorry, Sullen."

"I . . . I . . ." Sullen stood up quickly. "I gotta go. I promised I'd meet her."

"Sullen, she's gone."

"It doesn't matter. I promised."

Sullen quickly turned and went out the door, leaving Simon alone in the office with Carissa.

"Well," Carissa began as Simon put on his hat and coat, preparing to go to the club. "Seems someone's back on the market."

- - - - - - - - - -

Sullen and Torchy had first met at Al's, a burger joint. That night, the place was packed and every seat was taken. Except for the booth where Sullen sat eating his burger and fries, which Al had given him on the house because Al was a nice guy and Sullen made him laugh.

Then she walked in, and his life changed forever. Torchy Blaze, a well-known singer at Silvershoes. The entire restaurant stopped eating and stared at her when she entered. Well, except for Sullen. Don't misunderstand. He was smitten with Torchy instantly, but staring was rude. And the cheeseburger was amazing.

Then she was standing by his table.

"Mind if I sit here?"

Sullen looked up with a mouth full of food, and no words would come. He quickly swallowed but still said nothing.

"Mind if I sit here?" she asked again.

"Why?" Sullen asked.

"Well, this is the only seat available, so . . ."

"Right," Sullen said. "And sure."

Torchy smiled and sat down. She ordered a burger and a beer, and after a few minutes, Sullen relaxed enough to talk to her. They ended up staying at Al's long after everyone else had left.

That night, Sullen walked Torchy home. When they got to her door, he wanted to ask her out, but never got the chance because she asked first. Though Sullen didn't know that's what she was doing.

"Sullen, I'm off tomorrow night."

"Great, me too. I was thinking of going to the carnival."

"Oh, I do love elephant ears. Maybe we could share one."

"I don't know. I don't think they stay fresh that long. I mean, I guess I could bring one to you the next time . . ." Sullen stopped talking as Torchy gave him a look. "Oh, you meant like, as in, you'd like to go with me."

"Unless you don't want me to."

"No, no, I mean. Yes. That would be great. Amazing."

She leaned in and kissed him on the cheek. "Pick me up at seven?"

Sullen could only nod yes. Torchy smiled and walked inside her apartment.

He stood there for a while, unable to move. He gently touched where she had kissed him and swore he would never wash that cheek again. (Which wouldn't be a problem because his water had been cut off earlier that day.) As he walked home, Sullen couldn't wait for tomorrow and all of the tomorrows that he imagined them having.

And they had a lot. But not enough. It would've never been enough even if their tomorrows had gone on forever, and now they had run out of them. Something he never believed would happen.

He didn't quite know why he was still heading to Al's. She wouldn't be there. She would never be anywhere again, and that thought destroyed him. There was now a hollow spot inside that he knew would only continue to grow. Still he kept walking as the rain poured down around him while the thought of failing her again, one more time, haunted him. What made it worse? He would never get the chance to fix it.

Sullen arrived at Al's around nine that night, three hours after Torchy's show had started. The sounds of sirens in the distance echoed in his head as a constant reminder. He tried to open the door, but it was locked. He then noticed the lights were out. A sign said that due to a family emergency, Al's would be closed until further notice. Then Sullen remembered that Al's youngest daughter sang at Silvershoes too.

He turned around, feeling lost as the rain fell harder and harder, and looked blankly into the night. He thought of walking to Silvershoes but didn't think he could bear it. Then he considered walking to Torchy's house, but that would be even harder. He stayed in front of the place where they'd first met, where they'd had all their important "talks," where Sullen had hoped to one day propose to her.

As Sullen sat there in the pouring rain, he began to relive all of the "firsts" in their relationship. From that first meeting, to the first time he kissed her, to the first time he said "I love you," to the first time they . . . made cookies. As the memories continued and they faded from first moments to everything moments, a realization hit Sullen. He realized that it wasn't the big moments, the so-called important ones, that haunted him the most now. It was the little ones, the millions of little ones that happened every day, the ones he often missed. The fleeting smiles, the stories they shared as they talked the night away, the puns that Torchy loved and always had to explain to Sullen, the many shoulder rubs he gave her after rehearsals, the many times she tried to teach him proper English, the times that they simply sat or walked together in silence holding hands, and all those millions of other moments that Sullen had experienced but had not seen their importance at the time. Now he did because he realized that those were the ones that he'd miss the most. The ones he had taken for granted. The broken watch. Ah. That's what Carl meant. If he could go back, he would treasure every moment. Because at the end, once the fog was lifted, they were the ones that truly mattered.

But what would haunt him the most was that he wasn't there with her at Silvershoes. Like he had promised. He had disappointed her one final time.

In so many ways, Sullen felt like every day he'd disappointed her. He tried to get it right, get something right, but he couldn't. He thought about how for his entire life he had never been able to be what someone needed. Always came up short. He had never wanted to come through for someone more than he had for Torchy though. Now, sitting here in soaking clothes, he realized he could never be what she needed no matter how he tried. She was the most amazing person he had ever met. She deserved so much more than he could offer. She deserved better than to die onstage. If he could take her place, he would in a heartbeat because the world would be better for it. A lot better. Because she was everything, and he was . . . something else. Sullen suddenly broke down in sobs as the rain cascaded down around him, not noticing that he was no longer alone.

"Sullen. You came."

He looked up, clearing the water from his eyes and saw Torchy standing there. She was as beautiful as always. He tried to hide the fact that he had been crying.

"You know it's raining, right?"

"I, um, yeah," Sullen said, struggling to speak as he stood up.

"I can't believe you're here."

"I can't believe that you're . . . I'm a little late. Sorry."

"Figured you would be."

"I, uh, got lost on the way to the office, and then Carissa threw a chair out my window." Torchy stared at him, confused. "She was jealous of a pen."

"Sounds about right." They both laughed quietly and then fell silent, just looking at each other. "I'm glad you came." Torchy smiled at him, a smile that made Sullen happy and tore at him at the same time.

"You're so . . . you," he said, unsure of what he was seeing. "How was the show?" He realized after he said it what a stupid question it was.

"Besides the fire? Good. You heard about the fire, right?"

"Yeah. Silvershoes got a call."

Torchy nodded and considered the window of the darkened restaurant, not seeing her reflection. "I didn't make it, did I?" she asked without looking back.

Sullen couldn't take his eyes off her. "No." He took a step forward, reaching out for her instinctively, but something stopped him.

"I figured," Torchy said, turning around as Sullen was pulling back his hand. "Not many people survive a burning ceiling falling on top of them." She tried to laugh, but couldn't. "When I saw you, though, I had a little hope that maybe, but then I noticed that you had been crying and saw the look on your face." She turned away from him. "Guess we weren't meant for a happily ever after, were we?"

"Well, to be fair, I made a pretty crappy prince."

Torchy turned back to him and smiled. "No, you didn't." She looked Sullen right in the eyes. "If you knew that I was dead, why did you come here?"

"I promised I would." A moment passed between them.

"Sullen, I need to tell you something."

"Are you still breaking up with me?"

She chuckled at that. "No. I never was. I want to tell you before I go to wherever, or nowhere, that no matter what you may think, you were always my ace private eye, Sullen Summers, and I'm so sorry that I'm not going to get to see you solve your first case, or marry you, or have children, or grow old with you. You were my only dream that mattered, and I'm going to miss everything about us. About you."

Sullen, never much of a crier, was now crying again. He smiled. "Me too. I mean, I'm going to miss everything. More than you could ever know. I'm so sorry that I was . . . me."

"No. You, Sullen, were always enough, and my heart was always completely yours." A longing smile passed between the two of them. "Goodbye, Sullen," Torchy whispered. Sullen could barely hear her over the rain.

She kissed her fingers and put them close to Sullen's lips, stopping short. Then she was gone.

CHAPTER 12

Claire's sobs were heard throughout the forest. Vanessa turned to her.

"Uh, you okay over there?"

"Oh my god, that was the best story ever. And so sad. He finally kept his word, and she was dead." She tried to speak more but was overcome by her emotions.

"Good story, Dani," Vanessa said. "You have proven to be a great addition to our group."

"Thanks."

"Not scary, though. But it did continue tonight's bizarre theme of overly emotional stories," Lindsey added.

"Well, I said it wasn't scary, but it did have a ghost," Dani said.

"You wrote that for your dad?" Claire asked through her tears.

"Yeah." Dani stood up and walked away a little, casting her gaze through the clearing towards the lake. "See, my dad never felt like he was good enough for my mom. Not smart enough, not successful enough, not handsome enough, just not enough. You know? And on the day she died, they had a big blow-up where they said some things, and he got angry and left. Only needed time to think, he said. Mom, putting on her brave face, asked me if I wanted to go out for dinner. I said no, so she went out to get some groceries, and on the way to the store she had an accident. If I had said yes, she wouldn't have been . . . and then she wouldn't have died. But I didn't. That was the last time I saw her. My dad didn't tell her goodbye when he left. The last thing she got from him was a slamming door." Dani turned away from the girls. "By the time he made it to the hospital, it was too late. I watched him hold her in the hospital. He was crying. I stood there and stared because I didn't know what else to do. Then there was the funeral, which sucked. Everybody sharing funny stories and their memories of Mom, and I got why they did it, but it only reminded me that she wouldn't be making any new ones. And don't get me started on those people who said it was 'God's plan.' If it was God's plan, then God is a dick."

Dani stopped talking for a moment as the other girls looked on silently. Then she turned back to them. "Dad carried a lot of guilt after what happened, and I guess he tried to fix things through me. About a year after my mom died, when both of us were still aimlessly wandering through life, he had the grand idea that I should start going to summer camp where I'd finally find friends and fit in while he would paint that masterpiece that had always eluded him. And, you know, everything would magically be better."

"I'm guessing it wasn't?" said Vanessa.

"Well, let's say that not every fairy tale ends happily ever after."

"None of them do," Lindsey said.

Claire turned on her. "Yes, they do. Almost all of them."

"No, Claire, they don't," Lindsey corrected. "That's the part of the story you hear. It sucks because it gives us this false hope that all our lives are going to end happily ever after, which is crap because endings, by their very nature, suck. Face it, we'd find out that happily ever afters are a lie if we read the rest of their stories. Because if we did, we'd see everything fall completely and utterly apart."

"Stop!" Claire got up and looked at Lindsey. "Why, Lindsey? Why do you have to destroy happy endings for me?" She looked down, unsure what to say next. "I need to be alone for a moment." She ran off behind a tree.

"So why write this story?" Vanessa asked, ignoring the new round of sobs coming from Claire.

Dani stared out for a moment, unsure of why she was being so open with these girls. It seemed like once she decided to share, the floodgates opened. "I wanted him to know that Sullen came through in the end. That he had always been enough for Torchy."

"That's really nice, Dani," Lindsey said. "And yes, Vanessa, I feel you looking at me, and you can suck it."

"No, thank you," Vanessa said. "And see, Lindsey, this is what sharing looks like." Before Lindsey could reply, Vanessa turned back to Dani. "Did you let him read it?"

Dani looked into the fire. "Um, no. I, uh, no. I never got the chance." This was getting to be a little much for Dani. Sharing time had come to an end. Vanessa, looking at her, seemed to understand and was about to help her out, but Lindsey didn't give her a chance.

"I don't understand why you still don't give it to him. I mean, we can go dig it up if you want."

"No," Dani said firmly.

"Oh." A change came over Lindsey. She took a deep breath. "God, it must be awful to be you."

Vanessa cut her off with a look. "What the hell, Lindsey?"

"What?" Lindsey asked. "Oh, I didn't mean it that way. I meant that it must be awful to be Dani. If you'd let me finish, I would've explained what I meant."

"It seemed pretty clear," Dani said.

"Right. But what I meant is that it must be awful to know that even when you try to do the right thing, it's not going to work out. I mean, even with that Sullen character. He didn't come through. He should have been at the show. Maybe he could've saved her or something. I don't know. And his alter ego, your dad, I'm sure he's a great guy and all, but he sounds like he, I mean, I think that there are some people that will probably never be what someone needs or wants. Or 'not enough' as you say. No matter how hard they try, they won't be. For whatever reason. And the disappointment is always there in their eyes. Always."

"Ouch," Dani said quietly.

"Only telling the truth, and it's not like I don't understand that feeling completely."

"How?"

"What do you mean, how?"

"I mean, how would you understand that feeling?"

Lindsey stared at Dani for a moment and seemed ready to say more. Then she turned away and stared into the fire. "I do, okay? Because I've seen that look directed at me. A lot. And not just when I look into the mirror. Can we leave it at that?" Everyone went silent as all eyes went to Lindsey. "I know you're both staring at me, and you can stop that shit."

"Wow, Dani," Vanessa exclaimed. "You got honesty out of Lindsey. Miracles do happen apparently."

"Shut up," Lindsey said, sitting back down. She was greeted by a big back hug from Claire.

"Great, you're back. And I swear if you don't let me go, I will throw you into this dying fire."

"Oh, I'll let you go," Claire said, sitting beside her after one final squeeze. "Physically. But I'll never let the friendship hug go."

"God almighty. And you wonder why I don't share stuff. This night has been so freakin' weird."

Claire then went over to Dani, who looked up at her.

"Are you about to hug me?"

"I sure am." Claire hugged Dani. "I can't bring your mom or fix your dad, but I can give good hugs." To Dani's surprise, she hugged her back. Claire turned to Lindsey triumphantly. "See? Someone appreciates my hugs."

Lindsey, predictably, rolled her eyes, but she couldn't suppress a small grin as Claire walked back to the log to sit by her. The four of them sat together around what remained of the fire in silence. Dani's moment of honesty and Lindsey's moment of near-honesty had changed something within the group. They watched as the last wisps of fire faded from view. Dani noticed that both Claire and Lindsey seemed to be looking at Vanessa, as if waiting for directions, though it seemed none were coming. Dani cleared her throat.

"I want to tell you guys something. Tonight has been fun and something that I've needed for a long time. So thank you. I wish that my dad could see this, though it'd probably give him a heart attack or something."

Lindsey, looking quite uncomfortable, spoke first. "You're pretty cool. Now, never say anything like that again, because I've had enough of all these 'feels' tonight."

Dani laughed. "Okay. I only wanted you to know. I suppose it's getting late and you have to get back to camp?" The hope that they didn't need to leave yet clearly came out in her voice.

Claire saw, knew, what Vanessa was about to say, and she couldn't let her. Especially after what Dani had said. She jumped up.

"Yeah, it's super late, and the three of us are one more mistake away from getting in big time trouble, so we should probably get packed up and get a move on!" She started walking over to the cooler.

Dani was about to help until she watched a moment pass between Vanessa and Lindsey, and something in that look struck her as odd, making her stop dead in her tracks.

"Leave the cooler alone, Claire." Claire turned back to Vanessa. "Because we're not leaving yet. We still have one more story."

Claire reluctantly let go of the cooler and looked at Vanessa. "We're still doing that? Even though . . ."

"There's no 'even though,' and why wouldn't we, Claire? Right, Lindsey?"

Lindsey stared at the fire. "I don't know. I don't feel like it anymore."

"It doesn't matter how you feel. Now, both of you get over here." Lindsey shook her head but got up quickly, while Claire cast a glance at Dani and winced at the confused look on Dani's face. She walked slowly over to where Vanessa and Lindsey were standing. Lindsey, noticing that the fire was still hanging on ever so slightly, found an unopened water bottle and dumped the contents on it. The girls watched as the fire slowly died, leaving Vanessa's flashlight the sole light in the darkness.

Dani shifted uncomfortably. "What's going on?"

Vanessa brought her flashlight closer to her face and smiled at Dani. "Well, Claire is right. It is getting late, but no one would miss us anyway. And now we know that no one would miss you either, so I'd say that we have time for one more story. Right, you two?"

Claire took a deep breath. This Vanessa was the one that had always scared her. The one that didn't care about anything but whatever she was after, and tonight she was after the perfect story. In the past, Vanessa had always been content with making up or retelling disturbing stories, watching their faces intently for signs of "true fear," but lately she hadn't seemed satisfied with their responses and was determined to push her stories to the next level. The next level was this story, and Vanessa had told Claire and Lindsey they had to be involved. Lindsey had been on board from the beginning, and Claire said she was (even though she wasn't). But what did it matter? The odds of having the chance to do it were so small because they were so far out, and why would someone be in this part of the woods at night?

They wouldn't. Then they'd come upon Dani. Like she'd been waiting there for them. For this story.

Claire turned to Dani and watched her pull her hoodie further over her face. Then she looked at Claire in a way that seemed to be seeking a way to avoid whatever was coming.

"I asked you a question," Vanessa said. "Don't we have time for one more story?"

Lindsey, now fully playing the role of the loyal foot soldier, nodded. "Yep. Claire's on board too."

"I don't know. I'm kind of tired, and . . ." She wasn't able to finish the sentence.

"No, Claire," Lindsey interrupted. "It's what we came out here to do." The looks that Vanessa and Lindsey gave her were very loaded, and she wilted in front of them.

"Yeah. We have time for one more story," she said meekly. Lindsey and Claire turned on their flashlights, Claire's half a beat behind Lindsey's.

Dani looked at her three new friends where they stood side by side with the glow of the flashlights on their faces, and she grew more and more confused. "You guys are being super sketch right now. What's going on?"

"Nothing," Vanessa said. "Except our final story."

"The only one that Claire knows," Lindsey added, laughing half-heartedly.

"So . . ." Dani began, looking at the three of them suspiciously. "You three are going to tell this story together? To me?" The three girls nodded. "Like some performance art or something?"

Lindsey stared at Dani. "Yeah, in a way. Wanna hear it?"

Dani nodded, even though the vibe she was getting from the girls was bringing back bad memories from long ago. "Sure."

"Good," Vanessa said, moving closer to Dani. "Because you don't have a choice anyway." Vanessa stared at Dani for what Dani considered an abnormally long time.

"Are you trying to creep me out?" Dani asked. "Because it's not working."

"Give it time," Vanessa said, smirking.

Then Vanessa sat down on the log across from Dani and motioned for Claire and Lindsey to sit down beside her. They did so silently. Dani, though sitting close to the other girls, felt like she was miles away and growing more and more distant. And more alone. Almost like she was . . . Dani pushed the thought aside.

"Now, Dani," Vanessa began. "I want you to understand that this isn't like the rest of the stories we told tonight. This one is different. Because it's not made up. It's real, and it happened right here, in these woods, and in that very lake." Vanessa pointed over Dani's shoulder. The girls, minus Claire, laughed as they saw Dani visibly jump. "You see, there did use to be another camp. Now there's only one." Dani looked at her strangely. "That's right. Camp Espantosa closed. But at one time, it was the most popular camp in the state, and it would have stayed that way if it hadn't been for that one fateful summer. The summer when three new girls showed up. They weren't expected, hadn't even signed up, but for some reason, the camp, already filled, let them in. Which would turn out to be their worst mistake. Because what once promised to be a fun-filled summer instead became known as 'The Summer of . . .'"

"'. . . the Three,'" Vanessa, Lindsey, and Claire said together. Dani couldn't help but laugh. The girls stared at her.

"Is something funny?" Vanessa asked flatly.

"Yeah," Dani said. "The way you three said it all together. Like some choral reading or something." Vanessa, Lindsey, and Claire stared at Dani with no response. "What made these three girls so bad?"

"Not bad," Vanessa said. "Evil. Although no one could ever prove anything, stories about that summer pointed to these girls as being the most messed-up, meanest campers to have ever been at Camp Espantosa, or any camp. They tortured the other campers in such devious ways that no one could ever prove that it was them, even though everyone knew it was. Stuff went missing or was destroyed, journals were stolen and everyone's deepest secrets became common knowledge, fires were started that damaged cabins, campers got injured all the time, letters from home were found ripped up, campers suffered from mysterious food poisoning, dead animals were found in campers' and counselors' beds, and the youngest campers complained that someone was entering their cabin at night and threatening them. And the same three girls were often found lurking nearby when those things happened, but they always had an excuse. And even though everyone knew they were lying, they never had to answer for any of it. It was as if they had free rein of the camp."

Lindsey turned to Vanessa. "That was a little much, don't you think?"

"It would be if it weren't true."

"Shouldn't the camp have called the parents or something?" Dani asked.

"Oh, they tried," Lindsey said. "But the contact info they'd been given was fake, and they could never find any relatives or friends or anyone that they could tie to these girls. Like they appeared out of nowhere. With no other choice, they let them stay."

"How do you even know those things? What did the girls do? It sounds made up."

"Trust me," Vanessa said. "It's not."

"Besides," Lindsey said. "This story isn't about those things. It's not even really about them. It's about *her*. Samantha. See, Dani, this is her story. And Claire's going to start." She turned to Claire. "Right, Claire?"

Claire looked at Lindsey, sighed, nodded, and then began the story. "Samantha was the smallest and youngest girl at Camp Espantosa. It was also her first year, and things were not going well. Fortunately . . ." and here Claire cleared her throat, then at a pointed look from Vanessa, forged ahead, "she didn't have to worry about coming back for a second year."

CHAPTER 13

The Final Story

"What are you doing up there?" Hazel asked the little girl, who was sitting high up in a tree.

"I climbed up here."

"Your name's Samantha, right?" said Bella.

"Yep."

"Well, come down," she said. "We want to talk to you."

"About?"

"Come down and we'll tell you."

Samantha looked at them and, after a moment of hesitation, slowly started making her way down the tree. About halfway, she stopped and looked at the girls again, seeing them clearly for the first time. She knew exactly who they were. They called themselves "The Three," a rather silly name, Samantha thought, though she would never tell them that because they were scary and everyone at camp was afraid of them. They didn't look that scary right now. Bella, the tallest one, was fairly normal-looking. Blond hair and green eyes. Nose of a pug. Somehow always had a new outfit even though she was at camp. She was also clearly the leader of the group. The largest one, Hazel, had a face covered in freckles and always seemed to be scowling. The third, Erin, was the most terrifying because, even though she always smiled, she had the smile that Samantha imagined the devil would have if he were in the process of burning someone to death.

"Why do I feel like you're up there judging us?" Erin asked.

"Because I am."

When Samantha made it near the bottom, the girls helped her reach the ground. Then they started talking to her. Nicely, which was something that Samantha didn't often get from the other campers. Not that the other campers were ever too mean to her. Some were, but for the most part, Samantha's camp experience had been that of someone who wasn't there. Like she blended into the walls and disappeared. Except when she didn't. And most of those times were terrible. But this time, it wasn't.

It turned out that the three girls that everyone at camp was terrified of were okay. Samantha was stunned by this and even more stunned when they invited her to sit with them at their table at lunch the following day, where they told her some big news.

"Look . . ." Bella began, taking a bite of her sandwich that she had pulled out of her back pocket. "We want you to be part of our group."

"Why would you want that?" Samantha asked.

The girls laughed. "Because we do."

Samantha sat silently, unsure of what to think.

"We get that you don't have any friends," Hazel said. "It's your first year at this camp, which is highly overrated by the way and features the biggest collection of tools ever assembled anywhere. And we get that you're trying to make it through until you can get home and lie to your parents about what a great time you had."

"You're not giving me a reason why you want me to be part of your group. It can't be out of the kindness of your hearts."

"You're right. As you've probably heard, kindness isn't our thing. The reason we want you in our group is because we have a lot more in common with you than anyone else here," Erin said. "Let's go talk more outside."

"I'm not finished with my sandwich," Hazel said, standing up and snatching some boy's sandwich as he looked meekly away, "or this one either."

"Eat it outside," said Bella, leading the group out the door. Samantha sat there for a moment, trying to decide what to do. Bella paused at the door and looked back. "You coming?"

Samantha jumped up and quickly followed, hardly believing that she was doing this. Or that it was happening.

But it was.

From that day on, the group that at one time was known as "The Three" now became known as "The Four," though no one called them that because it apparently didn't have the same ring as "The Three." Privately, Samantha thought the new name was amazing, because she was the one that made them four. She hadn't been this happy in her life. For the first time at camp, or ever, she had friends. She was part of a group. Someone to be partners with, someone to eat with, and to gossip with. She wrote letters home talking about her new friends, and she smiled when her parents' letters back changed from "Put yourself out there more. You'll make a friend." to "We are so happy for you. It's about time everyone found out what we always knew!"

Things were perfect. Well, almost. The one thing that still bothered Samantha was how all the other campers still talked about her new friends. For a couple of weeks, she didn't see what they were talking about.

That is, until the night of the "Cabin Brawl," when several campers got injured. Erin, Bella, and Hazel were found elsewhere, and while there wasn't any proof and no one directly blamed them, they had all been sent to the nurse's station for some lame made-up reason with the truth being that no one wanted to deal with them at Field Day. This was the equivalent of being thrown in the corner for a time-out for the day. Samantha had been sent too even though she was in her room reading at the time and didn't even know anything about what happened. She hadn't complained because they were her friends, and to be honest, she couldn't have been happier. Well, for a little while.

While in the nurse's station, though, she started to question the intentions of her new friends as she watched them "explore" the building. Bella calmly broke into the files of the other campers, Hazel started pocketing medication that should've been locked up a little better, and Samantha watched as Erin calmly slipped a scalpel out of a drawer and pocketed it. She turned and saw Samantha watching her, smiled, and then walked over to a cot and lay down on it.

"So, Gretchen's got to pay for this," Bella said, sitting on the floor while continuing to go through the files and staring out the window watching the other campers participate in Field Day events. "And pay big time."

"What do you have in mind?" Hazel asked.

"Something huge. Something that will force her head counselor ass to go home."

"I'm down with that. But what?"

"Wait," Samantha said. "It sounds like you're talking about hurting her."

"Maybe," Erin said. "Look, you don't understand. No one messes with us. Especially not some stupid, barely graduated high school teen who gets off on punishing kids who wouldn't even give her the time of day in real life."

"I don't know if I'm okay with this."

Erin smiled in that cold way she always had. "Samantha, you're one of us now, and that means you are okay with it. If you aren't, well, you can't hang with us anymore. Your call."

Samantha sat there and looked at the three girls, who were staring at her impassively. She thought of saying no for a moment, but then realized she couldn't. The punishment, though it wasn't called a punishment, was a little much. Field Day was the best day of camp, and they had to miss it because of what was essentially a food fight in the cabin that went overboard. Not to mention that there wasn't even any proof. And Gretchen was mean to them for no reason.

"I'm good. I'll do whatever you want me to," Samantha said, hoping that the payback wasn't too bad.

It was.

A few days later, Samantha watched the ambulance come and take Gretchen away. A rope she had been using for a tree climbing activity had frayed and broken, causing Gretchen to fall about 25 feet to the ground. The other counselors told the campers that she would be fine after a couple months of healing and therapy, but the way she fell told Samantha that what they said was probably not true. Either way, her summer was over. The reason she fell, the campers were told, was a freak accident, but Samantha knew there was nothing accidental about it. She had been there when they had done it. She had only watched, but by doing nothing to stop it, she was just as guilty.

After that, she acted like nothing was wrong, but everything was. If they would do that to Gretchen, did that mean that everything people had been saying about them was true? Samantha had to find out once and for all. One morning, when the camp was on a hike, she left her group and found Bella, who was walking behind everyone else. Samantha started walking beside her silently.

"Seems like you have something to ask," Bella said, wiping the sweat from her eyes.

"Don't take this the wrong way," Samantha began. "But that thing with Gretchen made me think . . ."

"That all those stories were true about us?"

"Yeah."

"What do you think?"

"I mean, I want to believe it's not true," Samantha said, stumbling over her words.

"You should go with that, then."

"That's not telling me that the stories aren't true."

Bella stopped walking and stood in front of her. "Listen, those stories are stories that I wouldn't deny even though they're not true."

"I mean, a lot of those things are horrible, and the Gretchen thing was really bad. She could've died."

"But she didn't, and we were responsible for what happened. Including you," Bella said. "As for those other things, well, let's say it's better to be feared than forgotten. Right?"

Samantha smiled nervously. "I guess. I'm sorry that I asked."

"Don't worry about it. If I were you, I would have asked the same thing. Remember though, you're part of us now. 'The Four' and all that." She smiled. "Now you better catch up with your group before you end up back in the nurse's station."

Samantha laughed and ran ahead, feeling somewhat better about her friends. There was still something sketchy about them, but you could probably say that about every teenager. They had, though, befriended her when no one else had, so that had to mean something. And it did mean something.

Samantha ran back to her group, not noticing Erin and Hazel running towards Bella.

"We've got her. Let's do it tonight." The three girls laughed and ran to catch up to the group, excited about the plans they had for little Samantha.

- - - - - - - - - -

"I don't like this story that much," Dani said nervously.

"Give it a chance. We're getting to the good part," Vanessa said, pointing the flashlight at Dani, who shielded her eyes.

"Could you at least stop with the flashlights in my face? I mean the whole time Claire was talking, you and Lindsey kept aiming your flashlights in my eyes. I get that you're trying to create the mood or whatever, but it's annoying, and it's not adding to a story where I already know the ending."

"There you're wrong," Vanessa said. "You have no idea how this story ends."

"Fine. What was their little plan?"

Lindsey laughed. She had moved past her initial hesitation. "It was something they had been planning for a long, long time. They only needed the perfect victim. And in Samantha, they found her." Lindsey smiled as she took over the story.

- - - - - - - - - -

Samantha, no longer having to find somewhere to sit in the cafeteria where she wouldn't be picked on, starting heading to her new usual table and noticed that Bella, Erin, and Hazel weren't there yet. Thinking nothing of it, she put her bag down and went to get her lunch. She was fully aware of everyone staring at her, and unlike in the past when she was surrounded by gawking eyes, it felt good. Maybe Bella was right. Being feared is much better than being ignored.

"Can we talk?"

Samantha turned and saw Paige, one of her almost friends at camp at one point. She stood there awkwardly, wearing the same ridiculous long-sleeved rainbow dress she wore every day. Some people have security blankets, while Paige had a security dress.

"Sure, what's up?" Paige shifted nervously as Samantha put her tray down and sat. She looked up at Paige. "You can sit down."

Paige stared for a moment at the table that she was about to sit at. This table had been declared off limits to anyone because this was "The Four's Table," and Paige was already nervous enough talking to Samantha. Sitting at the table seemed a little much. Samantha looked at her.

"Hurry up. Before they get here."

Paige took a deep breath and slowly put her tray down. "Okay." She sat down and nervously looked around.

"So, what do you want to talk about?" Samantha asked.

After seeing no sign of Bella, Erin, or Hazel, she stopped looking and turned back to Samantha. "What are you doing with those girls?"

"What do you mean?" Samantha asked, a little more defensively than she intended.

"You know what I mean. Hanging with Bella, Hazel, and Erin. They're really bad."

"You mean my friends?" Samantha said angrily. Paige tried to continue, but Samantha was having none of it. "Stop. I know what this is. You're jealous because I don't talk to you anymore, and I'm sorry. If you want to hang out sometime, we could."

"It's not that. I'm scared for you."

"Well, don't be. They're my friends. And if anyone should be scared, it's you. They don't like you very much, and they wouldn't think too kindly of you saying these things. They'll be here soon, so you better leave."

"I'll go, but let me say one more thing. They're not your friends, and you can't trust them. They will hurt you. Believe me, I know." Paige rolled up the sleeve on her left arm, and Samantha noticed cuts across her forearms. Paige saw her looking at them.

"Yeah, that's my work. This is theirs."

She continued rolling up her sleeves, and Samantha saw

a huge "X" cut into her skin. "They did this to me. Said I disappointed them, and if I told anyone, no one would believe me because of my other cuts. They also said that if I even tried they would hurt me worse." She pulled the sleeve back down. "Guess that answers the question of why I always wear this dress and never go swimming." Paige got up and started to walk away.

"Wait," Samantha said.

Paige turned, but then she saw something behind Samantha. A look of fear crossed her face, and she quickly scurried away from the table.

Suddenly trays surrounded Samantha as Bella, Erin, and Hazel sat down.

"What did that toxic waste of space want?" Erin asked.

"Nothing. I think she missed me or something."

"I bet she does. You were her only friend. Glad she's your ex-friend now," Erin said, and the three girls laughed, making Samantha uncomfortable. "But now that you're not a loser anymore, she can be a loser on her own."

"She's not that bad," Samantha explained. "She's a little different, that's all."

"Doesn't matter," Bella said. "Because we have something special to talk about."

"What?"

"Well," Hazel continued. "You've been our friend for a while now, and we decided it's time to make it official."

"You mean like a matching tattoo or something?"

The girls laughed. A gleam filled Hazel's eyes.

"That's a good idea," Hazel said. "Matching vulture tats. On our backs."

Bella shook her head. "Maybe later. What we have in mind is something so, so much better."

The girls proceeded to tell her that she was to meet them out in the woods by the lake at midnight for a little "initiation." Samantha instantly hated this plan because she was terrified of the dark. At campfires, she would sit so close to the fire that she had singed her clothes a time or two. She had no interest in this little initiation if it meant going out into the woods at night.

But she didn't say anything because one part of her did want to go. The part that liked this feeling of being part of something. That feeling of belonging.

"So . . ." Erin asked. "You going to be there?"

Samantha took a deep breath. "Absolutely."

"Awesome. We've got to go now. Plans to make for tonight." Bella got up, followed quickly by the others.

"But you didn't even finish your food."

"Ah, this food sucks anyway," Bella said. "Besides, we're too excited about tonight to eat."

"I'm not," Hazel said, dumping the rest of her food in her pockets. Samantha almost gagged.

"That's gross."

Hazel shrugged. "Pockets are clean. Almost." They laughed. "See you tonight, Sam." Then they loudly headed out the door. When Bella passed Paige, who was sitting alone, she walked up to her, picked her tray up, and dropped it to the ground. Samantha watched and thought of helping Paige, but when she saw that Hazel was watching her, she quickly finished her lunch and quietly headed to her cabin so that she could read before her softball game.

In the cabin, she quickly realized that she wouldn't be able to read. She was too excited and scared about what was going to happen at midnight. She also thought of Paige and what had been done to her, by herself and her friends. Samantha's mind became completely ravaged by a storm of thoughts, some good and some not. She soon found that she had no control over them and decided to head to the field early and warm up in hopes that a little physical activity would quiet the noise. Unfortunately, the thoughts continued, even during the game. This led to her not noticing a ball coming her way and said ball smacking her in the face, which caused her to awkwardly step on a rock, which then led to her twisting her ankle. She then had to spend the rest of the afternoon in the nurse's station, which was quickly becoming her second home.

Night finally came, and after being released to her cabin to rest with wadded up tissues in her nose along with ice for her ankle, Samantha was still unable to relax or sleep, so she lay there and thought. And thought. She remembered her grandpa once said, "If you can't get away from the storm, you might as well soak in it." So, with no other choice, she soaked in them.

Much later, after her bunkmates had returned and quieted down, Samantha finally allowed herself to look at her tiny clock radio that had been her mom's. She saw that it was almost midnight, so she sat up quietly and listened, making sure that everyone was asleep. After she was sure they were, she slipped on her shoes and her jacket and quietly headed out the door, picking up her flashlight on the way out.

She walked quickly past all the other cabins, hearing a lot of laughing and noise in the counselor cabin. She made it to the entrance of the woods and looked back. She could easily say she had forgotten. They would have to understand. But she knew they wouldn't. So, believing she had no choice, Samantha turned back to the woods and stepped onto the trail. The moment she did, it was as if the darkness had swallowed up whatever light there was, and her flashlight offered very little resistance. She began walking as fast as she could to the lake where she was supposed to meet them, hoping she would make it there before she died of a heart attack.

After walking for what felt like forever with her ankle beginning to throb, she made it to the meeting place and was greeted by silence. No one was there. No one. That she could see, anyway. No matter where she shone the flashlight, there was nothing but woods. And of course, the lake. She looked at the ground and couldn't make out any footprints. Tension began spreading through her. A gust of wind made her jump.

"Bella?" Samantha called out to no answer. "Erin? Hazel?"

No response came, and no responses were forthcoming no matter how loud or how many times she called their names. The only noise she heard was the blowing of the wind.

- - - - - - - - - -

As if on cue, the wind in the woods picked up around the girls. Dani, remembering a night she would rather have forgotten, looked around and tried to smile. "Nice effect." Then Vanessa was in Dani's face, placing a finger on her mouth.

"Shhhh," Vanessa whispered. "No talking." She stayed in front of Dani a moment longer, and for the first time, Dani noticed something in Vanessa's eyes that she hadn't seen before. Something missing. There was none of the earlier Vanessa who had seemed nice. What she saw now was almost dead. No, that wasn't right. Or was it? Vanessa slowly backed away from Dani, turned, and walked back over to where Lindsey and Claire were standing, though Dani could barely make out her silhouette in the meager glow of the flashlights. She did not look at Dani as she began. "Samantha now grew more afraid and broke out into a cold sweat. She wanted to run but couldn't. She thought that maybe she was overreacting. She tried slowing down her breathing and started telling herself that everything was all right and that her friends would be there soon. Why wouldn't they be? They were the ones who told her to come out here and said that she was one of them. They couldn't have been lying. Unless Paige was right, which would mean something bad was about to happen to her. Then she heard her name whispered, almost as if on the wind."

"Samantha, Samantha, Samantha," Lindsey and Claire said with a singsong quality.

Dani stood up. "Seriously, I'm done."

"Suddenly," Vanessa continued without acknowledging Dani, "something ran into Samantha, knocking her to the ground and taking her flashlight." At that same moment, the girls turned off their flashlights, leaving the woods in darkness. Dani heard someone running and then she was forcefully knocked to the ground.

"Ow, why did you do that?" Dani asked. No one said anything as she felt someone looming over her. All those old feelings had come back, along with something else bubbling deep below the surface but rising quickly. Dani didn't know which she was more afraid of. The three girls she was starting to trust had now proven untrustworthy, it seemed, and she was now stuck with them. In total darkness. "Could you turn your flashlights back on?"

"No!" Lindsey hissed in her face. Dani could feel Lindsey's breath on her as she continued the story, almost in a whisper. "As Samantha lay there on the ground, crying, scared, and hurt, she heard laughter that seemed to come from all around her." Vanessa and Claire began laughing. "The laughter mocked the girl, who now realized that she had never truly been part of the group. Bella, Erin, and Hazel had never been her friends. Everything that had happened before, everything, was about this moment. Samantha covered her ears to shut out the noise, but to no avail. The laughter grew and grew to an almost inhuman level until there was nothing. No more laughter, no more footsteps, no more wind, no more anything. Samantha was alone again. Alone in the big scary woods."

Dani pulled her knees to her chest, fighting hard not to cry but also feeling something else rise through her. Anger. No, rage. She took a deep breath. "Stop," Dani said, surprised at how calm she sounded. "This isn't funny anymore. You need to stop."

"I don't think so," the sneering voice that Dani recognized as Vanessa's said. "Samantha was more scared than she had ever been in her life, and that's saying a lot for a girl who spent most of her life fearing her own shadow. The dead silence of the woods somehow echoed in her head. Then the chanting of her name started again."

"Samantha, Samantha, Samantha." Dani assumed it was Lindsey and Claire but perhaps it was voices from the past in Dani's mind.

"Until finally, she could take it no more. She got up and started to run away. It didn't matter where. She had to be away. But without her flashlight, she couldn't see where she was going, and she didn't make it far. She tripped over a root, falling and hitting her head on a rock. She didn't cry out. She only lay there as the blood flowed freely from her wound."

"Hearing her fall," Claire continued, "the three girls walked over and turned their flashlights on her." Vanessa, Claire, and Lindsey turned their flashlights on Dani. "There they saw Samantha, unmoving, with a huge gash on her forehead that was staining the ground red. The girls had never seen so much blood. They stood there, transfixed by the sight. There was no sadness in any of their eyes. More like shocked amazement. Bella checked Samantha's pulse and felt nothing. They hadn't meant to kill her, but they had. The girl known as Samantha lay dead at their feet." The three girls stared at Dani, who stared right back at them, though she could barely make out their darkened forms behind the beams of their flashlights.

For a few moments, no one spoke. Then Claire continued. "Now, they knew they couldn't leave her there. They also knew they'd have to take care of the blood that was on the ground. Hazel picked the lifeless body up and carried it to one of the camp's boats, being careful to lean Samantha's head over the water so the blood wouldn't get in the boat. While Hazel was doing that, Bella and Erin cleaned up the area where Samantha had fallen. When they were done, they carried the large rock that Samantha had hit her head on over to the boat and joined Hazel. The girls were so methodical with it, so precise; it was like they had done this kind of thing many times before. Who knows? Maybe they had. When they were done, no one would have ever suspected that a young girl had died there. While Bella and Hazel guided the boat out to the middle of the lake, Erin tied the rock to a rope they had found in the boat and tied the rope around Samantha's body."

Vanessa smiled at Dani and took over. "As they rowed, they talked as if nothing had happened. Like it was a typical night at camp. Once they had made it to the middle part of the lake, the deepest part, the three girls tossed Samantha's lifeless body into the water and watched her slowly sink to the bottom. Where she would never be found. Never seen again. And that lake, Dani, is the very one that's behind you."

Dani stared at the three girls as they stared back at her, saying nothing. She waited a moment but was greeted only by more silence. Finally, Dani couldn't take it anymore. "And?"

"And what?" Lindsey said.

"Where's the ghost?"

"There is no ghost, Dani. This isn't a ghost story," Vanessa said.

"We told you for a different reason," Lindsey added.

"Which is?" Dani said, standing up and dusting herself off.

Vanessa, Lindsey, and Claire, who had taken their flashlights off Dani, now trained them on her once more.

"You see, Dani," Vanessa began, "when I heard this story about the girls and what they did, I realized something. Or really, Lindsey and I did. We realized that we liked what they did and that we wanted to be like them."

"Do what they did," Lindsey added. "And see, we were already a lot like them anyway. It was always the three of us, playing tricks on the other campers, the campers who thought we were off. Well, who thought me and Claire were off. And once we saw the connection, we realized that we could be them. We only needed one more thing."

"Which was?" Dani asked, growing nervous.

"We needed our Samantha," Vanessa said, now holding the flashlight under her chin, causing her face to be cast in a chilling light. She smiled, and Dani shivered at the sight. "We needed you, Dani."

Dani didn't back away. "That's not funny."

"Of course not. It's not meant to be. You're our Samantha. The lonely girl who wanted to fit in. Too bad the only place she would ever fit in was at the bottom of the lake."

The three girls turned off their flashlights again and ran at Dani, who was too shocked to move. She felt arms go around her, and she was thrown to the ground. She screamed as she fell.

"Stop, you're scaring me!" That wasn't true. She wasn't afraid. She was becoming something else, and if they didn't stop soon, they would regret it. She had felt this way only once before, and it did not end well. For anyone.

Vanessa and Lindsey laughed. Vanessa turned on her flashlight, and Dani saw that Lindsey was holding her down and Vanessa was standing above her. Dani looked for Claire and found her behind the other girls, looking uncomfortable.

Vanessa laughed. "Why, there's nothing to be afraid of, Dani. You belong there. With her. Where neither one of you will ever be hurt again. Pick her up, girls!" Vanessa moved behind Dani's shoulders, grabbing them and starting to pull them up as Lindsey grabbed her by her legs. Dani kicked and screamed, trying to break free, but the more she fought, the more the girls strengthened their hold. Vanessa, realizing that Claire wasn't helping, turned back to her. "Get over here, Claire! Now!"

Claire looked at Vanessa and then to Dani. This was not what they had said they would do. This was messed up. But if she didn't, then what would Vanessa and Lindsey do to her? She didn't want to find out. Because she was a coward. For the first time in her life, she legitimately didn't like herself. She slowly started walking over.

"Would you hurry up?" Lindsey shouted.

Claire got in the middle and reached down, about to help hold Dani, but then she looked at Dani's face and stopped dead. She recognized that face. That fear. Because she had seen it before. In herself. She couldn't do this. She couldn't. She backed away suddenly.

"What are you doing, Claire?"

"We're messing with you, Dani!"

"What?" Dani screamed.

"Put her down! It was a joke. A stupid joke! We were never going to . . ."

But she never finished that thought. Vanessa, who had harshly dropped Dani to the ground, ran over and threw Claire to the ground. She reached down and grabbed Claire by her shirt.

"It wasn't the time for that, idiot! God, you ruin everything!"

"Couldn't you have waited a few minutes?" Lindsey added, letting go of Dani.

"No," Claire said. "She was scared, and this isn't what you told me we were going to do. If you had, I never would've agreed to it because I could easily be her! I mean, seriously, what's wrong with us?"

"Shut up, Claire!" Vanessa pulled back her free hand, ready to punch her. Claire tried to pull away but couldn't.

"You're hurting me!"

"Calm down, Vanessa. It's over," Lindsey said, pulling at Vanessa, who reluctantly let go and walked away, cursing Claire.

"All of this for nothing."

Dani, looking at the three girls with a mix of fear and hurt, had a moment of clarity. "You did this to make fun of me?"

The three girls looked at Dani.

"Well, no," Lindsey said. "It didn't even matter that it was you. It could've been anybody. Matter of fact, we didn't even think that we would get the chance. I mean, at the spot it supposedly happened? And you're here, feeling rejected. Talk about perfect."

"You're like the rest of them."

"No, we're not," Claire said. "I mean, I guess we are, but it was meant to be a joke, and it got out of hand. That's all."

"Besides, we wouldn't have actually gotten to the end of it. We were going to get to the part of throwing you in the lake and then stop."

Vanessa, who had calmed down, turned to Lindsey. "Not making it better, Lindsey, so can you stop talking?"

"Sure, boss, whatever you say. It was your stupid plan anyway."

"But you went along with it." Vanessa walked over to Dani. "Look, Dani. I know this won't mean anything, but we're sorry. I'm sorry. Claire was right. It was a stupid joke, and we should never have done it. When I heard that story, I thought it would be cool to come up here to see what happened, and then you were here. It's almost like . . ."

"It was meant to be?"

"I guess," Vanessa said awkwardly. "I mean, we were going to create the perfect real story." Dani continued to stare at her. "But none of that matters. Sometimes I don't think when I come up with these things. I see now that we shouldn't have done it."

Dani smiled at her. "You're right. You shouldn't have. But it doesn't change the fact that you did." This time, something in *Dani's* smile made Vanessa take several steps back.

Dani turned away from the three girls and looked out over the dark lake. There was no longer a battle going on inside of her. The victor had been declared. "I can't tell you how many times I've heard 'I'm sorry' in my life. And, oddly enough, none of them ever made things better. When Mom died, people came up and said they were sorry, but it never changed the fact that she was dead. I could almost see the relief in their eyes that it wasn't their mom. When Dad said that he was sorry that he wasn't a good dad, it didn't make it better. It made it worse because I felt that it was my fault. That if I was better then maybe it would be easier to be a good dad. And all those other times, the forced 'I'm sorry' from the kids who picked on me. They wouldn't even make eye contact. They would mumble it and go on doing the same thing day after day. Because apologies are easy. Said in a moment and carry no weight." Dani stopped talking as she continued looking out at the lake, her mind filled with a thousand thoughts.

"This sorry . . ." Claire began.

"I'm not done," Dani cut her off. "And you three made me feel like you liked me. Brought me into your stupid little ghost storytelling group. Talked, laughed, had a food fight. Who even has a food fight in real life? And for the first time in a long time, I felt like I belonged. Like I mattered. I even shared things with you that I've never shared with anyone. Like my story for my dad, the one thing I thought would fix things, and he never even got to hear it. But you did. So, good for you three. Good for fucking you. You took a pathetic lonely girl and demolished her. That's awesome, and you should feel super proud."

"I like you, Dani. I wasn't faking," Claire said.

"We all like you," Lindsey added.

"You guys have a really funny way of showing it."

"Well, we never actually said that we were good at being friends."

"And to be honest, I didn't even think you'd fall for it," Vanessa said. "I mean, clearly we all go to the same camp."

"Have you seen me there? Ever?" Dani asked without turning. The girls looked at each other. "You haven't. Because I haven't been at camp in a long, long time."

"Very funny," Lindsey said, trying to sound brave but failing miserably. "You don't have to try to scare us now, Dani. We said we were sorry, and we mean it."

"It's much too late for being sorry, Lindsey. And I'm not trying to scare you. I'm trying to help you, all of you, understand. You see, your story was good, even got most of the details right, but I could never be your Samantha. Because I was already theirs."

Dani turned to them, and the girls' flashlights exploded in their hands. Yet even in the darkness, they saw her clear as day.

234

CHAPTER 14

Vanessa, Lindsey, and Claire could only stare at the girl with whom they'd spent the last several hours. Her skin was now pale, a grayish blue with an unearthly glow to it. Her clothes were tattered, and there was a rock tied to her waist that wasn't there before. The girls watched as Dani, smiling, slowly reached for her hood and removed it. Her hair was tangled, full of twigs and debris, but what drew the girls' attention was the large cut across the side of Dani's forehead, still fresh and bleeding profusely.

"Oh my god," Lindsey said.

"God left this story a long time ago. He had his chance. Now it's my turn." Dani began walking towards them. "I wanted to fit in. That's it. Have friends. Finally be able to write to my dad that he didn't have to worry anymore. That I wasn't the kid sitting alone in the corner. The one being laughed at. The one being forgotten. They said I was their friend. I trusted them, and they lied to me. They hurt me. Like so many. Like you."

"It was just a joke," Vanessa said meekly.

"That's what everybody always said. Just a joke. But you know what? I never laughed. Never even found it funny." Dani walked a few steps away and looked at the ground. Images began floating in her mind. Running away, tripping, hitting her head, the splitting pain, the fog. "I wasn't dead when they threw me into the lake."

"What?" Claire asked, her voice barely above a whisper.

"I wasn't dead. I suppose they thought I was. Or they didn't care." Dani sighed and looked out into the lake. "After they threw me in, I sank to the bottom and opened my eyes. I tried to swim up to the surface, but the rock they tied to me made that impossible. I tried to untie it, but I suppose they took the knot-tying class at camp super seriously. I kept trying, though. Trying to save a life that I long ago had been done with. I wasn't fighting for me. I was fighting for my dad. So he wouldn't be left alone. As the water filled my lungs, I kept seeing his face. I fought and fought, but no matter what I did, I wasn't going to make it back home."

"That's awful," Claire said.

"You should try living it," Dani replied bitterly. She looked down at the rock still tied around her waist. She snapped her fingers, and it was gone. "After, my eyes opened again, but it was different. I saw myself there below me. Lying there, on the bottom of the lake. It was weird. On some level, though, I knew it wasn't me anymore. I was now free. I thought I would move on or something, you know, being dead and all. Not heaven, though. I had given up on that long ago. That being said, the little girl in me still had hope that maybe I would see my mom again. I didn't. I was just there, floating. But then, little by little, everything around me began disappearing until there was nothing left but my body. Then that faded away, and there was only darkness. Some kind of abyss, I assumed. I don't know how long I was there, but the voices brought me back. Their voices. In the boat. Laughing. Making fun of me, even in death. Hearing that caused something inside of me to change. I was no longer afraid. Nor was I the lonely little girl who only wanted to belong. Something was coursing through me, a rage that I never felt before. And as I gave in to that rage, that need to belong and all those feelings that had haunted me when I was alive ceased to be. Because there was only room for one feeling. One need. And that's when I knew that they would never make it back to camp."

- - - - - - - - - -

"I can't believe we did that. We killed someone."

"Stop talking so loud, Hazel, and keep paddling," Bella said.

Erin laughed. "Relax, Bella. No one's out here this late, and it's not like she's going to be missed."

"She will be tomorrow, and everyone thinks that we're her friends. Speaking of friends, we might have to take care of that Paige girl too."

"Maybe."

Hazel looked at Bella. "Wait, we're going to kill her too?"

"I didn't say kill. I said take care of. Which I suppose could mean kill if necessary." Hazel shifted uncomfortably. Bella smiled. "Look, we'll go back to camp, and in the morning, they'll find us in our beds, and we haven't seen her. Then they'll search, which we'll help with while always playing the worried friends, maybe cry a little, and she'll never be found, and who knows, maybe since our dear friend died, we might be popular."

Erin looked at her, shocked. "That's a strong plan. It's almost as if you knew that she was going to die."

"Yes, Erin. I knew that she was going to hit her head on a big ass rock and die."

"What if she's not dead?" Hazel asked.

"Well, then she would've drowned by now, so still dead." Erin's laughter took Bella and Hazel by surprise. "Lighten up, guys. It's not like we killed her. We only had a hand in it. And we're going to get away with it. No harm, no foul."

They didn't know that Samantha was there. Not the Samantha they knew. This Samantha was different. As she watched them laugh and talk proudly of what they'd done, the last remaining bits of humanity in her burned away. All that she once was, was gone, and something new filled the space. And this something new would relish making the three girls pay for what they did.

She calmly floated to the shore and waited for them.

Hazel shivered. "Did you feel that? Like a cold breeze."

"A cold breeze at night on the lake. Shocking," Bella said, laughing.

The girls paddled on in silence, each lost in her own thoughts. Erin joyfully relived everything that had happened. Bella wondered what they might encounter tomorrow morning and brainstormed ways to make sure that they could get away with it. Hazel's thoughts were a little mixed: on one hand, she was excited that they'd pulled it off, but on the other hand, Samantha had died. And if she hadn't died when she hit her head on the rock, well, that meant that they had drowned her. Hazel pushed that thought aside. Kids died every day, and it wasn't like Samantha would be missed by a lot of people. Yeah, Hazel thought, that's it. I need to think more like Erin. It's only a story. She then laughed out loud but stopped suddenly when she heard Erin yell.

"Oh shit."

Bella and Hazel looked to where Erin was looking and couldn't believe their eyes.

There she was – Samantha – floating in front of them at the water's edge, with a rock still tied around her and blood flowing from her wound. She tilted her head slowly to the left and smiled at them.

"Let's get the hell out of here," Hazel said.

The girls started paddling as fast as they could, but a gust of wind began blowing so strongly that there was no way they would make it back out onto the lake. There was nothing they could do. They were heading to the shore. Where Samantha was. Or whatever she'd become.

The girls tried to jump out of the boat but soon felt their bodies being lifted and drawn to the shore. The boat ripped apart by some unknown, unseen force into thousands of pieces. The girls tried to scream, but their voices had gone silent.

They found themselves stuck to three trees, side by side by side, unable to move. Then she was suddenly in front of them. Samantha watched them quietly for a moment before speaking.

"Hey, guys. Miss me?"

That was the last thing the girls ever heard. The last thing they ever saw was Samantha's piercing red eyes as she tore into them. They never saw their flayed bodies being taken down from the trees and hauled away, thought to be the victims of some animal attack, or heard the other campers' sighs of relief, never saw the undeserved memorial, and they never saw the girl in the lake watching it all.

- - - - - - - - - -

"You killed them."

"I did. Because they deserved it. They hurt me. They took me from my dad." She paused and looked straight at Vanessa. "You got that part of the story wrong. My mom was already dead." Dani started moving slowly around the girls. "I was there when the camp director told him. They thought I was dead, but they couldn't find the body. He didn't believe them. He came out searching every day. For months. The woods, the lake, everywhere, but of course he never found me. I wanted to appear to him, tell him that I loved him and that I was sorry I was me. But I didn't. I guess I didn't want to take his hope away. And then one day, he stopped showing up, and his little girl went home. To the bottom of the lake. I've been there ever since. You can't imagine how lonely I've gotten." Dani moved to where the fire once was. "I started waiting here most nights. In the same spot where you found me. Waiting, hoping, for someone, anyone, to come and be my friend. But every night always ended the same. Until tonight. Because now the lonely girl finally has friends." She looked at them and smiled. "Three of them."

Lindsey started to move. "Okay, you win. We're creeped out now, and we will be heading back to camp." Vanessa started to follow, Claire remaining oddly still. Dani raised her hands, and Vanessa and Lindsey froze, unable to move.

"You're never going back to camp again."

"Please, Dani . . ."

"Dani was my mother. My name is Samantha."

CHAPTER 15

"Let us go, please!" Claire pleaded. "We don't deserve . . ."

"To die?" Samantha yelled. "Neither did I. My only sin was being different. And I paid with . . ." A tear slowly rolled down her cheek. She wiped it away angrily. "And to think, I was going to let you all go. I only wanted one night of feeling like I belonged, but I couldn't even get that. I can't change my fate, but at least I can make sure I'm never alone again."

"The counselors have to be looking for us," Lindsey said. "And they'll, I don't know, do whatever counselors do when their campers are being threatened by vengeance-seeking ghosts."

Suddenly, Samantha was in front of Lindsey, her piercing red eyes forcing Lindsey to look away. "What do you think they'll do, Lindsey? Find you? Like they found me? Trust me, they won't. Because it's really hard to find a body where I'm taking yours."

Vanessa took off running, and Lindsey started to follow. Lindsey looked back and noticed that Claire wasn't running. She came back to her and grabbed her arm.

"Come on, Claire!"

Claire broke out of her shock and followed Lindsey into the woods.

Samantha remained, no urgency at all. "No matter where you go, you'll end up here. Every time. With me." And then she disappeared.

"What the hell, what the hell, what the hell?" Vanessa yelled through her tears. She was running faster than she ever had, but unfortunately, she had no idea where she was going. And the quickly descending fog made it worse.

She never even saw the tree. She smacked into it and fell to the ground. The shooting pain in her nose made her realize that she had probably broken it. She reached up and felt wetness that she hoped was not blood– knowing all the while that it was. There goes the perfect face.

Vanessa pulled herself up and leaned on the tree as she tried to catch her breath. She wondered if Lindsey and Claire had gotten away. They would probably be pissed that she didn't wait for them, but who cared. They would have done the same thing. Wait, that wasn't true. She had seen Lindsey go back for Claire.

Whatever, she was safe now.

"You're not."

Vanessa jumped and slowly turned around.

There Samantha was. Floating in front of her, her eyes growing redder by the moment.

"Now you're a mind reader as well?"

"You said it out loud."

Vanessa considered what to do, then took off again. She ran right through Samantha, who only laughed in response.

"Oh, Vanessa, friends don't run through friends."

"I'm sorry, but . . ." She didn't finish that thought as she focused on running back to camp. Only she wasn't running back to camp. She quickly realized that she was running back to the lake.

When she got there, she heard the water hitting the shore and shook her head. "Oh, crap."

She started to run again but was thrown forcefully against a tree. Vanessa slumped down, unable to move.

Samantha suddenly appeared in front of her.

"Got you," she whispered. "One little piggie down, two to go." She disappeared again.

- - - - - - - - - -

"Hurry up, Claire!"

"I'm trying!" Claire yelled, out of breath. "But I can't see anything."

"Keep listening to my voice, okay?"

"Okay."

The girls continued running as fast they could through the fog-covered forest. Occasionally Lindsey would say something, and Claire would answer her. Claire wondered if Lindsey had a clue where they were going.

"Ow!" Lindsey cried out as Claire heard a loud sound.

"Are you all right?"

"No, I think . . . shit!" Lindsey screamed out in pain. Claire ran to where she thought the sound was coming from, then tripped over Lindsey, causing both to yelp in pain.

"Smooth, Claire, smooth," Lindsey said, grimacing.

"Are you okay?" Claire asked, still barely able to see Lindsey even though she was almost on top of her.

"No, I think I broke my ankle. You have to get out of here."

"Not without you I'm not. Let me help you up."

"You'll never be able to carry me fast enough. Just go. Find Vanessa and get back to camp. Send help once you get there."

"What if she finds you first?"

"Probably what I deserve. Now, go!" Claire remained frozen. "I don't hear your feet moving." Then she felt Claire's arms around her in an awkward and failing attempt to pull her up. "Nice try, now get the hell out of here." Claire got up and started to run away. "Hey, one more thing." Claire's footsteps paused. "Um, you were right about me. What I said earlier, about, you know . . . it wasn't a joke, and . . . maybe when we get back . . . we can talk about it. Or something. I mean, if we don't die, that is."

Claire smiled. "That would be awesome, and by the way, I always knew. Even though you think I didn't. And I feel the same way. I know you can't see it, but I have a big smile on my face."

"Figured. Now get out of here. And don't trip."

Claire turned to leave but then turned back.

"What the hell are you doing, Claire?" Lindsey screamed.

"I'm not leaving you. I can't. I, uh, don't want to. I won't."

"Dammit! Get the fuck out of here. If one of us has to die, it should be me. I suck, okay?" A tear rolled down her cheek. "But you, you don't. So please, for me, run. I promise I'll find you."

Claire stared at Lindsey, her eyes saying what her words could not. "I will, but you better keep your word."

Claire leaned down and kissed her gently, then pulled away

and smiled. She squeezed Lindsey's hand one more time, and then, in an instant, she was gone. Lindsey watched her go and hoped she would make it back. But with the fog, Lindsey had no clue if she was heading in the right direction. As she sat there, her leg throbbing, she thought of everything that had led to this moment and wondered if she and Claire . . . what did it matter? She had to make it back, and to be fair, who knew if she could get past her multiple issues with herself to be what Claire needed.

It was so quiet, and Lindsey was tiring of this introspection. Fortunately, she didn't have any more time for it.

"Lindsey. Lindsey. Lindsey." Lindsey heard the voice whisper in the wind. She looked around to see where it was coming from but saw no farther than a few inches in front of her face.

"Well, this is pointless." She struggled to push herself up, falling several times. Finally, using the tree to lean against, she managed to stand up as the chanting of her name grew louder and quieter at the same time. How was that even possible? Either way, if the goal was to scare her, it was working. Normally, Lindsey would have appreciated it more – she always did like a good scare – but not this time. She tried to put pressure on her foot, and it hurt like shit, but she could do it.

"Guess it wasn't broken."

Then her ankle snapped, and she fell to the ground.

"Now it is." Lindsey turned over and saw Samantha standing above her.

Lindsey rolled back over and began crawling away, the pain growing worse by the moment, as Samantha's laughter followed her. She had only gone a few feet when the fog suddenly cleared and she saw . . .

The lake.

"That cannot be good."

"Lindsey."

She looked toward the sound of the voice and saw Vanessa slumped against a tree, a pained expression on her blood-covered face.

"Now, that definitely isn't good."

"It's not."

Lindsey turned and saw Samantha.

"Oh, hi, Dani. Sorry, Samantha. Really a fan of the red eyes and your ability to snap my ankle. Guess there's no chance you'll let us go, huh?"

"I'm thinking no."

Suddenly, Lindsey found herself flying through the air. She screamed out and felt a crushing pain as she was slammed into the tree beside Vanessa's. She tried to move but couldn't. The two girls watched as Samantha floated towards them, enjoying every moment of this.

She stopped in front of them.

"What are you going to . . ." Lindsey's mouth suddenly snapped closed.

"Shhhh," Samantha said. "You talk too much while saying very little. But to answer your question, nothing right now." She pointed to the other tree beside her. "You have a table for three." At that moment, Claire came through the woods, saw the lake, and looked confused. Lindsey saw her and fought with all her strength to open her mouth and yell, "Get out of here, Claire!"

Claire looked at Lindsey and Vanessa. "This can't be."

"But it is."

Claire then saw that Vanessa and Lindsey were slammed up against two trees. Claire remembered the story Samantha told and knew what was coming next if she didn't think of something. She looked at Samantha, who was smiling at her. Samantha flicked her wrist and in an instant, Claire was against the third tree, unable to move.

"Look, the band's all back together, and we're almost to the last song. I don't think you're going to like it though." She turned away from them. "It's funny, in a not-funny kind of way, that this was not the ending I wanted, not even close, but sometimes you have to go with what you've been given." Claire began crying, which started all the other girls crying as well. Samantha turned back and saw the complete and utter terror that was radiating through them. If there was anything left of the other Samantha, the girl that she once was, she might have felt something. Perhaps even let them go.

But that Samantha had burned away again, perhaps permanently this time. The last fragments destroyed tonight. Now all that remained was what had ripped the flesh off of the ones who had hurt her before. And now she would make these three pay as well.

"We are so sorry, Samantha."

Samantha turned to Claire. "It's much too late for apologies, Claire. Much too late."

Samantha reached out her hand and gently touched Claire's cheek. Then her eyes became bright red again, and the heat from her now-burning hand caused Claire to scream in anguish.

"Leave her alone!" Lindsey yelled.

Samantha turned to Lindsey. "Of course." Samantha

withdrew her hand. She left Claire for the moment and drifted over to Lindsey's tree. "Oh, Lindsey, I feel sorry for you."

"Seems reasonable."

Samantha laughed. "Always one for the clever line. But no, not because of this. You caused this."

"No, she didn't. And neither did Claire," Vanessa yelled. Samantha turned to her. "It was me. It was all me! Not them. Kill me. I deserve it. Let them go!"

"Well, look at that. Guess you weren't heartless after all. Don't worry though, I'll make sure you suffer the most."

"C'mon, Samantha. You don't want to do this."

"Oh, but I do."

At that moment, the girls began struggling to breathe, gasping for air that would not come. Samantha watched as their faces began turning blue, the oxygen in their bodies replaced by foul-smelling water. Their bodies convulsed more violently, lake water seeping from their mouths.

"Fatal Drowning, the technical term for what's about to happen to you, is a terrible way to die. You fight and fight for a breath that you will never find because once your body forces you, craving that oxygen, to try to breathe, the water quickly rushes in, filling up inside of you until at some point, your body gives up and you die."

Samantha watched as their lives slowly seeped away, water filling their lungs, the girls fighting for a breath that they would never find. She thought that it would bring her pleasure to watch them die, to make them suffer as she had. And for a moment, it did.

But then it didn't. Something unexpected happened.

Something she didn't experience with the other ones. Her mind began to fill with images that were not her own. Images of all three girls, from their lives, that she hadn't heard them talk about. She struggled to maintain control, but now it was as if someone else was taking the reins and changing the story.

As the girls hung there in a state of drowning that neither advanced nor dissipated, they watched as Samantha seemed to be watching a film that they could not.

The scenes attacked Samantha's mind. Scenes of Vanessa, Claire, and Lindsey that she had never seen, couldn't have known about, but were there nonetheless. Of random days, parties, injuries, family trips. When they were babies and opening their eyes for the first time, their entire lives ahead of them. Seeing the love and joy in their parents' eyes as they held their new babies, like she imagined her parents had held her. Then the stories started to separate, and Samantha stepped into each of their lives.

She saw Lindsey's first, a baby with white-brown hair and the biggest, most awkward smile she had ever seen on a baby. Her father was holding her with tears flowing freely. Samantha then saw a rambunctious, tiny, very tiny little kid with now dirty blond hair, who was surrounded by tons of other kids, playing happily. The image then switched to a church, where Lindsey sat quite happily in the pew with her mom and dad, singing all of the hymns loudly. Samantha watched as her parents covered her with affection because, and Samantha heard this clearly, she was a "good, God-fearing child."

And perhaps it was this very fear that caused the hue of the scene to change, as Lindsey started to realize that she wasn't what she thought she was, what everyone demanded that she be, what she couldn't be. Samantha watched as the once happy childhood became full of Lindsey's mom telling her that "it must be a phase" because "that is not what God intended." She watched as Lindsey tried to argue that if God made them the way that they were, then clearly God had made her the way she was. She watched in horror as Lindsey's mom slapped her across the face and told her that she was bad and would burn in hell if she didn't be the person Christ had made her. She watched as Lindsey looked up, tears in her eyes and a hand to her cheek, to her dad, who turned away from her and looked off silently, too timid to defend his daughter.

This, then, was the moment that the Lindsey who Samantha met tonight came to be. The one who, at one point, was happy and had so many places that she felt like she belonged, but now only had one. And that one was locked up tight and seen by no one.

That final vision of Lindsey was quickly ushered away and replaced by perhaps the cutest baby that Samantha had ever seen and one that she instantly recognized as Claire and her big brown eyes, her smile lighting up the room. Her parents were holding her as if she were the greatest gift in the entire world. The pages turned quickly, and Samantha watched as Claire and her parents lived out the most perfectly bizarre life that Samantha had ever seen. It was also the most wonderful and one that reminded her most of her life with her parents. Every day seemed to be filled with games, songs, adventures, laughter, and love. Lots and lots of love. All the while, the centerpiece, Claire, in her loud and mismatched clothes, happily existed, dancing to a song that only she could hear.

Then, as with Lindsey's story, came the part where the twist happened. The part, the turning point, that changed Claire forever. When she was called "weird" and "loser" for the first time. And then many times after that. Samantha watched as she tried to talk to her parents and they, with good intentions, told her not to let it bother her because people depended on people like her to let nothing keep them down. She watched Claire as she gamely accepted her role. She was going to be the Claire that everyone expected her to be, the one who never cared what anyone thought because that's who she was. Even though she did care, she wouldn't let anyone know. Because it was her job, to be what people needed her to be. Carefree Claire, an idea, not a person. Samantha watched as Claire got up each morning and looked in the mirror, telling herself to put her brave face on. And she did. Every single day.

But Samantha could feel what Claire was feeling on the inside, the unbelievable pain of doing what was expected.

- - - - - - - - - -

The girls watched on, powerless to do anything except slowly die. Despite their intense fear and pain, they watched with extreme interest. Something was happening to Samantha. Vanessa imagined that she was perhaps having second thoughts. Claire saw the sadness in Samantha's eyes and only wanted her to be happy. And stop killing them. And Lindsey, being done with all of this, wanted Samantha to get this over with and kill them already, seeing it more as a gift than a punishment.

Then it was Vanessa's life that Samantha saw. Her parents loved their little girl, who was the most perfect baby, then child, that Samantha had ever seen. She watched her take her first step at what looked like two months old (was that even possible?) as her parents cheered her on. She saw her read her first book to her parents at the age of two. The images that flashed so quickly in front of Samantha did not in any way reflect Vanessa's story of her parents. They were almost as loving as her own parents. They would move the world for her if they could. What was Vanessa talking about?

The next shot showed Vanessa holding her new sister, and Samantha was amazed by the way that the now older Vanessa stared at the baby's eyes. It was so human. And beautiful.

The next image was not. A tiny grave. Vanessa stood sadly by her parents, who seemed miles away. Vanessa was reaching for hands that would never again be there to hold. Samantha recognized the look in her parents' eyes because that's the same look her dad had.

And that look never left Vanessa's parents in every scene after that. They focused on everything else, while Vanessa pulled further and further away, understanding that what she needed from them they were no longer able to give. The last shot was of a teenage Vanessa staring quietly at a picture of her sister and gently packing it away.

Samantha then saw the four of them from earlier, talking around the fire, having fun together, being friends. But this time, she saw beyond their masks and a moment of clarity struck her. They weren't like the other three. They were like her. Damaged.

She looked at the girls that she was slowly killing in a new light. Whatever rage was left instantly fell away, and Samantha's eyes returned to normal. The three girls dropped to the ground and began coughing up the water that had previously filled their lungs.

Samantha simply floated there, watching them as they started to recover. Claire was the first one to look up at her, followed by Lindsey and Vanessa.

She smiled sadly at them. Then she turned and started back to the lake.

Claire struggled to stand up. "Dan . . . Samantha, wait!"

"What are you doing?" Vanessa hissed.

Samantha turned. She looked at them and something started happening to her. A bright light radiated from her. The girls shielded their eyes, and once the light faded, they looked again. Samantha had changed. She was younger and no longer wearing a hoodie or bleeding. She wore a t-shirt with shorts, her dirty blond pigtails blown by a nonexistent wind.

She smiled gently at them and then disappeared.

Samantha was gone.

The world slowly came to life as the sun began rising over the lake. Vanessa and Lindsey sat with blank expressions. Claire looked out at the lake.

"She didn't kill us."

"Thanks for pointing that . . ." Vanessa, standing up shakily, started to say something but changed her mind. "No, she didn't."

"Why?" Claire turned to her. "I mean, we did exactly what those girls did."

"Well, not exactly. We didn't kill her," Lindsey said from the ground, not even trying to get up, wincing as she massaged her ankle.

"I guess," Claire said, looking out.

Vanessa crossed to Claire while wiping off the blood from her nose. "This may seem like another obvious question, but did that really happen?"

"Well, my broken ankle happened and so did your busted-up nose, nice look by the way, so there's that," Lindsey said. Claire slowly walked to the shore. "I don't think now's the time for a swim, Claire."

"I'm not. Look." Claire pointed out to the center of the lake. "The lake's still dark."

"What were you hoping for?" Vanessa asked as she walked to stand beside her.

"I don't know. Something different, I guess."

Vanessa sighed. "Like that part of the lake would've become clear or something?" Claire nodded. "That would've been nice. But . . ."

"There aren't happy endings, huh?" Claire asked, still not looking at her.

"No, I was going to say that this part of the lake has always been dark. Way before Samantha. It's a depth and soil thing. I added that part about the lake turning dark for . . ."

"Effect. Right," Claire said. "I'm sad for her. Really, really sad." Vanessa awkwardly poked her shoulder. Claire turned to her. "Thanks for that."

"Hey, Claire, stop with this maudlin shit. We're alive, and before everything went to hell – because of us, yes – we all had fun. Even Samantha had fun. She felt like she belonged. Sort of.

That's a happy ending, right?" Vanessa and Claire turned and saw Lindsey crawling awkwardly over.

"You look like a crab."

"Thanks, Vanessa, for not acknowledging my wise words and only focusing on my awkward movement. And I would love not to be crawling like this, but I have no choice. Because I have a broken ankle, and my friends left me in the sand."

Claire and Vanessa went back and helped Lindsey walk to the shore. They stood there, silently looking out. Then Vanessa started laughing. Lindsey turned to her.

"Why are you laughing?"

Vanessa laughed some more. "You know, I wanted an epic story, and I think this kind of qualifies." She then paused and took a deep breath. "I'm sorry I ran off without you guys."

"Yeah, you're a pretty horrible friend," Lindsey said, laughing.

"Never knew how much though. Until tonight."

Vanessa felt an arm go around her. It was Claire, who had moved from holding Lindsey to beside Vanessa. "Oh, don't be so hard on yourself. We're all pretty horrible. We should probably go about fixing that." The three of them laughed. "Do you think she knew we liked her?"

"I'm guessing yes. I mean, she didn't drown us."

"There's that. And at least there's a chance she's free, right?" Vanessa asked.

"Yeah, I think so. I hope so," Claire said.

"There's something I don't get," Lindsey said. "She was a ghost, right? So how was she all corporeal and shit? Like how did she eat food? Or sit on a log. Or really do anything that she did?" Vanessa and Lindsey didn't answer. "Anybody?"

"Well," Vanessa began. "I think that everything we know about ghosts is of the made-up ghost variety. You know, the stories and rules that were simply made as a way to create some semblance of reality, so people would be more likely to believe that there were ghosts, thus giving people hope of the possibility of something after death besides rotting in the ground."

"Nicely put."

"Thank you. My point is . . . Samantha, whatever she was, was real and played by rules that we don't know nor understand."

"So you're saying that Samantha could do whatever she wants?" Claire asked.

"I guess."

"Thank goodness she decided not to kill us." Claire smiled at the rising sun. "I feel like we've been given another chance. You know, to be better."

"Yeah," Vanessa and Lindsey said at the same time.

They grew silent as images of the previous night flooded their minds. This reminiscing didn't last very long, though, because the distraction of the memories caused Vanessa and Claire to forget another role they were also playing. A supporting one.

Lindsey, now having no one to hold her up because Vanessa and Claire had forgotten to hold her up, fell face-first to the ground.

"Nice support system I got here." Claire and Vanessa turned, laughed, and then helped her back up. "Glad you both chose to laugh first. You know, I'm enjoying the bonding time, but maybe we should go back to camp before my leg falls off."

At the mention of camp, a nervous look came over Claire. "Oh crap, we are going to be in so much trouble."

"No, we're not," Vanessa assured her. "We'll go back and tell the counselors that we encountered the ghost of Samantha, who we befriended, then were dicks to, and then she tried to kill us, decided not to, and then she went home. Hopefully."

Claire smiled. "Oh, good. I thought we wouldn't tell them."

"We're not telling them, Claire," Vanessa said.

"I think we should," Lindsey said.

Vanessa turned to her. "Wait, what?"

"Yeah, let's tell the truth. Look, they're not going to believe us anyway, so why not tell the truth? Besides, Samantha needs her story heard. The true one."

"When did you become a fan of the truth, Lindsey?"

Lindsey smiled at Claire. "Recently. Maybe even started to believe in happy endings." A moment passed between Claire and Lindsey that didn't go unnoticed by Vanessa.

"Did you guys have a moment? Because I feel like you did," Vanessa said, grinning.

"Shut up," Lindsey said.

"Just so you both know, I'm cool with being a third wheel. With my messed-up nose, third wheel may be my best option."

"Whatever, your parents will probably buy you like five new noses."

"Why would I need five new noses? Wouldn't one suffice?"

"I don't know. Rich people are strange. Anyway, I have an idea. Remember how Samantha talked about writing that story and burying it near her cabin?" The girls nodded. "What if, after we survive our coming ordeal, we come back to the old camp and look for it?"

"How are we supposed to find it?" Vanessa asked.

"No clue. We'll dig around, and hell, maybe we'll even get some ghostly help. If we find the story, we could give it to her dad."

"That would be the perfect ending," Claire said. "But how would we find him?"

"Google him, dummy. Shouldn't be that hard to find once we find out what Samantha's last name was. You guys in?" Both Vanessa and Claire nodded. "Cool. Now let's get back to camp before we tick off another ghost."

The three of them started their trek back but stopped suddenly when Claire, removing herself from Lindsey, almost causing her to fall again, jumped in front of her and Vanessa.

"What, Claire?" Vanessa asked.

"Do you think those other girls, the ones Samantha killed, are ghosts too?" Claire asked.

"God, I hope not," Vanessa said. "If they were that awful in life, I can't imagine what they would be like in death. Or after death. Not to mention, if they were as powerful as Samantha was then . . ."

"Then it would be a real shitstorm," Lindsey said.

"Oh," Claire said nervously. She then rushed back to Lindsey's side. "Let's get as far away from here as we can and, just so you know, Vanessa, next year at camp, we are not coming here."

"Seems reasonable."

The girls laughed as they began the long trek back to camp. Behind them loomed the lake, still dark, but perhaps not as foreboding as before.

STEVEN STACK has been writing for young audiences for over a decade. During that time, 30 of his plays and scenes have been published, racking up over 300 performances in 44 states and eight countries. He also has decades of experience working with students ages 7-18 – in public schools, in a studio environment, and in immersive theatre summer camps.

When he's not writing, Steven enjoys watching *Supernatural*, *Phineas and Ferb*, *Bones*, and *Boy Meets World* – sometimes with one or both of his daughters. They live in the troll capital of the world: Mount Horeb, Wisconsin.

This is his first novel, an important milestone on a journey that began in the second grade with Steven's first story, "Dumb Pilot." (Longtime fans will agree that his writing style has not changed very much since then.)